in the province of saints

in the province of saints

A NOVEL

Thomas O'Malley

Little, Brown and Company
New York   Boston

Little, Brown and Company
Time Warner Book Group
1271 Avenue of the Americas, New York, NY 10020
Visit our Web site at www.twbookmark.com

FIRST EDITION: August 2005

The characters and events in this book are fictitious. Any similarity to real persons, living or dead, is coincidental and not intended by the author.

Chapters from this novel, in somewhat different form, have been previously published: "The Road to Emain" in *Shenandoah;* "All the Way from America" in *Crab Orchard Review;* "The Hidden Country" in *Blue Mesa Review;* "Play the Reel Slowly" in *New Millennium Writings;* "The Banshee" in *Ploughshares;* "The Sowing Season" in *Natural Bridge;* "Wake" in *Glimmer Train;* "Maundy Thursday" in *Mississippi Review;* "Martyrs of the New Republic" in *Vanguard.*

Excerpt from "A Small Farm" by Michael Hartnett, from *Collected Poems* (2001). Reprinted by kind permission of the Estate of Michael Hartnett and The Gallery Press, Loughcrew, Oldcastle, County Meath, Ireland.
Excerpt from "Stopping to Take Notes" by Michael Smith, from *Selected Poems.* Reprinted by kind permission of the author.
Excerpt from "She Moved Through the Fair" by Padraic Colum, from *The Poet's Circuits* (Dolmen Press, 1981). Reprinted by kind permission of the Estate of Padraic Colum.

Library of Congress Cataloging-in-Publication Data
O'Malley, Thomas.
    In the province of saints : a novel / Thomas O'Malley. — 1st ed.
        p. cm.
    ISBN 0-316-11039-6
    1. Boys — Fiction. 2. Ireland — Fiction. 3. Sudden death — Fiction. 4. Fathers and sons — Fiction. I. Title.

PR6115.M347I5 2005
823'.92 — dc22   2005003824

10 9 8 7 6 5 4 3 2 1

Q-MB

Book design by Fearn Cutler de Vicq
Printed in the United States of America

For my mother,
Bridie Lennon,
and my father,
Bartley O'Malley

As much as the living
the dead make their exactions.
Someone we have not met
sent us on this journey.

— MICHAEL SMITH

All the perversions of the soul
I learnt on a small farm,
how to do the neighbours harm
by magic, how to hate.
I was abandoned to their tragedies,
minor but unhealing. . . .

— MICHAEL HARTNETT

in the province of saints

in the dead of winter

IT was nine the year winter came in spring, and Cait Delacey's mother, Mag of Slievecorragh, died; the winter had come and gone and surprised us with its return — sneaking furtively back to us like a fox during the night. The storm turned the sky black, the mercury plummeted, and everything beyond New Rowan froze. The snow fell so heavily and quickly it was like a hand wiping the land of every distinguishable feature. In the morning the fields were blanketed by soft-packed snow that sparkled all the way to town.

No one was prepared for snow, most especially the distraught farmers. The sudden deep chill killed livestock as well as crops. In the morning the small frozen bodies of lambs lay shrouded in white all across the hillsides and fields; clusters of sheep, their fleece now suddenly and noticeably yellow against the backdrop of white, moved in and around them, bleating softly. I stared from my bedroom window, disturbed but in awe of the storm's strange beauty.

It was the same night that Mag Delacey died quietly in her sleep as her heart ruptured but continued pumping and spilling her blood throughout the cavity of her body while her husband, John, slept beside her, only awakening when he heard a long final death rattle from her lungs and noticed the blood about her mouth, while the children down the hall, Cait, the youngest, her two sisters and four brothers, and the rest of us in the parish slept in a world of dreams, numb and oblivious to death during the soundless fall of snow covering the land beyond our curtained windows.

In the morning, when I saw Lugh McConnahue, the farmer's laborer, tracking his way across the far field, I dressed quickly and rushed out into the cold bright morning to join him. Snot froze in my nose. My breath whistled high in my chest. Ice crystals sparkled on tree limbs where crows were already gathering. Lugh was kneeling before a lamb, his thin angular frame bent, cords of tight-wound muscle flexed in his shoulders and back. His black shaggy head was flecked with silver frost.

Howya, Lugh, I called. Jaysus, it's cold so.

Lugh looked up, squinting. He had hard drinking eyes, bleached and pale, like I remembered my father's. At times I wondered if I actually remembered Father or had merely created an image of him in my mind and clung to it, and dreamed of him instead. He was in America these last two years working on the construction, and always, it seemed, on the point of return. Lugh's face was wan and pinched. He smiled grimly.

'Tis that. He looked back at the lamb.

Ah, the poor little lambs, I said, leaning forward, resting my hands on my thighs.

Feckin shame, Lugh agreed. Paddy'll be fit to be tied.

He tenderly brushed the snow from the lamb's face. Its brown eyes stared back, and I was waiting for it to blink; it seemed that if you touched the lamb it would still be warm, the fleece still soft, the heart still alive within, and that it might awake. Lugh grasped its rigid hind legs, and in one quick movement hurled it into the back of the lorry with a loud resounding crack of bone against metal.

How many do you think there are? he asked as he reached for another carcass. I looked about the field and up the slopes of the valley, and I thought about Paddy Flaherty's fields that lay beyond the road and on the other side of the hill, all covered in white death.

I shrugged. There's got to be a hundred or more.

Lugh nodded and grimaced. Oh, he'll be on the tear after this all right.

In the pub? I asked and he laughed.

In the pub, on the horses, with the women.

I nodded seriously as if I understood this.

Lugh paused and cracked his back. I had gloves on but my hands were numb.

How's your mammy? he asked.

She's well, I said without ever thinking whether she was or not; she hadn't been up when I left. She'd been sleeping for days it seemed, only rising late at night while Molly and I lay awake in bed, listening.

We grunted together as I helped him swing the next body into the lorry, balancing my short-limbed swing with his large one, my smaller hands wrapped around their narrow legs, my fingers pressing in the narrow spaces between their small bones so that when I squeezed really hard I could hear them splinter and crack. I looked away from their eyes.

It's a terrible thing, Lugh said and I agreed.

I headed back to the house to light the fire, to feed the dog and let it out, and watched from the kitchen window as Flaherty's other laborers arrived and gathered up the small bodies. All through the day the lorry made its slow progress through the fields and up the hills, leaving behind deep black furrows in the white snow, so deep it seemed as if nothing might be able to touch that spot ever again.

The church was filled for Mag's funeral. People who'd come in from the country stretched out the door into the vestibule and then out onto the road. Even as Father O'Brien began, there were coughs and shuffles, stamped feet or the dull slap of Wellingtons on stone as more people pushed into the church. People shook the snow that still lay across the country roads from their feet; their breath smoked the air. The radiators in the church pinged and hissed and shunted water through baseboards. Everything was gurgling and steaming, but if there was warmth it didn't seem to touch a thing.

Everyone looked cold but Cait. Her face was flushed and her eyes wide — not the squint that people had from being pressed in by a chill. Her hair shone dark as the lacquered pews. Each time Father O'Brien looked up, he glared toward the back, and only after a long still silence, in which he craned his neck to the rafters as if he were searching for strength that only the divine could provide him with, did he begin.

Throughout the Mass I looked at her; sometimes she stared at the coffin, at other times she turned and searched the back of the room. She leant close to Aisling, her eldest sister, who wrapped an arm about her. Aisling gestured with her head toward the coffin and whispered. Cait stared at the coffin again, perplexed it seemed, and I knew that she was wondering where her mother was.

After the Final Commendation, John Delacey and his sons came forward, dipped their knees, and hefted the long box atop their shoulders. One of Mag's cousins, a large woman from Roscommon, stood before the altar and began to sing the Ave Maria. Someone opened the doors of the church; the heavy wood resounded as they thumped the walls. Coins fell from pockets as people staggered to their feet; knee rests slammed against pews. The heaters kicked in as the cold rushed down the aisle: wick-smoke of extinguished candles; rustle of clothing; smell of wax and incense and the thick doughy odor of old women.

The coffin passed down the aisle, the pallbearers' feet scraping the tile. John Delacey clean shaven, his face scrubbed so hard it looked like polished stone; Martin holding back tears; and JJ, his head bowed, long, lank hair hanging before his face.

And lastly, Aisling holding Cait's hand. They followed the coffin out into the gray silver day, their heels shattering what was left of the silence, and we followed them. People spread out like a fan against the wrought-iron gates to allow the funeral procession to pass. It was blustery still and a few strakes of windblown snow threw themselves across the road and the distant fields, dashed the top of the coffin so that the pallbearers squinted and bowed their heads.

To our right, down the hill, lay the Barrow and the bridge that crossed over into Rowan. Boats moved sluggishly before the quay. Cars motored back and forth, slow and hesitant over the bridge, and then along the white stretch of waterfront, exhausts smoking the air. Someone had spray painted UP THE PROVOS! BRITS OUT! on the wall by the rusted old railway tracks that ran alongside the black riverbank. In bright red letters three feet tall the words glared at traffic coming into town on the Waterford road. The doors of the hearse slammed closed.

I blessed myself with holy water from the font, then dallied in the vestibule adjusting my scarf and buttoning my anorak. Two men stood by the arch, finishing their cigarettes. They watched the funeral procession moving off down the hill. When the hearse and the cars were gone, they threw their butt-ends to the gravel and ground them into the crushed stone with their boots.

Do you think John knew? one of them said. He was from the town and I couldn't place him although he looked familiar. The other, his wide back to me, shrugged and hacked phlegm. Then I heard my father's name, *McDonagh,* hissed like a curse and I shrank against the stone, moved back into the shadows against the wall.

A'course he knew, sure isn't that why she's in the ground right now instead of off with your man?

Well, there are other reasons for that.

He'd be daft not to know, the whole town knows.

Still.

I expect it will be a cold day in hell before we see *his* face again.

I doubt we would, but sure when he hears about this. . . . The man shook his head again.

I waited in the shadows until I heard their footsteps receding on the road. They were heading down the hill toward the pub, their shoulders hunched against the wind. Across the river, upon the far hill, the funeral procession moved in a staggered, uncertain line up Mary Street. The river a black sheet of glass. The fertilizer factory stacks pumping gray. The last of the snow dropped in soft lumps from tree branches above the sedge, thumping the macadam in an incessant and awkward rhythm, and then slowing as everything froze once more. My hands and feet were numb, my head aching with the cold. I stood and watched as the snow, turning to ice, slowly darkened into pools at the edge of the road.

fter Mag Delacey's funeral, Mother didn't move from her bed for days. It was Thursday and she was supposed to go into Rowan to collect the dole but sent me instead with a letter from Dr. French.

The dole office was in an old building squeezed between derelict tenements on the Bosheen Housing Estate. Across the road St. Bridget's massive spires blocked all sunlight and the dole office was so dark that you had to stand in the dim light squinting; the wooden floors echoed as you stepped across them to the desk, and everything smelled of mildew and dust burning black on the radiators and Dettol disinfectant coming in from the outdoor toilets. When you said your name it resounded off the wood and the stone and narrow walls and splintered desks so that everyone in the room heard.

The last of the snow had melted and rushed through the gutters, flooding the cobbled lanes and tenements in the Old Quay. The clouds looked bright and hard as stamped metal so that you had to squint at them, and there was a coolness in the air that suggested autumn and not spring at all. A fierce wind howled down the narrow streets, pushing empty crisp packets before it, and I was glad for the coat I was wearing.

At nine in the morning it was crowded; people queued down the street. Those that had already gotten their money lounged outside with others, smoking cigarettes or waiting for someone else to be done. The country people nodded at one another, spoke silently, and headed toward the bank or the shops with their money when they were done. Those without cars would ride back into the country on their push-bikes. The townsfolk were raucous and happy. They threw their cigarette butts into the gutter and called to one another from either side of the street as they made their way down to the pubs along the quay. I turned my face toward the wall and hoped I would see no one who might recognize me from school.

Color rose to my cheeks as I looked at the woman behind the desk. *Moira McDonagh,* I whispered and still my voice seemed to carry and echo beyond and around me and I willed myself to stand straight and to look strong and proud, no matter what I felt inside.

Where's your mammy? the woman asked.

She's not well, I said, and slid the paper across the desk to her. This is the doctor's note.

She glanced at the paper, and her mouth puckered. What's the matter with her then?

Heads turned in our direction. It seemed as if talking had stilled. Outside someone hollered and then there was laughter. A wireless somewhere was playing a football match. I shrugged.

You're too young to be in here, she said. Why aren't you in school? Whose son are ye?

Mammy's too ill to come. I'm looking after her.

What's the matter with her? she asked again.

I don't know. What does the letter say?

The woman grunted and made me wait at the far side of the room, against the wall, until she called me.

I've talked to the manager, she said as she handed over the pound notes. She stuck her mouth forward when she said this and pursed her lips, showing her teeth so that *manager* sounded very impressive and official-like.

Can I have me letter? I asked.

She hesitated, looked at the letter in her hands, then stared at me coldly. Wha? Did ye think I'd want to hold on to your silly paper?

She tossed the letter onto the counter and I folded it carefully into my pocket. Will I need to bring it next time? I asked, but she had already turned away and was pointing to me as she spoke with another clerk.

It's all right, a voice whispered at my shoulder, and I turned and there was Lugh grinning. She's a right bitch, that one. Has been since she was a schoolgirl. He put his hand on my shoulder and leant in close. His breath was warm with whiskey. Look at her, Michael. No, go ahead. Look at her and tell me what you see.

He turned my body slightly with his strong hands so that I was looking back at the woman. Now that Lugh was with me she didn't look my way. An old man held himself at the desk with a dirty, muck-encrusted cane. It looked as if he'd come in from the country. She shoved some papers back across the table at him and shook her head. She looked incredibly satisfied. When the old man shuffled from the counter, spittle covered his chin; he looked as if he were drooling but couldn't help himself. His mouth was sunken in on itself, his eyes as small as pips, and he shook. Mrs. Kelly adjusted her hair, compressed it with her palm into a tight bun, then stared off into space with her lips pursed tightly. I suddenly felt sorry for her although I couldn't explain why.

Lugh followed my gaze. Will you look at the puss on her. She's been like that her entire life, do ye understand? Her entire life.

He stood straight and he seemed taller in that small room; he shrugged his shoulders slowly, rolling the muscles. You've always got to hold your head a little higher than them, yeah?

He took a bent hand-rolled cigarette from his shirt pocket and looked at it; it seemed in sad shape but he tightened the roll with a lick and lit it anyway, squinting as he inhaled. He stepped toward the polished wood counter. Howya, Katherine, he said loudly, exhaling a plume of thick blue-gray smoke, and the woman turned.

By God, you're looking fit today. Sure how does Niall keep the men at bay at all? Jaysus woman, you'd tempt a monk in that dress, wha? All the men must be after you.

Like fleas on a dog.

Aye, you have it right there sure enough, Katherine. Ahh, there we are, grand, grand so. The Republic's reward to the people who served her well all these years. Lugh kissed the pound notes, bowed, and, taking my shoulder, led me out into the sunlight.

September 1976

e didn't get to go to the beach often although it was only a short drive away. But Father was home from America and there were all sorts of things he had planned for us. The beach was deserted because it was the end of summer and much too cold to be swimming. We had sandwiches wrapped in wax paper and a large flask of tea. Father bought us pink rock candy from the only shop that was open in the village; I wanted to play the penny arcades but everything was boarded up and closed. Besides me and my father and mother and sister, Molly, I saw only two other people on the beach. An old couple, in blue anoraks, bundled up from the wind and the sea spray, treaded carefully around tide pools in the distance, every once in a while peering and pointing, then holding each other and walking on. It seemed natural to be cold all the time when you were old; mother was cold all the time but I'd never thought of her as being old.

I ran up and down the sand dunes whooping and hollering, sending birds lifting in great flapping crowds. All the way along the beach, one end to the other, I was leading the armies of the West into Ulster. I was Cuchulain defending Ulster from Queen Maeve and the Connaught invaders. I shifted allegiances and heroes and outcomes. I was Queen Maeve and I'd come into Ulster with my men, come for revenge and for the great Brown Bull while the Ulstermen dozed beneath a magic spell of sleep or lay down helpless, crying with women's cramps. What if Cuchulain came too late, what if all of Ulster was destroyed? I was Finn McCool and his son Oisin; I was Caoilte, the fastest man in all Ireland. I swung a great cudgel and crushed the fleeing Fomorians before me. With a sling I drove a rock through the big eye of Balor, turning his eye back in his head so that he stared at his own men and turned them all to stone.

I dove and flopped on the sand, mortally wounded, then back up on my feet cutting great swaths of air with my sword. Gannets shrieked above the cliff tops, echoing my war cries; they rose into the low gray sky and became specks out over the waves before they wheeled back toward their mossy crags.

Mother was sitting up near the rocks with my father and sister, together, sheltered from the wind. Father had been home from the construction in America for a month now, and it seemed as if he might stay. He said all the jobs in America were done. Mother was as content as I had seen her in a long time. She stretched her legs and arched her back toward the sun and looked young and strong again, the way she looked when Molly and I were little, before Father left. She had her sandals off and was curling the sand with her toes. She winced momentarily, a small tight exhale whistling through her clenched teeth. Father looked up. Are you all right? he asked.

She nodded and tried to smile, but her teeth were still clenched. After a moment: I'm fine, just an old muscle ache is all. Father shifted closer to her on the sand, pulled up the bottom of her jumper, and began to massage her. Mother drew her knees up to her chest, dropped her head as Father's strong hands worked her back.

From here I could see the tower of the Knights Templar standing above Ballyhack Harbor and all the colorful boats pressed in against one another as if awaiting a storm. Shearwaters dipped and rolled above the whitecaps, raking the crest and coming up with fish angled silver in their claws.

Mother lifted her face and closed her eyes, a smile playing on her face. The small wireless was tuned to Radio 1, which was counting down the top forty. Telly Savalas was singing "Lovin' Understandin' Man," sounding, I imagined, like a New York drunk rolling in a gutter, and Father laughed.

Is that what it's like then? Mother asked, teasing him — but there was a slight edge to her voice.

He grinned and shook his head. No place like America. That's for sure.

The skin pinched between my mother's eyebrows. She stared at her toes moving through the sand. Her lips pursed and she nodded her head. *No place.* Molly was next to her, chewing on her stick of soft rock, her mouth stained pink as if she'd just been slapped.

Father began fiddling with the lure at the end of an entangled fishing line. The rod's cork base had crumbled; he held it daintily with three fingers, his little finger curled in midair as if he were holding a teacup. Each time he looked up, the tide had receded further. He grunted and worked faster on the lure but it was futile, and he laughed. Jaysus, he said when the water had made the breakwater at the outer edges of the rock scar, everything turning the color of a dirty washcloth.

Finally he threw the rod behind him. And sure I wasn't meant to bring home the supper today, he said. What on earth shall we do? I suppose we could get chips in town, and some battie burgers? He raised his eyebrows questioningly. But I don't know so, sure everyone was counting on me catching some fish. He looked at Molly seriously; I paused halfway up the beach.

Father laughed and pulled Mother close to him. The small bleached skeleton of some unrecognizable thing jutted up from the sand. Mussel shells scratched at the bottoms of my feet. I looked back toward the drying sand, darker where my feet had pressed.

I stood in the pools as the tide receded, the sharp brine of the sea high in my nostrils, the sound of the gannets and shearwaters filling up the sky as my parents kissed.

Molly wrapped up what was left of her rock candy even though the plastic was covered with sand. Father helped Mother up, and then collected the towels and blanket. Mother carried the flask and what was left of the sandwiches in her Dunne's Stores shopping bag. They wiped the sand off each other's backs and made their way up the beach to the car, and I followed them, ignoring the pain in my feet, but by the time I reached them, something had changed. The radio was on and it was announcing that the government had declared a state of emergency following a summer of sectarian violence in the North. Catholics and Protestants were killing one another on the street, in the pubs, and in one another's homes. The latest were ten-month-old Brigeen Dempsey and her brother and sister killed in their home by a petrol bomb.

Mother sat motionless in the front seat, staring straight ahead and crying, and at first I thought it was because of the murders. The sky had turned darker beyond the glass, and low clouds had come in with the waves. I cupped my hands over my feet, squeezed my toes tight; I'd left my socks on the beach.

You know what they've said about you and Mag, she said. You know what I've had to listen to this entire time, me raising two children on my own and not a word or care from you.

This town, this bleedin town, Moira, you know as well as I that they live to spread muck like this. I can't believe you of all people would listen to such rubbish.

Even her own husband believes it.

I can't take this. I can't.

Did you cry when you'd heard she'd died, John? Did you cry in America thinking of her?

For fucksake, Moira!

The sky darkened and the beach lay empty; even the old couple was gone. Wind whipped against the dunes and rain began to fall, hard and fast. The birds retreated to their scraggy nests. I waited for Father to start the car, but he sat in his seat unmoving, his hands on the wheel and his head bowed. The radio crackled and spat. Rain rattled and thrummed upon the roof and Mother was speaking again but sounded far away as if she were trying to see into Father's bedroom in America all those years without us, of pictures that might adorn walls, of clothing in closets and bureaus, and of all the letters she told us she sent him and he never answered: *Did you cry thinking of her, John? Did you cry? Well, did you?*

I sat next to my father at the bar munching on crisps, listening to Uncle Oweny talking about gunrunning during the War of Independence, and of swimming the English Channel from France during World War II with top secret information hidden in a waterproof pouch about his waist, and being shot at by a British submarine that suddenly breached like some great whale off to his right as he paddled into the dark Dover-peaked twilight. And although I knew he had done none of these things, Oweny had a way of making you believe his stories, and I'd missed hearing them since Father had come home. Uncle Brendan was there as well, but he and Oweny had been fighting over the price of a fishing catch they'd split, so I sat between them. Whenever Oweny ordered a pint Brendan raised his pint as well, then winked at me. When the two pints came, Oweny paid. Brendan nodded and, with a scowl, drank the offering, and then a second and a third. Oweny sighed.

The pub was crowded because it was a Thursday night and everyone had gotten the dole and some of the men were talking of the North and of the shootings and bombings and of the murder of young Majella O'Hare by British soldiers, and I was laughing at the expression on Oweny's face when I heard the word *Hoor,* and then a pint glass shattered and bar stools were squealing and Oweny was wrapping an arm around me as tables were overturned and bodies banged against us as they surged toward the door.

Oweny took me by the hand and led me outside. Men were gathered in the road cursing and spitting, and we stood back from them. In their center, spotlighted by the streetlamps, stood my father and Flaherty. I went to go to my father but Oweny held me. Stay by his side, Michael, Brendan said. Your father won't want you out there.

Flaherty was much bigger than Father, but when Father moved I'd never seen anyone move so fast. His sinewy muscled forearms snapped and his large fists worked like sledges as he battered Flaherty into the gutter, and then, once Flaherty rose, his trousers muddied and stuck with a single fluttering crisp packet, Father raised his fists again and drove him all the way across the road into the far ditch. Men tried to call him off but it was no good. One man pleaded, Sure, he didn't mean it, Padraig. It's only the drink talking. Another shouted, Sure, what is Mag Delacey to you, McDonagh? Sure, what effin business is it of yours at all? Go back to America where you belong, sure no one wants you here. But none of it stopped my father, and gradually the crowd became silent.

The lights of the pub spilt out onto the dark road. I could hear a boat blowing its horn down along the quay, and buoys clanging softly, and the sounds of Father's fists working Flaherty's face, and his harsh breathing and then Flaherty's own voice, small and moiling like an animal in terrible pain.

My father stepped back. His large hands hung by his side, his breath steamed through his nostrils. Someone came out of the crowd and he turned on them with his fists raised, but they were rushing to Flaherty, who lay still and quiet in the muck, the bottoms of his boots mottled with shadow and light.

Father reached for me, but I remained still. Give me your hand, he said.

But I could not move.

Michael, he said, and his jaws clenched. Give me your hand.

His eyes were small and bright, his face suffused with blood. I imagined if Flaherty were to stir, Father would be upon him once again. I prayed that Flaherty would not move, that he would stay where he was, and that no one would say a word to my father.

For fucksake, Michael! Give me your hand. I turned and looked to Oweny, who'd let go of me, and then to Brendan. Then Father took my hand and I was aware of blood on his knuckles as he dragged me up the street, his long legs tamping the road like metal bars, and I looked back at the pub and the town and Oweny and Brendan and all the staring faces until they were gone and the only light came from stars glittering dimly atop distant hedgerows.

Spring 1977

Father stood in the scullery with the shotgun in his hand. He jammed shells into the gun breech, his jaw working relentlessly. Blackie howled from the shed, a long and painful sound to hear, and I felt I would be sick. It was twilight and the fields spread out into the bruised evening light — a vast undulation of valleys furrowed by black plow lines stretching farther and farther away for miles.

Even at this late hour men still moved on the slopes, calling to one another as they turned toward home. Harvesters sprayed the drills with seed as tractors growled up the hillsides, their lights bobbing softly. There was the smell of rich earth and the turmoil of crows circling above fresh-turned drills.

Our footsteps crackled on twigs and brush as we climbed through the ditches. The sounds of men and machinery faded. Everything seemed very still and silent. For a moment I thought that perhaps I had made a mistake, that there had been no sheep, and that I had merely imagined Blackie ravaging it. Could I have been wrong? My heart hummed on a thin wire of expectation and fear. Father spat into stagnant ditch water. I smelled rot beneath the undergrowth, and the fetid odor of hog wallow drifting over from Milo Meaney's pigpens.

I had been waiting for Father to return home. Waiting for the light to fade, for the cover of night to come. But the day seemed to prolong itself and the sun made only a slow track across my bedroom wall. It was as if I could hear the sound of the sun roaring in my ears, the explosion of gases on its surface. I listened as Molly traipsed down the hall in her Wellingtons and out to the fields with the slop buckets. Her boots sounded on the cobblestone and then passed the shed. I had not told Mother about the dog attacking the sheep and I'd made no attempt to clean him up; I could not explain why, except, perhaps, that I knew they would find out sooner or later, and when they did, there could be no excuses. Father would check in on the dog when he came home from the foundry; it was one of the first things he did of an evening, and then I would be punished. And although he wasn't the type of man that would strap me — my mother would do that — he had an unpredictable temper that I feared.

The sound of the Angelus and of Lugh cycling into the pub told me it was just after six. The milking pumps from Meaney's farm across the way hummed to life, and one of his men brought the cattle up from grazing, their hooves clacking on the macadam, and then the rattle of Brid Long's Cortina returning from Easter novenas told me it was sometime after seven and then eight. I heard the sound of the telly and Molly listening to *Top of the Pops*.

I dozed and woke to my parents' voices. They seemed to be arguing all the time these days. My cheek was numb from the pillow; nausea tumbled in my stomach.

Come down here, you! Mother shouted, and I treaded the stairs slowly. The telly was off and the house was strangely silent. She was waiting at the bottom and grabbed the sleeve of my jumper, pulling me from the last two steps. The flesh around her eyes was swollen as if she'd been crying; she spat when she spoke.

Why didn't you tell me about the dog? she hissed, and I heard Blackie howling from the shed, his blunt nails scrabbling at its door. Father stared at me; his long shadow reached across the lino.

What have you done with Blackie? I asked.

I've done nothing with that blasted dog. Yet. The bloody fool. Father shouted through the walls as if the dog could hear him, Shut up, would you? For fucksake, shut up!

Why didn't you tell your mother what the dog had done? he asked. Did you think we wouldn't find out?

I was scared.

You've a good mind to be scared, Mother began, but Father silenced her with a look.

Sure, the dog is covered in blood, he said. You didn't even have the sense to clean him up. What kind of fool are you, altogether? What in God's name were you thinking? Were you thinking at all? Did you think that this would just all go away? Jaysus, boy, I thought you had more cop on than that. He shook his head and chewed on his bottom lip. What was he at this time? he asked.

A sheep — a lamb. I shrugged.

Is it dead?

I don't know.

You don't know?

I don't think so, I said.

Where?

Flaherty's.

Ah, Jaysus. Father sat heavily at the table and stared at his large fire-scarred hands. He nodded and scraped his knuckles against his stubbled chin. It would have to be Flaherty's. Just what I feckin need. How in God's name are we going to pay for this? You know the bastard has it in for me as it is.

He stared grim faced into the dusk night beyond. The Sacred Heart glowed red on the mantel above the fireplace.

He'll get this out of me in blood, he muttered.

You lied you lied, Mother said over and over again. She stared at the floor and spoke around the tear-damp handkerchief she had balled against her mouth, and I had the sense that it was not me she was referring to at all, but my father, as she suddenly struck me about the head and I stood there unmoving looking at Father, who remained tight-lipped, his jaw set, ignoring the both of us.

When he and Mother spoke these days all I heard was America, America, America. When he came home after a day slogging at the foundry down in Waterford it was all that was on his mind. He was already there, he had just to leave, and it was with the pending sense of his leaving that things had changed between them — I could not say what it was really, other than a kind of loss from which it seemed they could not recover. Father stared at the Sacred Heart as if it might offer strength, or succor.

You lied you lied you lied —.

For fucksake, that's enough! Will you be quiet! Father shouted and they stared hard at each other, Mother's face red and pinched, her eyes blinking rapidly. Father exhaled slowly and reached out to touch her arm, but she brushed his hand away.

We'll talk about it later, he said, but Mother just glared at him. He turned and stamped into the scullery for his shotgun. Mother held the sleeve of my jumper.

Go on, boy, she said, her face a grimace of disgust, her hand squeezing my arm tightly so that I winced. Go after your father, sure, aren't you and him the same.

Get out of my sight, she spat. America would suit the both of you. Her throat convulsed, and she pushed me from the room.

Michael, Father called, his voice already drifting out into the night so that it was fading before I reached the door and asked, Da? And he said my name again.

It was a beautiful night, and not yet fully dark. The distant town lights shimmered through a ghost mist of soft rain. The animals in the fields and pastures were still. Lilac and hyacinth filled the air.

The gun caught the rising moonlight through the mist, and slivers of moon swam on the barrel. I'd seen Father raise the gun in similar fashion before. We could have been rabbit hunting at midnight; his hair stuck out at angles from his head as if he had just risen from the bed.

Amidst the dew and the mist, the fading, peculiar light offered only fanciful suggestions of what lay beyond. A quilt of starlings thrummed almost soundlessly into the air.

We went up the field in the graying and the silence. Dew slicked the grass. Everything shone. A hare burst from the ditch above us and shot across the purple plumb line of the horizon. There was the hare and the low sky and the horizon and nothing more so that the hare seemed to take forever to pass out of sight. The bottoms of clouds tumbled silver above us. We were still. Father raised the gun and tracked the hare with the barrel's sight until it was gone.

Tadhg Dolan says the rabbits have run wild on Murphy's Flats, I said, imagining Father and me spending the rest of the bright summer nights down on the Flats and him forgiving me everything.

What's Tadhg Dolan doing in Murphy's fields?

Huntin with his da.

Father grunted and waded through a ditch full of rainwater where a fox floated belly-open in the scum. All manner of things had been at it. Maggots wriggled in its blackened viscera and I eyed it cautiously as I crossed.

Da, I called. Da.

Will you come on.

The fox, Da.

It won't bite you, come on.

I climbed the far side, breathless, still imagining us rabbit hunting: the moon high above the Flats, a curlew crying out beyond the bulrushes, old men out on the Nore fishing for eels, their cigarettes burning like sparks of naphtha light, while Father and I hid in the furze. I would hold Father's gun while he poured hot tea from a flask, its pungent steam rising in the warm night as we waited and watched rabbits poking their small, soft heads above the wild grass.

Da, Tadhg and his da go huntin down the Flats every weekend, I said. I'm sure Murphy wouldn't mind if we —.

I'm sure, Father snapped, Murphy'll be huntin the both of them if they're not careful. Now, would you whisht.

He hoisted the gun deliberately as he pushed forward through thicket. I blinked and everything began to lose shape and sound in the forming mist. A wind pushed clouds across the moon, creating movement in the changing light, and I wished that Father would say something. He cleared a sty without slowing; using one hand for balance, he leapt high above the rock. It took me a moment to climb over and then longer to make up the ground that I had lost. Father moved further ahead. I kept an eye on the back of his head. In the damp his hair began to curl, dark ringlets raised like horns.

He paused at the entrance to Flaherty's field and waited for me. I ran to catch up.

When something is hurt like this, in the country, we must kill it, he said. It's the only way. You can't have an animal suffering. Do you understand? And you can't have an animal that you cannot control. That effin dog will have to go.

I looked at him. Sure you'll not hurt Blackie so.

Father remained tight-lipped. He ground his teeth and stared off across the fields.

You'll not hurt Blackie, I said.

A'course I won't hurt the feckin dog! He exhaled. But I don't know how I'll pay Flaherty for this at all. Where is it now?

Just beyond. Along the wall by the ditch.

Jaysus, right behind his bleedin house. I'm surprised the miser didn't hear the racket.

Tall, yet lithe, he snaked easily through the barbed-wire fence into Flaherty's pasture and waited again, holding the barbs apart, as I climbed through. A barb caught my anorak but he unhooked me quickly and I stumbled forward, down from my torn jacket blooming.

The lights of Flaherty's farmhouse shone from the lane. In the courtyard, Flaherty's daughter, Dodi, was singing as she walked the Black Hunter — I recognized her voice — and the Hunter's shod hooves snapped the cobblestone as if it were a snare drum.

Father shifted the gun and cursed. Right behind his bleedin house, he muttered, and shook his head. Sure, this feckin country will be the death of me.

He'll make me pay for this in blood, boyo, in blood, Father said. He stared at me then, and for a moment I thought he might have forgiven me.

What are you crying for? he asked.

I'm not crying, I argued, and wiped at my eyes with the sleeve of my jumper.

It best not be for yourself and that blasted dog. Anything's more deserving than that. The poor sheep should get your tears, or bejesus, a few my way wouldn't hurt either if you're in the mood for crying.

Father spat and his expression darkened. Without speaking we descended the gentle slope of the valley. Trees rose up, their high canopies rustling at their peaks with a gentle wind above, and deeper into the glen the dark, fresh-plowed fields brought the night down, full of crows and other scavengers uprooting the new seed for struggling grubs. The dark patches of earth glinted like scars.

We came across the lamb in the half-light, its white coat stark and shimmering, and Father's face tightened. He stared at it for a moment, still counting all the different ways in which Flaherty could make him pay for the sheep, all the different ways in which he could afford to pay him. He spoke aloud to himself, and the words fell together like a desperate prayer: I can fix his pig sheds, they're in need of work. The gates and posts on the fields down beyond Murphy's need mending. The corrugate on the milking stalls are near rotted away. And I'm sure when the turnips and beets come in I could give him a few days of free labor, but Jaysus, knowin that man, he'll take as much as he can get. He'll want feckin blood. How in God's name will I satisfy him at all? This feckin country makes everyone so bloody miserly. If he'd wait I'd get the money back to him in spades . . . but he won't wait . . . not for me . . . Jaysus.

He placed the barrel of the gun over the head of the lamb, which was still moving, although just slightly, its eyes closed as if asleep. When Father looked at me I knew that I was the one who should be doing this and not him but that he would not make me do it, and I should be glad. Small gasps of air passed through the lamb's parted mouth, its life sliding away in a broken half whistle, and I wanted to ask Father if we could wait and let it die in its own time instead of doing this, or perhaps it wasn't really as bad as he thought and after it rested for a while it would be better, perhaps the vet could fix it yet — and then its head was gone, and I jumped with the gunshot. It took moments to properly hear it coming back off the hills, a wash of sound with blackbirds lifting from the trees it seemed for miles, and nothing left but the bloodied stump of the lamb's neck pooling into the grass.

White bursts of discharge danced before my eyes. Everything shone brightly: the hillocks and paddocks, the high hedgerows, the plowed fields, the hills covered in gorse, and, higher up, the usually dark heather. Father's face, full of checked anger, was bright as burnished tin; he was a negative burnt upon film, shining with brilliant violence, and then his figure, too, receded into darkness.

He raised the gun with the recoil, hand and arm and gun in one quick gleaming movement as if he were shoveling earth. He stared at me coldly as he plucked out the shells and threw them to the ground, a gesture I did not understand.

Flaherty will get his blood later, he said. Then he tramped away, leaving me standing there.

Time came back slowly. Blackbirds settled once more in the trees. Flaherty's dogs barked. The voices of the farmer's laborers echoed on the road, a woman's high laughter amongst them, all seemingly unconcerned by the close gunshot. In the country no one cared about a gunshot fired in a field.

Although there was sound again it all seemed very far away. Lights came on in the farmhouses. A wild hen called from a far thicket. Everything seemed to be narrowing, converging to a single point of light surrounded by a growing darkness at its edges.

Mammy will have the tay on, so, and she'll be mad if it goes cold, I said aloud into the boreen and the empty thicket.

I stared at the spot where the lamb's head had been, and knelt, the dew grass wet on my knees. I touched the body, felt its still warmth. I stroked the wool, the odor of suint rising, the blood beneath my fingers black in the fading light.

There was the sharp-sweet smell of honeysuckle, of fennel, and the scent of pending rain. The air had grown heavy. A dissonant sound like church bells at Mass jarred my senses. I gathered up Father's spent shell casings and placed them in the breast pocket of my anorak.

I imagined my mother and father sitting before the supper, accusing and condemning each other without ever saying the words, and I, smelling the lamb's blood-let on my hands and clothes, my heart still racing like a hare's, felt where Father's gun shells pressed tightly against my chest. Touching my hand there, the image of him still burning bright in my mind, I followed the flattened path his large footsteps had made in the wet grass, to the darkness at the bottom of the field, and through the dusk mist, the lights of our house shimmering beyond.

laherty's Rover was blocking the gate when Molly and I walked the road from school. We stood at the gate and stared toward the house. Oh Jay, she said, you're in for it now.

Will you not come in with me?

I will in me hole. Sure you know Daddy'll be in a right temper. He'll eat the head off anyone who looks at him. Flaherty's probably in there this very minute lording it over him for what your fool dog did to his sheep. You'd best stay out of his way, so.

Molly took jeans from the clothesline and went into the coal shed to change. There was the rattle of Blackie's chain and her voice came through the rotten timbers: Ahhh, Blackie, sure you're a fine little fool, aren't ye, and don't we love you anyway? I shook my head and waited for her to emerge. She sat on the overturned water barrel, bound up her long black hair, and pulled on her Wellingtons. She grinned. I'm off to the river. Shall I check your traps for you?

You're awful funny, aren't you? I swung my satchel at her and she took off running down the field.

I took my time feeding Blackie the dinner scraps that were waiting in a bucket by the back door and made sure he was locked in his shed before I went in. The smell of Flaherty seemed to take up most of the scullery. He was sitting at the kitchen table, wearing Wellingtons he hadn't bothered to wipe at the door. He'd traipsed muck all the way through the carpeted living room. Upstairs I could hear Mother moving about restlessly.

Flaherty was wearing his tweed cap, which probably meant he was on his way to the dog races. He seemed incredibly pleased with himself. As he sipped his tea his face had the look of a squeezed lemon to it.

Father sat quietly in the chair opposite, staring at his cup. He glanced up when I came in.

Howya, Michael, Flaherty said, and I nodded. Me and your daddy were just talking about the bit of work he's going to do for me, after what your dog did to my sheep. Flaherty took a bite out of a biscuit and then dropped it back to the plate. I was glad to see that Father had only put out the digestives for him, not the good Jacobs we normally kept for guests. Flaherty gulped his tea down and slapped his big thighs. Crumbs fell to the floor. He smelled of manure, silage, and stale sweat. He laughed. Ah, that's a grand dog, so. You might think of letting me bring him coursin, seems like he has it in him all right.

I stared through him and pictured Father leveling him back and forth the length of the road.

Well, then, he said, I'd best be off. Flaherty rose and, it seemed, was waiting for my father to do the same. Father tipped off the top of his tea into the saucer and sipped from it slowly. Flaherty stared down at him and frowned.

So, are we right then? Flaherty asked.

We are, Father said.

Tomorrow evening at six.

As soon as I get in from the foundry.

Flaherty grinned at the thought of it: my father slogging in the furnaces all day long only to come home and slog for him. Do ye like pigs? Flaherty asked with his lemon face.

Father remained quiet. I like pigs, I said, and my father exhaled deeply.

Flaherty laughed. Grand, so. Perhaps you can help your father.

After, I watched his car from the window. Rain misted the glass, shimmered on the road. A skein of geese tossed overhead, white through the swirling gray. When Flaherty was gone I said, Da, I'm sorry.

Father sighed behind me. He was watching the geese pass as well. He placed a hand on my shoulder and squeezed softly. He held his hand there for a long time as if he didn't have the energy to move. Ah, sure, it's done now, he said. It's no harm. I'll give him what he wants and be done with it. But there didn't seem to be a lot of conviction to his words. You have to pick your battles, son, he said. He laughed bitterly and shook his head. But I've never been much good at it.

He passed back through the living room, and when he paused, I knew he was staring at the muck Flaherty had tracked in. He seemed to be standing in one spot for a long time, then I heard him rummaging in the coal closet for the Hoover. I followed him into the living room. He was fumbling at the coils and the cord and suddenly he threw the vacuum to the floor; plastic splintered and cracked. For fucksake! he shouted. When he ran his hand through his thick hair, it was trembling. Da, I said and touched him gently on the shoulder. I squeezed softly as he had done. He stared at me, his eyes red-rimmed and pale, the blue washed from them.

Sudden movement beyond his right shoulder caught the edge of my eye. Through the window, a bird was flickering in the hedgerow. Thrashing its wings, it moved from shadow to sunlight like water flashing down a mountain. I saw that it was caught, a piece of glinting snare wire around its bloody claw.

I'll do this, I said. Don't mind it.

Father pursed his bottom lip, looked down at the muck, and, after a moment, nodded. His footsteps were slow and measured on the stairs and then they were above me in the bedroom. I heard him talking with Mother quietly. I turned on the Hoover and began grinding Flaherty's dirt out of the carpet.

After my dog ravaged Flaherty's lamb, Father was sullen. He had no patience for the dog or, it seemed, for me. He was tired all the time now. On weekends when he should have been enjoying his rest from the foundry, he was working for Flaherty to pay off the damages, and Father had been right when he said Flaherty would make him pay for it in blood. It wasn't just the loss of the lamb, Flaherty claimed, but trespass, and destruction of property that he'd charge Father with if he didn't satisfy his demands. I imagined Flaherty took almost as much satisfaction in watching Father labor silently for him as he would had he kicked his teeth in. This was for all the blows he would never strike at my father, and for all the pain he could never make him feel.

But finally, it was the last of the month and almost the end of Father's indenture to him. The day had darkened quickly, and as dusk turned, the sky burnt purple with storm clouds and the rains began. The dog dozed before the fire; the small room was crowded with the smell of him and of the cabbage my mother was boiling for dinner. When Father came in from the foundry, his clothes were drenched. He'd walked all the way from town in the rain and was in bad form. And although he didn't say it, I could also tell he'd been in Sullivan's on the quay.

No one had stopped to offer him a lift although he said countless cars from the country had passed him, including Flaherty's — that bastard. He swore they went out of their way to be mean and miserly. Great satisfaction they got from their little acts of spite. He could only hope they'd get theirs in one form or another.

He threw his overalls on the clothes rack and pulled the rack before the fire. He nudged at Blackie with his toe, but Blackie wouldn't budge. Effin move, will you? he growled, but the dog just rolled onto his back, baring his pale belly at him.

Jaysus, my father said, will you move! He put his boot into Blackie's rib cage and I flinched. The dog yelped and jumped to his feet. He eyed Father warily, circled about him, and then came to rest beside the sofa. He lay alert for a time and I patted him until he placed his head upon his paws and fell asleep. All the while Father continued cursing under his breath.

On Father's last day at Flaherty's, we all sat at the kitchen table waiting for him until twilight when the skies darkened and it began to rain again. Mother lit the lamp and we watched the high fields flatten and sway and finally I rose and went down the road in the rain and the wind moaning through the trees to greet him.

Father stood just outside Flaherty's closed gate, staring into the dusky shadows beyond, but looked up when he heard my footsteps on the road. I smelled a Woodbine, the scent of it came warmly through the rain, and when I approached I saw Flaherty standing on the other side of the gate beneath the shelter of yew trees, the glowing tip of his cigarette a spark in the dusk light as he drew on it.

Father stood with his feet planted wide apart, large work boots covered in muck — a black figure with the rain and the wind whipping at his collar, rippling the waist of his foundry work shirt with the embroidered name patch on its chest. Something had been said between the two of them, and Flaherty was smiling.

Father's face was rigid and set like stone. I feared a fight happening again, and I came up to father and held tight to his arm. His forearm was taut and wired with veins. He looked down at me, and though his mouth was set and grim, he squeezed my hand tightly. And then he reassured me with a brief smile that did not touch his eyes.

We're done here. Michael, let's go home.

Father turned away from the gate and began to walk slowly up the lane, his hand hard but reassuring in mine. I looked up at the rain slanting down over his brow and sharpening his already hawkish nose. His powerful jaws were clenched and they seemed to stand out terribly in the dimming light.

Flaherty called after us. You're lucky, Padraig. You're lucky I'm a forgiving man else you would have been in jail a long time ago and not just mucking up pig shit. After everything else, think of the boy, Padraig, and what else he'd have to be proud of.

The rain came down faster and harder and my father pulled up his collar and bundled me against his side. He lifted me with a tremendous strength I remembered from when I was a child; I was much too big for it now, yet he did it anyway. He staggered, half ran up the lane until Flaherty's voice fell away behind us. Father's heart thumped loudly as I banged against his chest and ribs, and his feet hammered the lane. He held me tighter, so tight the rain could not touch me, so tight I could hear nothing at all, and still in that impenetrable space, I could smell Father's fear.

eeks passed and, no longer indebted to Flaherty, Father's mood improved. The killing of Flaherty's sheep seemed a thing of the past. He even began to take Blackie rabbit hunting in the evenings as Molly and I did our homework at the kitchen table, and when Blackie didn't take to it, Father seemed strangely disappointed that there was nothing to bond him to the dog.

It was dark and a frost had descended upon the fields when they came in from their last hunt. I'd just turned the telly off and the clock ticked quietly over the mantel. Mother had been crying again and had gone to bed early; Molly stayed up with me watching *The Late Late Show* with Gay Byrne, and then after heating water for a hot water bottle, she, too, had gone to bed, dipping her hand in the font in the hall and blessing herself before climbing the stairs.

Do you still pray, Molly? I asked. The thought had come to me as I watched her.

Sometimes, y'know?

I nodded.

Yourself?

She stood on the first step, holding the banister. It was dark at the end of the hall, and darker still above the stairs, and in that dark space her nightdress shimmered. There was a draft coming in the back door and I imagined she must be cold, and yet still she waited. I couldn't make out her face, and turned back to the telly. Sometimes, I said. Sometimes I do as well.

Father looked cold, and I helped him with his damp Wellingtons. He took off his wool hat, and his normally bushy hair lay flat against his head. The thin legs of rabbits stuck from his gunnysack.

He handed me the gun as he rolled off his socks. What are you doing up? he asked.

It's Saturday, I said.

Oh aye, so it is. He seemed surprised. It's quare strange, all my days seem to be running together.

How was Blackie? I asked.

Father shook his head but smiled. Feckin useless, he said.

He put away the gun, hung three gutted carcasses in the scullery by the back door, and propped a metal drip bucket beneath them. From his pack he took a flask of tea laced with whiskey. Normally he would have cleaned the gun first. The dog followed him into the living room where a fire blazed in the grate, dropped himself before it, and closed his eyes. Father sat on the sofa and, as he sipped from his flask, stared at the dog.

Perhaps you'll do better with the pheasants, he suggested aloud, and Blackie lifted his ears with the sound. Father stretched his back, then twisted the cup onto the flask.

Ah, sure, you're a good dog, aren't you? he said. A good dog. He reached forward and stroked Blackie gently along his back, and Blackie stretched beneath the touch. I turned the telly back on, and Father put his feet up and lay back. Some time passed, and both dog and Father fell asleep. As the hours turned, I threw more coal on the fire, switched the telly off, and listened to the both of them snoring softly and pleasantly in the dark. Then, beneath that, came the sound of Mother moving endlessly across the floors above.

I traced her footsteps back and forth across the ceiling, back and forth in wider and then smaller circles and then there was silence as if she had finally become tired, as if she might have cried herself asleep. But as sleep overcame me her footsteps began again, faster and madder than ever.

October 1977

t was the end of the potato picking and farmers were looking for help bringing the turnips in. Yet when Molly and I
saw Flaherty's Rover parked outside our gate, I knew it was not a
good sign. Molly exhaled. Jay, he can't want any more from Daddy,
can he? What's it about this time?

He was at the kitchen table with Father again. Blackie lay quietly
on the floor before them. I saw that Flaherty was drinking tea and
that Father had the digestive biscuits out. Flaherty was wearing his
Wellingtons; once more, there was mud tracked all the way to the
kitchen. Flaherty eyed me as Molly and I hung our satchels in the
scullery.

Howya Michael, Howya Molly, Flaherty said.

Hello, Mr. Flaherty, Molly said. Blackie's tail thumped the floor
and I knelt beside him so that he would not rise and cause a commo-
tion.

How's the dog? he asked, and I saw Father's face tighten.

He's brilliant, I said.

Fine dog. Did you train it yourself? He smiled but I saw no
humor to it; he was enjoying himself. I was just telling your daddy
the difference between dogs and men, so I was. Of course he hears
me telling it to him all the time while he's working with me pigs, but
sometimes I have to remind him. Do you know what it is, Michael?

The difference between dogs and men? Father cleared his throat loudly and Flaherty looked back at him.

Well, then, Flaherty said. He put back his tea and rubbed his hands together. I'd best be on my way.

No rest for the wicked, Father said.

No rest, Flaherty agreed. We could always use another hand over at the yards if you're interested.

Father nodded, and I could tell he was thinking, But will you pay me, you bastard?

I'll think about it, he said.

Do that.

Flaherty rose from the table and gestured with his head as I patted Blackie.

Your daddy suggested that dog might have coursin blood in him, wha? He grinned. I'm always lookin for a dog that can go the mile.

He's no coursin dog, I said, and my father looked at me sharply.

You never know, you never know, but sure, you might consider it. Flaherty paused as if he were about to say something further, then nodded to himself and went out the door.

When he was gone I turned to Father. What was that about? I asked.

Father shook his head. Ah, it was nothing, Michael. Just the end of it, that's all. The bloody end of it.

A week later when Molly and I rode our bikes up from school, we saw Uncle Oweny's Morris Minor pulled into the ditch beyond our gate. It lay concealed beneath the overhanging hedgerows, its engine ticking over as it cooled. White petals from the cherry blossom trees had fallen across the hood and scattered the gun-gray metal, giving it a certain sense of sanctity.

We leant our bikes against the wall and I made for the gate. As we came down the gravel, Father and Oweny were leaving the house with Blackie. There was a sudden tightness in my chest and I ran to them. Not my dog! I shouted. Not my dog. I'll pay for what he did, I will, I swear — please.

I lunged toward the leash but Oweny held it tight.

Now, now, Michael. He squeezed my shoulder with his left hand; his arm was locked at the elbow and he would let me no closer to Blackie. It's for the best, he said. Your father is right about this.

I glared at Father and he looked at me for a moment before speaking to Molly. Go into the house and tell your mother to put the supper on the table.

But, Da —.

We'll be right in, so. Go on.

Molly slung her satchel angrily over her shoulder and stomped down the gravel. At the door she looked back to make sure I was okay and then entered the house.

I knelt and wrapped my arms about Blackie's chest and hugged him tight. He licked at my face and then squirmed and I let him go. Oweny gave the leash a tug, and although Blackie was not used to a leash, had never been on one, he obediently followed Uncle Oweny up the gravel, to the car.

The sun was setting above the hedgerows and the soft light of twilight forming; Blackie seemed eager to go off across the fields, as he had with my father all the last fortnight. If Oweny had his gun, it would have been the perfect time for the two of them to go rabbit hunting, before the light faded altogether. The road before them shimmered slick and shiny from an early rain.

Oweny opened the driver's door, and then looked back before he climbed in. Michael, he called, it's better this way. Blackie's going to a better place. Trust me, your father is right. This is the only way the dog can live, otherwise he'd have to be shot. Oweny settled into the car and then they drove away, off down the country road, the old Morris bottoming out in the potholed macadam and shuddering as Oweny shifted gears.

I leant against the gate stone. Father stared after the car. I expected a look of satisfaction upon his face but there was none. Instead, he seemed very tired.

Blackie was my dog, I said. You had no right. You didn't even tell me.

Sure, it's done now, the damage is done. The dog had to go, I wasn't going to argue with you about it. Flaherty wouldn't have it any other way, Michael. I'm sorry, but I'm bleedin sick of the whole affair. It's over, it's done, Flaherty has got his blood.

I hate you, I said but there wasn't much feeling to it.

Sure, doesn't everyone.

The car reached the bend of the road, turned, and was gone, but Father continued to stare nonetheless. I could hear it still, whining down the Rowan road.

Father sighed and ran a hand through his thick hair. Your mother will have the tea on, he said. You'd best go and wash up. He looked at me for a response, but I continued to lean my head on the stone. I sensed him near me, and then a hand was on my shoulder. I wanted to strike his hand away, but instead I turned from the wall, and he pulled me against him. He bent and rested his head atop mine as I shook.

It's done now, Michael, he said. He patted me and stepped back. His own eyes were red. I know you hate me, he said, and I looked at him. His eyes were open and waiting and expectant.

When are you leaving for America? I asked.

He inhaled deeply, turned his head as if he had just been slapped. Without another word, he headed to the house.

I stared at the fields, full and thick and in need of threshing. I tried to trace the distant roads Oweny would take home, the hills the car would sputter on, the glens where it would become cooler, the tractors and cows that would block his way as he turned the sharp bends and spirals. Once he crossed the Rowan bridge, the river would be on their right, and then, when they reached Oweny's, it would curl before them. Blackie would smell the river as it rose and fell and, perhaps, because he'd be so near to it, he'd even smell the sea.

A wind lifted at the undersides of the hedgerows. The sky was darkening. The sound of the Angelus came from the house, and all across the country everything seemed stilled by it. Lugh would soon be coming up the road on his old push-bike, and Flaherty's fool dogs would begin their baying. I headed in for the supper.

he foundry closed at the end of November and Father was made redundant. His boots remained muck encrusted in the scullery. Not even rabbit hunting interested him anymore. His gun rested on its hooks over the mantel and his clean work shirts remained in the hot press. He sat before the fire watching the flames, and in the evenings he'd put the telly on once RTÉ broadcasting had begun.

My mother's words sounded around the house with the cadence of a hammer striking: *I won't go back to it, Padraig, I won't. You promised that you wouldn't let it happen, you promised me. I won't have this town laughing at us any more than they already have. You won't put us on the dole again.* Only once did Father say something back to her — he told her to trust him, even though she'd never trusted him, to just feckin trust him now! — and then he said no more, and he stopped listening. Instead, he simply left.

He wandered off before dawn each morning and returned long after midnight, when I know he thought we were all sleeping. Some mornings there would be money on the kitchen table, rolled-up five-pound notes, and I knew he'd been working as farmer's laborer, and I wondered how far he'd traveled from Rowan. Other mornings there would be nothing, perhaps a soiled work shirt hung over the back of a chair, and then I knew he was drinking again.

It was Thursday and Mother always went into Rowan on Thursdays to get her medicine, but she wasn't able to get out of bed and Father seemed not to notice that she was ill, that there was no food in the house, and that there hadn't been for days. I waited until evening so that the dole queue that normally stretched up Mary Street was gone and the town seemed empty and still.

In the chemist, Prendergast smiled kindly at me when he handed me Mother's prescription; I was thankful for that, for the kindness he always showed. In the butcher's, Mrs. Walsh and Mrs. Kent were holding their shopping bags and talking about the weather or some such. I knew Mrs. Walsh's son, Liam, and I didn't like him much. They looked at me when I came in as if I were a bad cut of meat and then went back to their conversation. I handed Mother's list to Bolger, the butcher, and waited.

The women's voices reminded me of the way people prayed at Mass — there was something conspiratorial as well as reverent in their voices, as if what they were doing should be done in the dark. Every so often they glanced in my direction and their mouths made silent contortions, their tongues seemed to cut the air. I focused on the sound of the meat cutter, the blade spinning as Bolger drew it back and forth. I smelled the fresh-killed meat, the hanging carcasses, the polished and washed tiles, sawdust on the floor.

Smoke churned from the roofs of small terraced cottages. The lads of the Bosheen who usually sent me home by throwing stones at my back or trying to knock me from my bike were all in at their suppers. Not even a dog barking.

The hedgerows rose up; water gurgled in the fosse. I climbed the hill with my bike past empty, crumbling row houses and the church where the road began narrowing into the country, and that is when I saw Father in the graveyard off to my right.

I leant my bike against the stone wall and watched from the stile. He moved amongst the stones, pausing as he read the words here and there or touching another gently and then moving on. I thought of approaching him although I didn't know what I might say. Finally, he stopped and blessed himself. He began to trace the words on a stone, then knelt and lay his head against it and I realized he must be drunk.

He would come staggering into the house tonight, and in the morning he'd be off before dawn again. I thought of Mother sick and at home in the bed and in need of her medication. Quickly, I pulled my bike from the wall and pushed off on the pedals. At the top of the hill I glanced back: smoke rising over the Housing Estate, the graveyard stretching green and uncut down to the black Barrow, white mist boiling over the fields, and Father looking small and fragile and scared, bowed at Mag Delacey's grave.

We did not see Father to the airport; we did not even say good-bye. He left in the dark and we woke in the dark, sensing he was gone and already missing him. The fire had been lit but the house was cold and full of shadows. Buttered toast lay in the center of the kitchen table and a pot of tea was steaming on the grill. The smell of him remained as if he were still in the house somewhere and we had only to search him out. I brought in one of his old, torn donkey jackets from the shed and placed it over me as we sat in the kitchen; as it grew warm the smell of him rose off it. Molly and I cried as we chewed on the toast.

I pulled the shoebox of family pictures from behind the linen closet and Molly and I spread them out on the table and looked at them silently. The tea went cold and the toast turned hard. I put more coal on the fire and brewed another pot. Our chairs scraped the cold cement as we pulled closer to look at the pictures, as if it were important that we shared the same glimpses of him, and of him with us.

Mother padded silently into the kitchen. She clawed at her hair and smiled. Ahhh, the old pictures, she said, and nodded. She came behind the chairs and wrapped her arms about us, then laid her head upon our shoulders and stared at the photographs. After a moment she squeezed us hard. Did I ever tell you two I knew you were *puckawns* from the first minute I set eyes on ye? she said. Did I not ever tell you that? My wee *puckawns*.

The clock ticked above the mantel and I opened the curtains; gray light was coming over the fields from the east. Malone's dairy lorry was parked up the far hill at the Three Mile Cross, its head-lights the only thing on the narrow black bend of the road. Black-birds lifted from the trees as Malone moved farther down the valley, his lights flickering through gates in the high hedgerow. Soon Father would be at Shannon and then he would be on the plane for Amer-ica and thoughts of us would be gone from him.

Why do you think he left, Mammy? Molly asked. She was look-ing at a picture of him cradling the both of us, Molly and I wrapped in matching red blankets, one in each arm, on the day she'd been released from the hospital in Wexford. Molly had been in an incuba-tor for two weeks. Mother had said that we were both so small he was scared to hold us in case he dropped us. I thought of how soft our bones must have been, like the lambs that froze in the spring-time, and how he did not look scared at all.

He didn't leave, I said. He went to find work and when he makes the money he'll send for us, so he will.

What if he can't find work, so? Molly's face was pinched and pale, her eyes wide and dark.

Don't be daft, Mother said and wiped at her eyes. It's America.

I opened the donkey jacket and pulled my left arm out of the large sleeve and held it open. Molly squeezed in next to me and placed her arm in. Mother pulled the jacket tight about the both of us so that it covered us with the shape and the smell of him and then she poured the tea. I imagined his plane climbing through the rain over the Atlantic and the light falling away in the darkness, and I knew that if he just leant back to catch a last glimpse of the land and of everything he was leaving behind then he would return to us, sure he would have to.

the banshee

Christmas came and went but it didn't mean much without Father. Mother stopped going to church of a Sunday. Instead she walked the fields or the glen or made her way down to the river at dusk, or, if she'd made the tea, she'd wait until after twilight, when mist fell upon the low pasture, and wander the chary-lit fields in her nightgown.

Our mother was not right, and we knew it. Something was wrong and it was more than just Father leaving. After all, he'd left before. She began to cry, at night when we were supposed to be sleeping, her sobs sounded softly in the hall, the stairwell, on the old wood and stone. And in the morning she would say nothing of it to us, and we were too scared to ask.

In the evenings, after the Angelus, Mother lowered the flame on the paraffin lamps so that the fire was the only light in the room. The cats twitched in their sleep. And I'd watch the taut lines gradually ease from Mother's face as she slumbered. In an hour or so she'd wake and head out into the fields. The one time I'd pressed her, asked her where she was going and why, she'd looked at me as if I were mad. I have to get out of this house, she said. Do you not understand that?

My sister and I drank our tea, chewed quietly on our biscuits, and when the fire died down I placed more coal upon it. Together, we watched over our mother as if something at any moment might steal the breath from between her parted lips, and we waited, as if by being there, we could prevent it.

March 1978

The clouds raced toward Rowan and I could see the twinkling lights of town as the sky darkened. I sat on the wall outside the scullery, waiting with Mother's shopping list for Pat Malone's dairy lorry crumpled in my pocket. Smoke curled up from the chimney and seemed to tether the gloom above us. The first drops of rain pattered against the sheets on the clothesline.

Culleton's old tractor was climbing the rise of his fields and I immersed myself in its sound. I did not hear Mother until she was pulling the sheets from the line, her white hands working like claws. When she spoke her voice trembled through the rain.

Desperate it is, they can't even get off their arses to bring the washing in from the rain. Soaked it is, soaked, and your man sitting on the wall staring at it like a feckin eejit. Sure that's all right, Mammy will do it, Mammy has nothin better to do, of course not, sure, Mammy will cook me dinner, Mammy will wash me clothes, Mammy will sew me jumpers, Mammy will wipe your feckin arse for you, too! Mary, Mother of God, grant me patience. She shook her head frantically. I don't know, I just don't know so, Lord Jesus, I don't.

Her eyes were swollen and red. Her cheeks streaked from where she had wiped at them roughly. I knew the word *sorry* carried little weight with her, would most likely send her into another rage, and besides, these days, I no longer knew what I was guilty of and supposed to be sorry for.

Mud spattered the bottom of the white sheets as she struggled to hold them; clothespins fell to the ground. She began crying again.

I rose from the wall to help, but when I reached for the sheets she yanked them from my hands and glared at me. Her tears had stopped. This is how she had looked at my father before he left.

I stared at water pooling in the muck. I'll go up the road and wait for Pat, I said, but did not move.

Aye, you do that, Mother spat. I looked up as she struggled into the house, the white washing falling down around her.

I went up the road and waited in the rain. For shelter, I stood in the ditch beneath the thick hedgerows. I shivered and listened as cows moved heavily through the fields. Finally, in the distance, I could see the lights of the lorry on the far hill as it threaded its way from stops at the Three Mile Cross. I imagined Pat Malone placing his deliveries, for the Culletons, old Mrs. Molloy, and the Walshes, in their roadside boxes. The thought made my stomach sick with hunger. I stamped my feet to keep warm. The fields were flattened and the sedge dark. The odor of coal smoke hung in the air, thick and weighted by rain.

The lights of the lorry came around the bend, its motor muted by the wind, and I stepped out into the road. As he came to a stop Pat rolled his window down. He sat high in the lorry with the motor running and his wipers ticking loudly back and forth, spraying water down upon me.

Howya, Pat, awful morning, I said, and he said, It is, Michael, it is. I stepped on the lorry's running board and reached up to him with my mother's list. He shook his head.

I'm sorry, Michael, but your mother is in arrears with me. She hasn't paid for the last two months. I told her last time she could have no more credit until she paid up.

I stared, my mouth agape. I wiped rain from my eyes.

I'm sorry, Pat said, I can't. He rattled the gear stick and jammed the lorry into gear. I stepped off the running board. The lorry lurched as Pat eased out the clutch and then it pulled away, its exhaust belching oil-smoke, its black tires flinging wet muck back at me. In a mist of diesel, I watched it clamber up the hill toward Listerlin. The macadam beneath my feet felt unsteady; my mother's list dissolved into small wet ribbons in my hands.

I looked up the road toward the Three Mile Cross and thought of the milk and eggs and rashers and sausages and bread left in the tin boxes in the ditch. The rain fell harder as I crossed the fields. I slipped on rocks as I traversed the swollen burn, and the grass I clutched at was thick and full, like a mossy head of hair, in my hands. A lone sheep bleated mournfully amongst the rocky sedge. I wiped the muck on my trousers.

I thought of old Mrs. Molloy, who had the shingles and whose brothers had been killed during the War of Independence. When I was younger and Lugh went on the bottle, I'd often led her four thin-shanked cows up from their grazing down by the Flats and she'd always invited me in. She longed for company but no one ever visited her. We'd sit by her smoky fire with a mug of tea and some braic. The inside of her house was black with soot and smelled like a dung heap. I felt bad that there was no one to look after her, and I felt guilty for thinking so much about the smell of her. Gradually, I stopped herding her cows and left it to Lugh, whether he was drunk or not. I stopped visiting, too, and the longer I stayed away the more my shame grew and prevented me from returning at all. The rain was lashing the slate roof of her house now, and in the graying, I could not tell if she had a fire going, but I hoped she had.

I climbed over the stone stile and searched the ditch. The Culletons and Walshes all had big lads working down in Waterford; they could afford what I would take. I watched the road for cars as I rifled through the boxes. I stuffed a loaf of bread, a pint of milk, and six individual eggs into my jacket; there were no rashers or sausages or black-and-white pudding. When I climbed the stile I looked back down the hill the way I had come and saw our house. Blackbirds rose from the tree line. Flaherty's hounds had finally woken. Smoke curled from our chimney, and I moved slowly; everything was becoming silent again, and in that numbing silence, our house offered no suggestion of warmth.

Mother was folding the washing in the kitchen. She had the scrubbing brush out and there was soapy water in the sink. The clothing that had fallen and been washed again was stretched across the clothes rack to dry.

I set the milk and bread on the kitchen table. The room was warm and dimly lit. Mother had yet to turn on the lights and I assumed her eyes were bothering her again.

Mother of God, she said, you're drowned to the skin. Quick, get out of those wet clothes. She reached for the sleeves of my jacket and began to pull it off me.

She glanced at the table as she huffed with the exertion of removing my jacket. Where's the rashers, and the black-and-white pudding? she asked.

I wrung the water from my jumper and hung it before the fire. Pat said he was out. He'll get us tomorrow.

Mother placed a mug of tea on the table before me and grunted. A fine lot of good that does us today.

I nodded.

She stretched the jacket upon the rack. Slowly, she pulled the eggs from the jacket pockets and turned with them in her hands. One was cracked.

What's this?

I looked at her and shrugged.

She held the egg up as if I might deny its existence. Pat didn't give you eggs like this, she said. Where did you get it?

Pat wouldn't give us anything, so I went up to the Three Mile Cross.

You stole these eggs, and this bread, and this milk?

I didn't respond, there was nothing to say, and then she slapped me, once, hard across the face. And I didn't move, not even when she slapped me a second time. She raised her hand again, and that's when I shouted, It was you that lied, and that's been lyin! Pat Malone said he told you you had no more credit with him until you paid him the two months' worth you owe. Did you forget that? Did that just slip your mind? And why haven't you paid him? I know Da's been sending you money. What have you been doing with it? Or are you planning on leaving as well?

There's been no money. Your father's sent nothing.

Of course he has, I know he has —.

There's nothing.

He must have sent you something.

I'm telling you there's nothing! Your father has sent no money since he's been gone. She laughed weakly, bitterly. Three months and not an effin penny. Nothing. What in God's name does he think I can feed you on? Ah, sure, I guess he's not put a lot of thought into that.

She sighed. I'm sure the whole town knows. Oh, and they'll have a grand old time of it when I sign up for the dole and the child allowance. Moira McDonagh this and Moira McDonagh that — "The poor bitch! It serves her right, her husband's left her and now she can't even feed her children" — and they call themselves Christians, all of them bloody hypocrites.

She turned and threw the cracked egg into the basin, where it rattled against the metal. She leant against the countertop with her back to me and lowered her head. I wished he'd taken you with him, she said. Oh God, do I wish it. Every single day looking at you reminds me of him.

old damp smell of ashes in the black hearth. Rain on the air. A wind sighing down the chimney, and Mother silent in her bedroom again. Molly was at the sink washing dishes, her sleeves rolled up, hands pink from the scalding water. I watched her features shimmering in the glass of the window; every so often she blew hair from her face. Beyond the angle of her flushed cheeks, gray fields bent, flattened by the wind.

Is she all right? I asked.

Molly held her forearm across her brow and sighed. I don't know, she said. She wouldn't eat this morning.

What's the matter with her?

Jaysus, sure how should I know?

I went out to the coal shed but there was no coal, only the cat and her kittens, who looked up sleepily from their warm tea chest of straw in the corner, the littlest ones mewling in their sleep, as wind whistled through the rotting timbers.

On the second day Mother still refused her food, and then again on the third. The following morning, before breakfast, I walked the fields and found a small tree that had been felled by the storm. I went back to the house for the axe, cut the tree into logs, and brought back as much wood as I could carry. It was wet but I thought it might still burn. The sun was glinting on the wet fields but a chill was in the air. As I'd worked, my body had warmed and I'd forgotten the cold, but all the way home I shivered and cursed that I'd forgotten to bring my anorak.

In the kitchen Molly was sitting at the table alone. Mother's breakfast was under the grill warming. It's no good, Molly said. She won't eat it.

Jay, did you try?

Molly exhaled and pursed her lips. Do I look like a jackeen? A'course I tried, aren't I just saying she won't eat it?

I began to stack the wood by the cooker. Molly was still staring at me. I looked up.

She puked as well, she said. It's all over the floor.

My aunt Una said that my mother had broken a *geis*, and that is why bad things were always happening to her. First with our father leaving six months before, and now with her sickness. A *geis*, she said, was a magical prohibition placed upon you, and you should never never break it. Once broken it was like a weapon, a bag of arrows cast at you but that might do injury to another if evoked. My uncle Oweny said it was rubbish. While he might have believed in lots of things, he did not believe for a moment in a *geis*. And Uncle Brendan seemed to agree. He sat at the kitchen table, shaking his dark head at his sister. For fucksake, Una, he kept swearing. For fucksake!

Whatever a *geis* might be, it seemed tragic, as tragic as the tale of the children of Lir — Aodh, Fionnghuala, Fiachra, and Conn — who we learnt at school had been transformed into swans by their jealous stepmother, Aoife. They were beautiful, but they were sad because they could never hug their father again, nor could they hug one another although they loved one another very much. The curse lasted for nine hundred years and in all that time their love was so great that they never parted. When one grew sick the others sheltered him with their feathers and kept him warm. When the curse was lifted they died and went to Heaven. But my aunt didn't talk about any of that; perhaps the thought of my mother dying and going to Heaven bothered her too much.

If Mother was anything, she was a swan, she was that beautiful, and if she was cursed, then it was to be beautiful like the children of Lir. But I considered why someone would place a curse upon her and what she might have done to break it. Whenever my uncle drove Mother to the doctor's up the country and Molly and I had to stay with my aunt Una, I worried. Each time my aunt recited her story over dinner, I was sure that it must be true; it seemed our mother was going to the doctor more and more frequently, yet she seemed less and less well.

It was June and the sky was almost cloudless. They were making the trip up the country again and Oweny held me at the car, his large hands firm on my shoulders. Mother sat in the front seat, bundled with blankets, but it was not cold. When she saw me staring, she smiled and waved good-bye; she'd lost weight and looked pale. I looked back to my uncle and asked him, Uncle Oweny, why does Auntie Una keep saying Mammy has broken a *geis?*

Uncle Brendan, who'd been circling the gravel and absently kicking stones, looked up. That effin bloody woman! He turned his back and continued cursing.

Oweny's grip grew tighter and he sighed. Is she telling you that nonsense again? Don't mind your aunt Una. She's a cracked one.

And for a time, that seemed to be the end of that. But in the country, ghosts, spirits, and faeries could take hold of one at any time. One always had to be aware walking the long unlit road from the town, or in the winter, after leading the cows to pasture after milking, of the Host who would at any moment take unwitting souls for their own. All they had to do was call to you, and if you listened — just once — you were gone. I convinced myself that my uncle was right, and perhaps that is why it came as such a shock to all of us, even to Aunt Una, when my uncle, pale and shaken, returned home alone.

unt Una stayed with us while our mother visited with the doctor, and at times Oweny and Brendan would stop in with food or news. Oweny made it sound like a holiday, like going to Butlins. Your mammy needs a rest, he said. Sure she's dead tired, has been run off her feet with the two of you and getting the house and the field in order.

He seemed more stern than normal, as if he felt he had to be, but we saw that it was only a guise for the tenderness that was always there and that became evident when he wasn't thinking about his new role. I guess he felt a certain responsibility as our temporary guardian and was not quite sure how to go about it; he was queerly not himself — at times strict and at other times overly attentive — and Molly and I did not know what to make of it.

We would wake together in the night and speak aloud, already knowing the other was awake and thinking similar thoughts: our mother wasn't holidaying; it was laughable to imagine her sashaying around some rural hospice on the edge of some peaceful coastal town. She had never been gone this long from us, and after a day or two we grew scared but told ourselves it was foolish to be scared. We were no longer little children, there was nothing wrong, and we would, after all, see her very soon. Uncle Oweny had said so.

꩜

Doesn't your mammy have the life, Uncle Oweny said at the supper table. Sure wouldn't we all like to be away at Butlins for this
long. But then he made us all say a prayer for mother before we
ate. We knew he meant well but we no longer believed him. We felt
as if we were slowly being singled out, isolated from other children; adults looked at us differently, a sad strange look that lingered on their faces. It was a look that frightened Molly and me,
made our pulses quicken and our chests tighten. *Cancer,* they
whispered in hushed tones when they thought we could not hear.
Cancer.

Una was placing stew on the plates when Oweny pushed back
his chair with a loud squeal and said he needed to go for a pint.
Molly and I looked at each other as the door closed behind him,
watched through the window as he made his way up the gravel, and
as he paused at the gate and stood there unmoving.

The weeks passed and the days grew shorter. Twilight came more
and more quickly, darkening the fields. Mother seemed to be gone
for so long that I feared she would forget us entirely. I imagined the
hospital in Carlow and Mother wandering the halls, her head losing
all thought and memory of us.

Now her name hung on the air at the edges of our lips as a prayer.
A soft breathy exhale. A hush. At night we dimmed the paraffin
lamp, climbed the stairs together, and whispered across the space
and divide of our separate beds in the cold room: *God bless Mammy
and make her well again. Amen.*

I'd wake and find that Molly had slipped into my bed sometime
during the night. She'd be snoring loudly and it would take me a
while to fall back asleep. I'd stare at the ceiling and listen for the
sound of cars out in the silent countryside, track one from miles off
and follow its journey through the night, mapping the roads and
hills by the sound of its engine revving and slowing until one or

another came to our road, and then drove on up the hill toward Tullogher, or bore east toward us. And then I'd wait for the headlights that would track across the ceiling as they passed, one sliding beam stretching the window sash across the ceiling and down the wall, and then gone. Only the sound of the car as it made its way down the bend, off into the country, and soon silence. And in the silence I'd wonder how far away mother was, how long it would take us to reach her if we needed her, if something were to go wrong.

I tried to evoke the image of Mother, of a recent memory, but nothing would come. When I thought of her I saw her far away in the dark: a flitting, shadowy silhouette at some candlelit window staring out at the black, unfamiliar Carlow night looking for us. I imagined something had spirited her away from us and that it must be in this house, in the coal shed, and in the fields beyond. We had not been watchful enough, and now this thing had our mother and she was dying. I could not see it but it was there.

And so I looked over my shoulder as I climbed the stairs, when I went out into the dark to the outhouse or to the coal shed; I searched the fields anxiously; I paused on the landing, holding my breath, waiting for a movement, a shimmer of light, a presence to betray itself, and, waiting to exhale, I searched my features in the mirror to see if anything moved across my face. I tried to fool my shadow as I walked and shake loose any clinging specter; I knew it was clever — although my sister seemed oblivious to its presence.

What's the matter with you? What are you listening for? What do you hear? she persisted, panicked, as if there were something there, beyond the silence, at the edge of darkness, that she could not hear — a chord, a tremor of music; a haunting, hypnotic chorus calling from a world away. Perhaps she was worried that I would go the way of our mother.

Ghosts, I whispered. And Molly rolled her eyes and said, Jaysus, will you stop that! and belted me so violently I held my arm.

I didn't mean to hit you that hard, she said after, and I nodded and looked away, for it was not me who was crying.

August 1978

tart a song, Michael. My uncle Oweny coughed and wiped his mouth with the back of his hand. I sat on the high stool next to him at the bar. We were in the Three Bullet Gate and outside it was falling to dusk; he handed me a packet of crisps and a bottle of Cidona. He took a gulp from his pint of stout, and when he put the glass back on the bar it was half empty. He coughed again, and this time, after he wiped the phlegm from his mouth, his eyes hesitated for the briefest of moments upon his hand. We were just off the Wexford road in the pub he always stopped at, and, outside in the old Morris Minor, the three plaice were still wriggling about in the back even though they'd begun to stink. Flat-headed and slick, and still alive though they should be dead, they scared the hell out of me. When I told him, he laughed and hugged me. I didn't understand but it was comforting to feel his arms about me, smelling of muck and fish and tobacco and alcohol. Aye, he said, ugly divils. He pushed his leather pouch of Old Magwyer's Brown across the bar to me and let me roll him a sloppy cigarette.

All along the Wexford road he had encouraged me to sing and had smiled but for once didn't join in. He just nodded and stared at the road ahead. The sound I made did not seem like enough without him, so I stopped, but he encouraged me to continue with a sad smile on his face. I knew something was wrong but I went on, singing as hard and long and clear as I could until my throat felt raw, and he reached over and tousled my hair. Grand job, Michael, grand job. His eyes glistened, and I fell silent; I felt as if I'd swallowed something large and it had lodged in my chest.

He said, Your grandfather is in my dreams every night now, so he is. I remember him as if I was a child again, and there's Sheamie Murphy, and JJ Burke, and Mick Culleton. Remember him, Declan? He sometimes called me Declan when he'd been drinking, it was the name of the son he had lost in a trawler off the coast — someone he rarely talked about. He was a right bastard with the young lads, he was quare mean, but he wasn't a bad sort sure he wasn't.

I munched at my crisps quietly.

He was in some state when they found him, he continued. His body had been down for over two weeks. Y'know, sometimes they do get caught on stuff and stay down longer. Well, all manner of things had been at him. You would hardly have recognized him at all. Oweny frowned and I had the sense that he could still see that body rising from the black Atlantic and it wasn't Mick Culleton he saw, but his own son Declan.

He shook his head and looked at his left hand. Years before, he'd been working on a fishing trawler and a line had caught him by the hand and pulled him overboard. He'd lost two fingers, sheared from the bone, in the struggle; the mark of the line burnt like a brand around his wrist. He had fought the sea and it had spared him and taken his son instead.

Driving home, the fading sun glancing blindingly off the high green hedgerows, I looked at my uncle's left hand. He had been lucky, the line had pulled him down but he had come back up. Some said he had cut his fingers off to free himself but no one ever asked him.

He leant his arm out the window and pressed his nubs into the wind, keeping his right hand on the wheel. Poor Mick Culleton, he said. He was a right dry shite, I don't think he ever had a good shag his whole miserable life.

We jumped the low stone walls, fell through brambles and gorse, and began running again. Cait was fast but Martin was faster. He was the first one through the bracken and into the other field. Jaffa took an angle on the left and Molly was heading for the stile. I was beside Cait, our breaths thumping in unison like a press. We glanced quickly at each other and pushed harder. I passed her shoulder and rushed toward an opening in the hedge. From beyond the hedgerow Martin was shouting, and I hollered as well. I dove into the brambles, leapt high into sunlight, and Martin stood there, madly waving his arms, the wide green field at his back, and before him, a silver bale of raggedy barbed wire curled open in the ditch. He was shouting but his mouth was a silent o. His elbow poked pink and raw through a hole in his jumper. A wisp of sheep scut curled delicately on a barb and floated off into the air. I closed my eyes and held my breath, felt the bale shuddering against my calf and then I was tumbling forward across the earth, and Cait was falling, shrieking at my shoulder.

Martin raced toward the hedge we'd just cleared, calling, Oh God, oh God.

Cait kept her arms across her face, away from the barbs, but she was caught in the wire. When she pulled her arms down, blood flowed freely from her neck.

Molly came running from the stile and we looked at each other.

Don't move, Cait, for fucksake, don't move, Martin said.

Oh Jaysus. Jaysus. We'd best get Milo.

I'll stay, I said, and the lads took off running across the field. I looked in the direction of Milo's house. Smoke from its chimney rose above the tree line, and it seemed very far away. Cait reached through the coils and I took her hand. She looked at the blood and moaned; her legs kicked at the barbed wire.

Look at me, I said. Just look at me.

Her eyes were large, her lips pressed firmly together. Sweat streaked her forehead. I began to talk. I talked about my rabbit snares, and fishing on the river and of eels. I talked about Uncle Oweny. For the first time I talked of my father and of his leaving for America; I talked of my mother's illness; I talked of Father O'Brien and of Lugh and Molly and of the master at school and my favorite classes and the books I had read over the summer and the best bands on *Top of the Pops*. A wind came up that sent the hawthorn waving, scattering its petals around us.

Bees moved sluggishly about a nest humming invisibly in the hedgerow. Now that the weather was turning cool, they searched out places of heat; they brushed against the wire, and I swept my hand at them. I looked across the fields for some sign of Milo. It wasn't yet dusk and I could see for miles: hills and straths of pastureland, cows and sheep and horses, farmhouses, all of it stretching down to the river. Sounds moved about us and I had an odd sense of them, of bees droning softly, a tractor grumbling up the road, lads at play crossing the field, a dog barking, cows being brought up from pasture, a herd of clattering hooves on the road. I felt as if I were floating away, as if I might be gone entirely if not for the feel of Cait's hand pressed into my own, the brittle glare off the wire, and her blood on my fingers.

I've ruined my blouse, she said. Daddy will have a fit.

I shook my head. Your daddy won't mind, so.

Finally, Milo came hulking across the field and the lads followed.

He looked at Cait, then at the blood. We'll have you out of there in no time, he said.

He'd brought a large bolt cutter and had given gloves to Jaffa and Martin, told them to hold the bales as he cut it, and to be careful because it would spring back with the coiled tension. He worked the head of the cutter over the wire, grunting as he squeezed the handles closed. The wire snapped and sprung back and the bale shook around Cait.

Milo inhaled sharply. Lads, he said, just mind the wire. Hold it steady, it's going to spring back some. You need to hold it.

He looked at Martin and Jaffa. Are you right? They nodded and he began again, swearing that whoever left barbed wire in such a way would get a sound thrashing from him. Milo spoke through clenched teeth as he worked the bolt cutter. If only I get my hands on the fucker that left this here, he said, I'll kick ten colors of shite out of him. Cait had become even paler; she stared at me and I squeezed her hand. Milo split the bale in two and Cait hollered as the barbs tore free. Her shout was a gun blast across the field, sending startled blackbirds up from a stretch of trees, their wings and throats all a clatter. Blood wrapped her neck like a scarf, there was so much of it. She held my hand tightly as they pulled the gleaming wire further and further apart, and I thought of her mother, not of her dying quietly in her sleep but of her waking, and struggling in the dark with the blood welling in her throat and of her husband and her children sleeping through that silent struggle — how alone and utterly afraid she must have been, her husband just an arm's reach away, her children on the other side of the wall, as she tried to speak to scream to shout their names and yet nothing but the fading sound of snow thumping softly on the slate, a wind moaning uneasily in the eaves, and the darkness pressing in upon her. Through clenched teeth Cait stared at me, her eyes narrowed in pain — I squeezed her hand tighter — and she did not look away and she did not move, and even after, she never cried.

October 1978

I t wasn't yet dawn and it was raining; a strong wind blew wet ragged gusts against the door and window jambs when our uncle Oweny woke us. *C'mon,* he said, *your mammy will be waiting.*

It was cold since it was October and we hadn't had time to light a fire. The thick cement floors were like slabs of ice through my shoes and my chilblains ached. Molly still looked half asleep and had barely touched her cold cereal. Our uncle drew her coat tightly around her at the door, stroked my head, and ushered us — half asleep, faces flushed and tingling from cold water in the pantry washbasin, hair quickly and roughly combed — to his old Morris Minor, already idling in the courtyard, white smoke drifting from its exhaust and smelling richly of oil.

In the backseat we wrapped blankets around ourselves. The old heater thumped out just enough dusty heat to defrost the windscreen. Molly fell asleep almost immediately; I stared out the window wondering how my uncle could see the road when I could see nothing at all.

Oweny wiped his sleeve against the glass and cursed. Behind and before us, there seemed to be nothing but fog. Oweny turned on the wireless. All across the width of the radio band there was static and silence. Finally, there came a commentator announcing more violence erupting in the North: a shooting in the Shankhill, a bomb exploding on the Belfast-to-Dublin train; then the fall in livestock prices, the banner year for wool out of the North, how badly the punt fared against the pound sterling, and an advert recommending farmers use Drexel fertilizer. The only other station was Radio Éireann. It gave the football scores in Irish. Oweny cursed and switched the radio off. Jaysus, he said, I don't know which is worse.

We were almost to Carlow when Molly woke; she blinked and stared ahead as if she were somewhere else. We passed the ruins of a castle along the edge of a riverbank and I knew that Oweny would normally have commented on it, known its history, and perhaps the songs that had come from its battles, its victories, or its defeat. Perhaps a young Irish queen had found asylum there from a cruel English king, and the people who sheltered her had died rather than give her up to him. I imagined the great walls bombarded by cannon shell, while the queen hid in some deep chamber of the castle. She would have taken her life rather than let the foreigner take her. Or perhaps she made her way through a secret passage and escaped into the West.

Uncle Oweny, I called, and he looked briefly in his rearview mirror. Did you see that castle?

I did.

Well? What happened there?

What happened?

Did they get the queen? Or did she escape?

Oweny shook his head. If I remember right, it was a stronghold of the Burkes. I don't know what happened there.

So, there could have been a queen and she could have escaped? Like the children of Lir, at the end?

Oweny was quiet for a moment, and just when I thought he would not speak again, he did. I suppose. He sighed. I suppose.

I nudged Molly. How about that, then.

Molly blinked and nodded and stared out at the passing fields. She squinted at the land as if she were trying to make out its geography, something that could tell her how close we were to reaching Mother. I knew the passing landscape meant nothing to her. I was the one who always paid attention on trips, who tried to remember as much as I could so that I could predict things before we saw them. I used to bet with her about what was coming around the next bend, what we would see before the next mile was up. She was always amazed, and then upset, because we had taken the same trips together and she remembered none of it. I reminded her that it was because she often slept the entire trip or read a book and that, in either case, she was smarter than me. How well she did at school proved it.

I poked her gently, and when she turned, her eyes were wide. She seemed stricken and ready to cry.

It's soon, I said. Only twenty minutes or so.

She nodded, and although she didn't smile, I knew she was trying to.

Our mother came out of the arched doorway of the hospital wearing a blue shawl. She paused beneath the archway's roof, sheltered from the rain and silhouetted by the blaze of a bright light set into a low girdle on the wall. The rain glinted through the electric light and for a moment she seemed horribly disfigured. When she saw the car she waved and we rushed toward her, clambering out of the doors breathlessly, our feet kicking up gravel. Oweny did not protest but merely watched. Her body seemed to crumple in upon itself as she took us in her arms and hugged us close to her, holding us tight as if she might lose her grip on us, as if we were already pulling away. I could feel the weakness of her arms and it alarmed me immensely so that I grew sullen and quiet.

After a moment she straightened, grasped both our shoulders, and at turns looked closely at Molly and me, stared into our eyes, which I knew must betray something. The shawl was pulled so tightly about her head it pinched the skin at the edges of her eyes. I was close to tears and I reached for her hand. A smile creased her face and she laughed. What? Go on out of that, she said, and playfully slapped my hand away. Your old mammy is fine, sure, you two big eejits, *puckawns* you! She gently pushed us ahead of her. I felt dazed and numb and unable to speak.

How are you, Moira? Oweny grinned as he hiked up his stained work overalls and gave her an awkward hug. Rain beaded atop his mass of curly hair.

I'm well, Owen, now that I have me children with me. She ruffled our heads. Thanks for taking care of them.

Not at all, Moira, not at all, my uncle muttered softly and ran a gnarled hand through his hair while he searched for words to say.

Fierce day, so it is.

I'll take any old day, Owen, as long as I'm out of there.

By God, Moira, I bet you would.

I won't be coming back.

Sure of course not, now why would you be coming back.

Oweny took her bag and led her to the car, where all the strength seemed to ebb out of her. She did not look rested at all — in fact, she looked exhausted, more fatigued than I had ever seen her, but still, somehow agitated, as if there were something beyond the rain that she was looking for. She turned in her seat and when she saw us she smiled, surprised. She reached out, touched us lightly with fluttering fingertips that barely made an impression upon our skin, and I shivered.

I had never seen my uncle so quiet; and my mother seemed to appreciate his stillness, and his silence. He could have been a tree offering shelter from the rain. And I tried to feel that calmness, distill it slowly from his close presence. He buckled her into the front seat, muttering, Not now, children, not now, your mammy needs to sleep, and she seemed to finally relax, and fell into a dreamy fitful doze.

In the distance, clouds were breaking; but no matter how far we traveled, we were never able to reach that point; it remained fixed on the horizon teasingly and we could get no closer to it.

Mother spoke suddenly, startling us. Owen, she said, and stared out the glass for a moment before speaking so that I thought she was asleep again, they put me in a cage, Owen, with the rest of them. They thought I was mad. Before they knew what it was . . . they thought I was mad.

Oweny reached over and squeezed her shoulder. It's all right, Moira, sure it's all right. And mother closed her eyes and fell back asleep.

My mother's breathing grew ragged and shallow, barely audible above the clatter of rain upon the car's roof. Oweny wiped condensation from the windows with a rag he kept down by the gearshift.

We were ghosts moving through a ghostly world, at the bottom of a great big sea from which now and again an ethereal church spire rose; a field of cows, bodies huddled together, turned in toward one another in shelter from the wind and the rain; the darkened center of a village, the desolate crumbling facades of a shop, a garage, a pub.

I looked at my mother's sleeping face and saw that she had aged noticeably. There were thin, deeply etched lines about her eyes and her mouth. Molly reached over and held my hand and, although I had not spoken, said, *Sssssshh, Mammy's sleeping.*

Oweny glanced in the mirror and the edges of his eyes were red and raw. He rolled down the window and hacked phlegm into the windswept rain. The car shuddered and bowed, then quickly slid across the road, but Oweny pulled it straight again, his hands gripping the wheel until the bones of his knuckles shone white, and we fled on through the rain and the wind and the perpetual twilight, all of us squinting through the glass, searching the dark churning horizon for some faint promise of light.

Summer 1979

The winter of 1978 wouldn't end, and with the meager dole Mother barely managed to keep a fire going in the hearth. Uncle Brendan and Oweny helped when they could, with fish and potatoes and coal and wood, but sometimes it took Mother's all just to make sure the house was heated. At night we took our hot water bottles and ran upstairs to our bedroom, jumped beneath the heavy wool blankets and quilts, and hoped we'd fall asleep before the heat of the fire had left us completely. In the mornings our breath frosted the air and we clenched our teeth as we plunged our hands into washbasins and splashed our faces with water so cold our skin would sting with the pain.

When summer finally came we were still waiting for a coal allowance that the government had promised for the hard winter everyone had endured, but as the weeks passed and no check came, Mother was convinced that we'd never see one.

We were at our tea in the kitchen watching the gray light sweeping across the fields when young Eileen Meaney came down the lane, the hood of her mac tightly bound around her head against the rain. She stood in the scullery, her cheeks the color of beets, her bare legs pink, and we sat at our tea and stared at her. Rain ran off the end of her nose and from the arms of her mac and the hem of her skirt. The water went drip drip drip on the floor. Howya, Moira, she said, breathless. Mammy sent me down. You have a call. From America.

And then the door banged behind her and she was running back up the lane toward their farmhouse because her daddy said she had to see to the horses and we sat in the silence and looked at one another. Mother's chair squealed as she rose and threw on her raincoat and Wellingtons and trudged up the gravel after her.

Molly and me waited in the dark kitchen where we had a view of the road. We'd been without the electric for a month because Mother couldn't pay the bill. Rain thumped the glass and everything was gray. I brewed tea and as it steeped we saw Mother walking fast, bent against the rain, a large sack of potatoes hung over her small back. The back door banged against the wall and then she was scraping her feet on the scullery mat.

Your father's coming home, she said, and threw the sack down. Potatoes spilt across the lino and banged against the baseboards; half of them were mealy and rotten. Mother eyed them as she took off her Wellingtons, and shook her head. When she looked up, her face shone wetly.

Michael, she said, you're going to go see your father.

Daddy's coming home, Daddy's coming home. We're going to see Daddy! Molly shouted and threw up her fists. She looked at me and grinned; her face was flushed.

Mother sat heavily and wrung her wet hair with a dish towel. She looked into it for a long time as if there were strands of her hair there so that I looked as well, to be sure.

Michael is going to see your father, she said. You're staying here. I can't lose you. If one of you stays here, he won't dare take the other.

What do you mean? Daddy wouldn't do that.

That man has broken too many promises for me to believe him now no matter what he says. You'll stay here, Molly, and Michael will go. Your father will be home again soon, and then, well, perhaps it will be different . . . but not now, I'm sorry . . . I promise that I'll make it up to you, Molly, somehow I will. But only Michael is going to see him.

But why? Molly's lip quivered. Why him and not me? Sure haven't I been good? Haven't I done me chores? Haven't I done well at school? What more could I do?

Molly, please. My mind is made up.

But why?

My mother placed her head in her hands, and Molly pushed back her chair. She had paled suddenly; sweat beaded her brow.

I think I'm going to be sick, she said, and ran from the room. A door slammed and after a moment the sounds of retching came from down the hall; it reverberated off the lino in the hallway, sounding harsher and much louder than it should, until I felt I would be sick myself listening to it.

After, I stayed in my room for some time; I lay upon the bed and stared at the mildewed ceiling wondering what it meant to see my father without Molly. How could I possibly see him without her? How could she not see him? It had been two years since he'd left. I couldn't imagine not seeing him, but I also couldn't imagine taking the place of my sister — and didn't know which was worse: not seeing him or going in the place of my sister. There was a gnawing in my guts as I thought it over. I didn't know what to do.

The kitchen was empty and the rear door leading from the scullery to the hallway open. The front door as well. Mother had left both doors open to let in the breeze. Washing was flapping on the line, and the smell of the fresh washed linen suggested good weather. The top of Sliabh Coillte was birch and heather-patched, straggling sheep along its dun western slopes; above, the sky was blue broken only by the infrequent cloud moving high and slow, drawn as if by an invisible hand. The air was warm and pleasant. You could smell the river, and the sea. Mother was burning refuse in the compost heap alongside the septic. At the far side of the field at its end, Molly sat upon the wall that stretched the divide between the fields.

I ran through the grass to reach her, but when she looked up I slowed.

Molly moved astride the wall and stared off toward the hills. She had a stone in her hand and was beating the rock with it slowly, methodically, and I listened and searched in that sound to hear something I might understand, something that might tell me what she was thinking or feeling.

I'd understand if you hated me, I said.

Molly shifted on the wall and pecked the rock with her stone, then threw the stone far into the field. Don't be daft. How could I hate you?

I sat next to her. Well, if you were going to see Daddy and not me, I don't know how I'd feel.

You'd probably feel the exact same, and you wouldn't hate me.

Will you look after my eel traps while I'm gone?

I don't know how.

If you have the time I can show you now. We'll go out on the river together.

Molly followed me down through the ten-acre pasture to the overgrown path and to the cove where my boat was tied. I pulled the boat from the rushes, and when Molly had clambered in, I pushed off through the Flats.

It was warm and thin streamers of mist had crept down to the water's edge from the woods above the fields. Sunlight flickered at the top of the trees along the banks and mottled the river, spotted with fallen leaves. It was warm and pleasant now that the rain had passed; steam rose from the rushes. A haze settled on the fields that came visible in the distance. Flying things hummed in the air about us dreamily. The oars felt good in my hands, and as I lengthened my strokes, I felt my shoulders stretch and warm pleasantly to the task.

Molly kicked at my creels. Jaysus, those things stink.

Are ye sure you want to do this when I'm gone?

The banks of the waterway became shale and stone, and a large stone rose like a quarry wall out of the waters. To our right was Mulligan's Rock, a chain running from a black ring imbedded in the stone from a hundred years before.

Mulligan's Rock, I said.

I know what it is.

Well, just in case you didn't.

I moved the boat toward the stone and glided alongside it until I was past the churning crosscurrent and into another series of shallows that would lead me to deeper hollows and darker places.

Will you remember this? I asked, and Molly looked about as if she was only now taking everything in.

I rested on the oars, breathing hard for a moment. The gorse was shimmering with twilight mist, the light was falling, and with its going, sections of the bank grew dark. We passed beneath canopies of trees and emerged into low sunlight again and Molly leant her head back to catch its warmth.

You have the life, coming out here when ye please.

Aye, but I didn't see you offering to help during the winter, or in the rain or the wind or the cold, ye loaf ye.

Molly smiled and shrugged. I pointed to my markers.

Take the gaff, will you, I said, and get hold of that line.

Together we heaved the pots in, pried the eels from the trap into the creel. Watch their teeth, if they catch hold you'll have a hell of a time getting them off. Make sure you wear the gloves. Are ye right?

Molly groaned, slammed the lid on them, and we sank the pots again. I blessed myself and watched as they sank slowly back beneath the water.

We did this a dozen times more until Molly said she was tired.

I won't be doing this every night, she said.

No. Only as long as you set the traps. If ye can't be bothered just pull them up so's the eels aren't rotting in their own juice when I get back. Then we can set them together.

What do you use to set them?

Fish bits. They like the heads and guts best, freshly killed. Molly grimaced, and I laughed.

I'll not set them.

No sure, you needn't. I'll set them just the once and then you can check them through the week.

Molly reached with the gaff and slowly drew a line in and we pulled the trap up, checked it, then sank it again. The boat rose and fell as she clambered across the seat. Water churned and slapped the black rock. The sun was sinking down through the trees along the shore and the gorse shone bright as gold. The last of the light played on the river in its own lambent ripples and undulations as the trees swayed and clouds raced in from the east. Molly looked at me and squinted. It's nice out here. I wouldn't have imagined it was this peaceful.

I nodded and rowed slowly toward the first of the stones I set for Mother, a praying cairn in imitation of the shrines throughout the countryside, garlanded with wildflowers, flowers which I knew had ancient meanings: pink thrift and sea campion, bog myrtle, flea-bane, meadow vetchling, marsh thistle, lichen and moss, the simple nettle and graceful Queen Anne's lace. I used the gaff to pull us close, then tied off. As I lifted stones from the bottom of the boat and piled them on the bank atop one another, Molly asked me what the stones were for.

They're for Mammy. I've been building these since she got sick.

Do they work?

She's well, so, isn't she? I snapped, and then regretted it. I shrugged. I think they might, I'm not sure. I like to think they do.

Could I lay a stone as well?

I nodded and sat back, watching as Molly took a stone from the bottom of the boat and set it atop the cairn. Light flickered amongst the trees; mottled shadow danced across her arms and face. She closed her eyes, and her mouth moved soundlessly. I rested on the oars and listened to the soft exhale of her words, lowered my head, and felt the water pressed and rushing beneath our feet.

The brake shifted and sighed and a bittern boomed from out of the hollow silence, startling us. For a moment we sat listening to its rare singular sound with the water lapping against the boat and the line bending back and forth, then drawing taut again. I played absently with a knot upon a seine that lay rotting in brine at the bottom of the boat.

How far do you think we could get if we just rowed for it, Molly? I said and smiled at her.

But she sat there in the half-light, distrait and silently considering it, listening, it seemed, to the sound of the bird. Finally she picked up the oars and banged them in the oarlocks so that the wood shuddered. I reached for them but she shook me off. Not far enough, she said, and began to paddle us home, but her strokes dragged and slapped the water and we went slow through the channel, bumping rock and shale. And that rare, lonely sound of the bittern boomed out of the depths of some secret dark place beyond the rising mists on the shore as we splashed our way down the dusk gray channel toward home.

Every month Molly and I had petitioned Father with badly spelled letters to which there came no response; at Christmas we had reversed the charges and pleaded on Milo Meaney's telephone until we were all in tears, but nothing would change Father's mind, nothing would make him return. He had returned once and it had sucked the life from him, he said. He couldn't go back to that, not after America. It would be a kind of death. It was ironic, then, that it was death that did finally bring him back to Ireland, to us. The death of his brother Rory.

Rory was the one who had never left, the one no one would sponsor in America on account he'd had the red fever as a child and had gone soft in the head, and who would never have done well in England or America, the places where you lost God. Rory, they figured, would either take to the drink or take to the women. So Rory stayed behind and looked after my grandmother, who was spitting black-blooded gob from her mouth with the tuberculosis, and then there were the cows and sheep, as emaciated as Rory had become herding them from pasture to pasture, roaming the fields and the mountains, searching for fit grazing amongst the rocks. But now, grandmother was gone and Rory had only to be put in the ground. After all these years, it was Rory to whom Father and his sisters and brothers were coming back with heads bowed in shame, returning to Ireland as if it were a penance for the sin of their having ever left in the first place.

In the predawn gloom Mother and I, holding tightly to our small suitcases, took the bus from Rowan to Dublin. Molly stayed at Aunt Una's with my cousins, and I both envied her and felt sorry for her. It was cold and the bus jostled and bounced along the empty country roads all the way to Carlow, where we waited for another bus to take us the rest of the way. We sat in an empty pub lounge that smelled of beer-sopped wood and cigarettes. The smell made me think of a circle of talking, laughing, shouting men, and it reassured me. Heavy, soiled red brocade curtains were drawn tight against the night outside, and one small light burned on the mantel above a hearth that hadn't been shoveled of ashes in weeks.

Once we boarded the second bus I was quickly asleep, my head nodding onto Mother's shoulder. She gently pushed me off. You're too old for that, she said, and I turned away, lay my head against the hard window instead, upset with her for no proper reason I could explain.

I woke bleary and confused, my head banging the glass. There wasn't much to see at that time of the morning, and nothing that I might reference or recognize. The stingy thread of the dirty Liffey as the bus passed over the bridge, early morning mist rising up off the slick gray-cobbled shop-lined streets pressed in upon one another, a stretch of tall glass office buildings, the grand statue of Parnell, a sleek church spire, and the distant dome of the GPO.

And then there was the train: dark, stained Naugahyde seats smelling slightly of manure. Jolting stops and sudden starts and long suspensions between short, stumpy fields, occasionally occupied by a sorrel, or a few raggedy sheep, fleece half shorn and dragging from their shanks, a small herd of cows chomping cud, a donkey hoofing the sparse gorse, and all wasting farther and farther away as the train staggered into the West. Yet I was filled with amazement at each scene that passed before my window — there was a wonder to the struggle of it all, and, as the land shifted and changed, hedgerow and valley and thick fertile field turning to stone and bog, I recognized the vast difference between the world I knew, and was leaving behind, and the one we were passing into. And for just that moment, I was glad of it.

The smell of burning came through the window at us. In the distance they were razing the fields down to the scutt — rows of orange flame moved across the land, leaving great black swaths behind and everything laid down like ashen snow and rising up in drifts and dirty billowing clouds against houses and sheds and walls and the train whistling headlong through the churning choking smoke, blowing in gaps across the tracks so that in the carriages it suddenly seemed as if it were night.

I sat heavily in my anorak and even when it grew warm I would not remove it; I imagined that I must look preposterous. The weather was mild and I sweated slightly. I bent into myself, slouched in my chair, dangled my feet, glanced quickly at the people who entered the carriage or passed the open doorway.

Mother had given me twenty pounds, tucked into an inside pocket of my anorak; it lay there, burning against my ribs. I feared that I would lose it, that as soon as I relaxed and allowed myself to take in the passing countryside or a girl in the vestibule or an old man talking — as soon as I allowed the slightest distraction — I risked it being gone.

Mother told me to Sit up straight, Stop acting the gom, Take my coat off — it would be useless when I really needed it — What is wrong with you? What's got at you? and What will your father think? That you've become a monkey?

I felt for the lump of money against my chest as Mother dozed, her head nodding back and forth with the rhythm of the train. We passed a ruined monastery with its high balustrades and vaulting arches, and then flat tea-colored plains of machined peat upon which a distant tinder light played like glittering glass, and which I imagined was a light drawing us closer and closer to Father.

At dusk a taxi brought us to a B and B on the outskirts of Shannon. Away from the industrial roadway with its lorries of coal and fertilizer and stout hurtling back and forth to Dublin and Cork, the silence seemed like a suspended thing dropped softly upon us. I spent the night in a strange bedroom, down the hall from my mother, stretched across the sagging mattress on my belly, staring out the parted curtains. The lights of planes shimmered over the Atlantic, magically sparkling out of a darkness of cloud and sea and sky — and then others, slowly burning alight in the gloom, one after the other, in staggered rows all through the night.

In the morning we rose before dawn once more and took a taxi to Shannon, passing fields glowing white with mist and quiet industrial estates and sleeping tenements and bowed corrugate hangars with their backs turned against the flat plains of the West beyond.

Do you think he'll recognize me? I asked. Even as I said it I thought Mother might snap at me, tell me to stop asking such stupid questions, but she paused and, considering this, smiled instead.

Of course he'll recognize you, sure you're his son.

At the airport I walked past sleeping bodies curled here and there in the rows of plastic seats, or lying prostrate on the carpeted floors. A young woman slept sitting against a wall, suitcase at her side, legs drawn up tightly to her chest. I stared at her dark head resting on her knees, the pleated skirt drawn tight against her hips.

As everyone slept, a cleaning lady worked a Hoover, her shoes echoing on the wide tiled floors, whispering on the lengths of worn carpet.

The fields beyond the wide glass windows were moored by mist. Everything was chill, yet waking and warming slowly. Light punched through the clouds in long slanting beams, and I hoped, as we waited outside customs, that such beauty would make Father come home to the South, and to us.

As we waited, my mother stared at me, and, no longer sure if her looks were of tenderness or contempt, I went and stood at the railings before the wide windows looking out at the runway. Over the darkness of the western horizon, a light emerged, pulsing urgently toward us. I rushed to tell Mother.

There's lights, there's lights.

Whisht, and sit down, Mother said. It'll be hours before his plane comes in. But she stood and took my hand and we walked toward the observation deck, and there it was, the plane from America, churning along the runway now — I could hear the whine and shudder of its jet engines reversing even through the heavy plate glass — and the plane was slowing, slowing, and then slanting toward us, its fuselage and burgeoning undercarriage gleaming with the first glints of sunrise.

I can't stay, Mother said — I can't face this man.

I stared at her, convinced that I had misheard.

What?

I said, "I can't stay." She clenched her hands; her brow furrowed. She looked about the airport, toward the long corridor, the hall and exit, the dark rain-misted dawn beyond.

He'll have you back to me in a fortnight, she said. He's not taking you with him, he promised. I shouldn't have come at all. What on earth was I thinking, she said, angrier now. Her eyes turned from the exit to the lounge and the waiting room, scanning the airport's width and breadth, and then she paused and exhaled, as if with relief. She took my hand and I held fast to my bag as she led me to a Guard who sat at a bench sipping from a mug of tea, his cap resting on the table before him.

She handed me to the Guard, muttering something about the boy's father coming in on the next flight and unable to stay because she desperately needed to make the Dublin train, and fled off down the walkway into the vast corridor beyond, her figure a racing shadow on the stone white walls. I looked at the stranger noisily slurping his tea next to me and waited for another — no less strange — to come like a crashing pummeling stampede or like a floating visitation through the doors of customs.

The Guard was a morose man with a bright bulbous nose who seemed completely unperturbed. The minutes passed and then it could have been hours. He stared at me for a while, then pursed his wet lips and gestured with his head. Is that your daddy then? he asked, and when I turned, the doors had magically opened and Father stood there with my aunts and uncles who'd come from America on either side of him, and I nodded, surprised. Father crossed the distance between us in just a few steps and took me in his arms and I thought of Mother's words: *He'll have you back to me in a fortnight. He's not taking you with him.*

I've missed you, Father said. His eyes were bloodshot. He shook his head as if he were holding back tears. The Guard stepped forward and asked him for identification, and Father untangled himself from me and brandished his wallet and it seemed the most natural thing in the world; while I might have liked a flourish, an indignant outrage, there was nothing — he didn't even ask where Mother was. McDonagh, Father said to the man in a way that only an American would say it, with the steadfast assurance that what one wanted could be gotten if one wanted it and only demanded it loudly enough. And the Guard, satisfied that my father was who he said he was, walked away, back to his tea.

My somber aunts and uncles from the West gathered about me

with their moans and sighs of melancholy and mourning and ineffable sadness and wrapped me up in it so that I felt smothered and trapped and small, but in that moment, I welcomed it all completely. Father took my hand in his — so familiar in its size and strength — and we strode toward the taxi stands, where a rental car was waiting.

play the reel slowly

Dark clouds that suggested rain held off all day until we had made it into the West, to Connemara, and then, when it did rain, it made the landscape look harsh and resolute, uninhabitable, in the manner I remembered it as a child. I watched through the car window as rain swept down the glass, in awe of it all.

A few sheep lay huddled miserably by the roadside. Others roamed around the remains of cottages, or squatted in the far barren pastures that dotted the mud-brown plains. Here and there a faded, whitewashed cottage with smoke curling thinly up from its chimney broke the vast windblown landscape, old dung heaps and a *cruach* of turf crumbling against its stone walls.

Colie was the only one who spoke in the car. He sounded like a tour guide, full of reading and history that he'd never known as a child, or as a man, here. This is the way it would have looked to the first Normans to travel beyond the Pale, he said, grinning. And as it had to the historian Siculus in his reports back to Rome. The Romans gave up after that, decided this island wasn't much use to them, that it wasn't worth the effort. We took their heads and put them over our doorways, for that's what we used to do. I don't suppose I'd stay with a welcome like that.

The car topped a rise and in front of us rose the expanse of the bog, mottled with gnarled and craggy cairns, straggled lines of mortarless rock walls, enclosing small fields no larger than animal pens —

the suggestion that each small pen had once held sheep or cows, or been a plot for growing meager vegetables. A wind swept across it all and shuddered against the car.

Finnoula crowed, They were clever, those Romans. The English could have learnt something from them. We could have learnt something as well. Colie, you can have your bog and your heads. Give me electricity and indoor plumbing please, and I'll be very happy. Thank you God.

O Dia, Teresa said softly, sure I didn't think I'd be coming back to this so soon.

The road grew more and more desolate as we wound our way inland, where nothing lay turned by the plow. We drove over russet, coal-colored slopes, and giant boulders pressed up from the bog against the side of the road. Now and then we passed a lone stone cottage, roofed with rotted thatch or rusted corrugate, and nothing about it, no trees or sedge to break its harsh, isolated outline.

We passed an old slate church with heavy mullioned windows and a single granite cross and if it hadn't been for the manicured graveyard at its side and the peal of the bell for Mass as we passed, I might have imagined there was no one left to pray there. Father stared out the window as the bell sounded and blessed himself.

For a while we climbed into a hilly country, over deep worn lanes, intermittently broken by recent yet potholed macadam, high sedge banks on either side, heavy with dripping moss and ferns and flowering gorse shining bright and yellow in the sharp slants of sunlight.

We descended once more and passed over a narrow stone bridge. Here and there along the edges of the stream broke woods of a sort of scrub brush and blackened fir. By the time we made it to the cottage, bronze bracken and mottled bramble gleamed with the sinking sun. A dull light came into the west and shone through the clouded windows. A narrow cow path wound its way across the bog. Nothing stirred over the vast expanse save a clotted tuft of sheep wool waving on a stretch of barbed wire strung between a gap in the rock walls. In the distance a plume of charcoal gray smoke rose from the seaweed processing plant beyond the island ferry station.

Squinting, Father looked out over the plain. *A mhac,* will you look there.

What is it? I asked.

A cow? No, it's a horse, by God, will you look at that.

Colie slowed the car and we looked toward the east. Across the brown undulating fields the rain-blackened knoc whipped this way and that, and in the middle of it all something lay writhing. The animal reared and stretched up its long white neck and bellowed. We could hear it plainly from across the bog — it sounded human — and I shivered.

What's happening, Da?

The bog has it, Michael. The bog is taking it down.

My aunts and uncles were silent. I couldn't understand us watching it and doing nothing.

Isn't there something we can do for it?

My father shook his head. No, there's nothing we can do for the poor thing. It's gone.

I looked through the glass again, and Father began to talk about all the sheep and cows they'd lost in the bog. How they'd often searched through the night for them but what the bog claimed was hers; she'd give everything up, he'd say, when she chose, when we were long gone and dead and buried in her ourselves.

He told me that when he was my age, or younger — ten, he thinks — his favorite pony, a fine brindle, wandered into the bog and when Father found him it was already too late. At first the animal thrashed and flailed and then its movements slowed until it became quite still, as if it had resigned itself to its fate. He saw its head for a time craning its white-dappled neck from the bog hole to stare at him.

I remember its eyes most of all, *a mhac,* Father said. It's the eyes I remember. For years I waited for the bog to give up that horse, and for it to come back to me. I was that daft as a boy. Sure isn't that soft altogether?

Colie pressed the accelerator and the car moved slowly forward but the image of the horse stayed with me, and the car became oddly silent. Even Colie was still. As we climbed the hills toward the dark mountains, I had a full view of the plain falling away behind us and I saw that the horse wasn't gone: it was still thrashing, its pale neck thrust to the sky, its mouth parted in rictus and one final horrific wail, even as the bog sucked it down.

Rory lay in the open coffin next to the bed I shared with Father, and I imagined that I could hear him breathing in the night, that his breath was Father's breath and the two were merged indistinctly from each other. When my father's chest rose I stared toward the window of the room and the open coffin with the meager moonlight slanting across it, revealing the white satin lining and the very top of Rory's chest. I imagined that it moved ever so slightly with Father's every inhale and exhale. The smell of camphor filled the small room. The candle flickered in the window. And I imagined it was Rory's hoarse breathing filling up the room, all the old, empty spaces of the house.

Earlier in the day Father had asked me all the ways I'd remembered Rory. He asked if I remembered the time Rory picked me up and I sang with him. You were only three at the time, Father said. Do you remember? There was an eagerness in his eyes as if my memory of Rory might in some way make him live again, or affirm all his own memories of him. I nodded, but I didn't remember. I knew Rory in the way that I knew fables and myths and folktales and superstitions. I knew him through the stories I'd heard Father tell of him, through the pain I now felt at Father's loss, and the vague, distant sense of someone familiar holding me as a child.

Rain banged on the tin roof. The house was cold and damp, although my aunts and uncles had had a fire burning in the hearth night and day since we'd arrived. It felt like a place only the dead could occupy. I closed my eyes and pulled the covers above my head, and trying to feel my father's warmth beside me, I lay one of my legs across his own, and then the queer thought came to me of Rory staring out from his coffin into the dark and he, too, afraid to sleep and in need of comfort.

Father and his brothers rolled the wet brackish earth over the coffin and the priest muttered the prayers in Irish. Thin-shanked heifers looked on, chewing wild grass. Wind moaned through the gorse, stirred bones in the black Connemara slough. The Maamturks and Twelve Bens rose still and dark to the north, lightning flaring on their heights like beacons. Father searched the road and the fields stretching for flat miles till the sea. He looked to the Atlantic, where gray rollers crashed against the rocks, and America must have seemed very far away.

At the house, neighbors came and went, smelling of whiskey, and I held the door for them. They touched my shoulder, tousled my hair. There's a grand lad, they said, sure you're the spittin image of himself, God bless us and save us. And with their blessings and the touch of their hands still warm upon me, I watched them swaying from the wind and the drink, down the narrow road, over the rise, and toward the gray sea.

The light faded and people huddled well past dusk by the crackling fire in prayer. Father stared at me closely in the meager light. I smiled but his eyes were empty, his face blank. The fire spat embers; they smoldered bright on the cement and then blackened. Through the window, distant rain was leveling the land flat.

The bogs were quiet; not even a curlew cried. The clouds that rested above the mountains held their place. A soft rain began to mist the rusted corrugate of the outhouses and cowsheds. It tamped the earth, pressed skin to bone.

The brothers and sisters that had come from America and England stood or sat stiffly drinking tea laced with *poitin;* they loosened ties, removed shoes and black or red shawls, and stepped upon the stone slabs as if they were cautious of sound.

Rory's red marbled accordion lay spooled by the hearth. Its silver and marble sparkled. The blood-red patina with the mother-of-pearl finish, the worn ivory buttons and the rich silver inlays all shone with a black, masticated matter that had stiffened between the grooves of the keys. No one would touch it.

Soiled lace curtains withered in the small cell-like windows, where candles sputtered and peaked. At the table with the red checkered tablecloth, my aunts and uncles spoke the Irish softly, their voices like flowing water. Father was amongst them but did not speak. He stared into the corners of the room as if there were something there, his eyes glancing quickly over the accordion and then moving away.

The pungent aroma of turf, dung, and oil from the paraffin lamps filled the room. Heavy wool jumpers steamed, drying after the rain. Rosary beads rattled like bones. It was cold yet no one sat by the fire. Rory's old black-and-white sheepdog moved to Father's side and would let no one else touch him.

Another bottle of *poitin* appeared on the table; soda bread and braic; a pot of steaming tea. A neighbor touched Father's shoulders briefly and offered him prayers in Irish. Father's shoulders were still and wide and straight, and I didn't have to see how guardedly he raised the bottle to his lips to know he was becoming drunk; I could tell by those straight shoulders and by the way his lips pursed and by the way his eyes grew hard. He had barely slept these last few nights and the lines around his eyes were drawn tight, the hollows of his sockets deeper and darker than I had ever seen, as if he was staring at me from the depths of some deep black well.

The turf hissed and spat and rain lashed the slate roof. Finnoula's hand was at my shoulder, strong and speckled with freckles like a young girl's.

Have you et? she asked.

I nodded.

She grasped my shoulder so that I had to look at her, held my chin so that I was seeing all of her — wisps of thick red-black hair falling into her face, the deep etched lines in the center of her brow.

She asked again and, looking into her eyes, I couldn't lie. No, Auntie Finn, I said, I haven't, but I'm not hungry, so I'm not.

Ye have to eat, she said, and shook her head, sighing. Sure, why would you be hungry, why would any of us be hungry? I don't know which is worse at all, the children or the grown-ups. She walked to the scullery to prepare something, her hair catching the red light of the Sacred Heart as she passed.

My aunts looked at one another across the table as Father drank. Bernadette, his closest sister, spoke first. *An diabhal, a buachaill,* that will do you no good at all. She slapped his hard, tensed shoulders. And then Orla, Maeve, and Finnoula: Sure you can depend on the men in times like these to go straight to the bottle. He wouldn't be actin out like that if Mammy or Daddy were here. God rest their souls. The sisters nodded and murmured blessings all around.

Ah, sure, what harm is a small sup of the whiskey? Finnoula dissented. Teresa, the quietest of them all, smiled sadly and nodded her head. She mouthed another Hail Mary on her rosary beads and reached out and touched Father's sleeve. He looked at none of them but twisted his face as he drank and continued drinking. He stared into the fire, at the chair, at the red accordion splayed upon the ground.

The sisters collectively murmured *musha, musha* and *diabhal, diabhal* as they talked about the brothers, how badly they had turned out, the sad excuses for men they had become. But their words were soft and filled with tenderness and seemed more to fill the slow, empty trawl of time than anything else.

Thomas and Maurteen had taken the pledge and did not drink; Colie, on the other hand, was on the tear again. He walked into the parish earlier in the day to Darby's Pub and was making up for lost time without them. It had been dark for hours now and he had yet to return.

Finnoula and I shared the small settle in the corner of the room. She snored softly as I watched Father amidst the shifting shapes the fire threw across the walls. His left hand worked into a fist and worried the knees of his black trousers; the bottle of *poitin* never left his right hand. Hours passed and the room grew cold and the shadows lengthened and became still, yet he did not move. The old sheepdog curled itself up at his feet. Candles flickered and waned in the deep windows. Wind howled down the flue.

The others were asleep in the loft when Colie finally clomped up the cobblestone and stumbled in. The door banged behind him. He stamped his Wellingtons loudly, and looking toward the room, where Rory had lain in state, his coffin open until yesterday, Colie blessed himself. Father looked at him and, without a word or gesture, leant forward to throw some kindling on the smoldering embers. The wood was dry and caught quickly, flaring about Father's face, illuminating his anger. Colie raised an eyebrow drunkenly and, ignoring Father, made for Rory's chair. Father stiffened. The drink had hardened the fine angles of his face, stretched skin across bone. The kindling burnt down and the peat smoldered wetly.

Finnoula's eyes fluttered awake in the candlelit dark. Her eyelashes were long and black like Father's, like Rory's had been. The blond tips caught the candlelight and curled to touch the hollow below her eye. The others were still asleep in the loft; I could hear Maeve snoring in harmony with Maurteen. I peered through my hands at Colie's bull neck, his wide-backed shoulders. He raised the accordion and its bellows sighed sadly.

You'll not be sittin there, *a mhac,* Father said.

Colie waved him away and, drawing the accordion in and out, began to play. He was much bigger than Father.

The tendons in Father's forearms flexed. His large hands clenched. Next to Colie he resembled angular sheet metal shaped by a press. Colie had spent the last two decades in England; I doubted he remembered what Father could do to men when he was on the whiskey, had done to men much bigger than himself.

Father pulled his back straight so that his sway was barely noticeable.

You'll not be sittin in Rory's chair, Colie, he said, his voice rising. Put his melodeon down.

Ah, give it a bleedin rest, would you. The house is asleep, keep your voice down, man. Colie continued to squeeze the bellows of the box.

Finnoula's eyelashes flickered. Her eyes shone wetly in the dark. She reached for my hand and held it tightly. Her breath was warm and pungent with milk and tea. Father shouted for Colie to move again.

Ahhh, hush, Padraig, hush. I'm not bleedin deaf. Sure can't I hear the grass growin in the field beyond. Rory wouldn't mind his own brother sitting in his chair playing one of the old airs.

Get out! Get out! Get out of his chair! And put down his blasted accordion!

The divil, Padraig, I'm too tired to argue. You're drunk, go to bed.

And with that Father was across the room, half stumbling but still faster than I expected. In two broken strides, he was upon

Colie, swinging his sledgelike fists and knocking him from the chair to the hard floor.

Finnoula screamed and pulled me close. It only took a moment for Maurteen and Thomas to wake and stumble from their beds. They clattered down the ladder from the loft, their faces cratered and washed pale like the moon. They hauled Father off Colie as if he were a great Basking they'd caught struggling in their nets. Father gave one great heave and seemed as if he was about to push them off of him, but then, just as suddenly, he collapsed into their hands, all his anger spent.

That's Rory's, Father sobbed, that's Rory's. He reached for the accordion with bloodied hands, and when that failed, he sank slowly to his knees but still Maurteen and Thomas held him back.

Breathing heavily, Colie rose slowly and stared at his brother, wide-eyed. His large arms hung limply from his sides, his fists clenched, but if there were ever fight in him it was gone now as he looked at Father. Colie's lips were split and his teeth were blood streaked. The flesh was already swelling on his cheek and around the bone of his eye. He spat blood.

In the scuffle they'd dashed the accordion to the wall. Finnoula picked it up tenderly, cradled it against her. Her nightgown hung loose on her thin frame. The bottom of the bellows collapsed and air groaned out. Finnoula poked at the divots razed upon the accordion's rich inlaid surface. She collapsed the bellows with a hiss of air and secured its latches tightly.

I stood in my pajamas, shivering. Colie hurried out into the starspun night, slamming the door behind him. It swung on its old rusted hinges and then remained open. Colie's retreating shape hulked over the dark windswept fields. The water of the bay glittered with the moon. Blue-white naphtha light sparked out on the bogs.

The brothers and sisters circled Father as he sobbed. He still hadn't risen to his feet and I was no longer sure he could.

Father looked up, his face streaked with tears. He reached out his hand and I took it. Maeve closed the door and the family climbed the creaking ladder to the loft. The candles were extinguished, and with the soft whisper of prayers Father and I were in darkness. The fire died down to embers; Father pulled me close, the stubble of his face grazing my cheek, and the sweet, sour exhale of drink, shame, and fear parted his lips in penance. *I love you,* he said, *I love you,* and I couldn't tell whether he meant Rory or me, but holding me close, he squeezed the life from me, and we shivered together in the dark.

I woke in the morning, once more in the bed I shared with Finnoula — as if I had dreamed it all. But I descended the ladder and saw the dark spot where the cement had been washed of Colie's blood. Bernadette was at the fire boiling the tea and burning rashers on a spit. Maeve was running some clothing up and down a washboard and spitting on the clothes for good luck. Maurteen carried an armful of wet turf in from the road, his boots tracking thick muck onto the floor that Orla had just swept. She watched him, eyes flickering angrily from his footprints to his face, her arms tensing on the broom in her hand; he threw a wet log of turf on the fire and dumped the rest onto the cement before tracking back out again, unmindful of Orla. Smoke billowed out of the hearth and Orla's curses followed him out of the room. I imagined how crowded this small space must have been with ten children, screaming, shouting, fighting, laughing — how full of life, and how empty this space must have been when they were gone.

In the light of day and a roaring fire of turf, the brothers' and sisters' pinched faces seemed desperate and furtive; they were looking for an escape. Even in the daylight it seemed the fields were pressing in on them with memories they would rather have left forgotten.

After breakfast Finnoula opened the door to let in sunlight; the sound of Radio Éireann on the wireless sputtered out the soft cadences of Irish in a way that mimicked the rise and fall of the fire's flames, and the soft murmurings of the family circled in genuflection on the hard floor in prayer once more, unwilling to release their hold on one another. Father's eyes were bloodshot and he swayed noticeably on his knees. He had not washed the blood from his hands. Teresa pulled me close and, sobbing, crushed me against her breasts. Her rosary beads pinched my skin. After prayers Father remained kneeling with his eyes closed. I sidled up next to him and took his hand.

My aunts and uncles could not make Father leave; he would stay on and board up the house and leave, he said, when he was effin well ready to leave. I knew that he wanted to spend some time in the space that Rory had occupied all these years by himself, and I thought Father was also looking for penance for having failed him, and wanting to be punished for what he felt he had done or failed to do.

The brothers and sisters packed quickly and quietly, and then, once again, were gone, and the two of us were alone.

ather prepared to bring Rory's stone to the grave with the old donkey and trap. He had a hard time putting the bit in the animal's mouth and I saw his legs shaking with the effort to move the stubborn thing, but when I came forward to help him, he shouted at me, Stay back, she's quare contrary and she'd sooner kick you and disembowel you as have you do this to her. The two of them struggled together, stumbling back and forth like old fighters, each vying for weight and balance. The donkey tried to bite Father and Father belted it one powerful blow square in the mouth that resounded off the bone with a crack like hurleys striking. The animal's feet slipped, and Father, holding tight, finally got the bit in. The donkey snorted, rolled its eyes to the white, drew back its thick black lips into a sneer, and worked its jaws to remove the mouthpiece. You would have thought my Father was killing it.

You effin bitch, Father swore as he leant his shoulder into its thin skeleton and brought it out the gate. The donkey's foal rushed up but I closed the gate before it. Both mother and child seemed to panic. Father struggled in the muck as he drew the blind over the donkey and led it down the path. I reached through the gate and stroked the rough back of the foal, around the hard bone of its brown eyes, in the tufts of thick hair around its ears. It stood, blinking its long dark lashes; I reached forward with hay but it moved away, sniffing the air as if there was something burnt or dead upon it.

In the courtyard, the tire tracks of the stonecutter's lorry had left deep sinkholes, now filled with black bog water. It seeped into everything. Father splashed through the holes to the wooden pallet upon which Uncle Rory's headstone was strapped. It was greenish-gray marble, cracked with veins of silver-white mica and quartz. He stroked the beveled edges, searching for any defect, ran his hand across the smooth polished surface, along the straps where they pinioned its sides. He asked me to read the words, and nodded when I was done. I had forgotten that Rory was the same age as Father, and I knew that thirty-six was a young age to die.

Watch your face now, he said as he raised the tamping bar and drove its blunt edge down. Wood splintered and the taut straps snapped and uncoiled like black whips. The donkey groaned and stamped its hooves. A shiver ran along its ridged back and I imagined its eyes rolling white beneath the blind.

On the road, a sleek new silver Audi sped past without slowing. It caught the narrow edge that dropped to the bogs and it slid momentarily out of control, its spinning tires throwing up muck, its young driver blowing his horn. The donkey trap lurched with the weight of the headstone.

You cunt you, Father said, serve you right ending up in the bog. He held the animal's shoulder absently, almost protectively. It shook itself, and its tarnished harness jangled with the sound of old metal. We continued on, and Father seemed lost in the simple rhythm of the trap's wheels, the clicking swivel of its axle, the old creaking bearings, the sagging lean of the springs trussed like two great arches beneath the small bed, and the beating of the donkey's hooves upon the road, striking the ground at angles as if it were made of iron. They moved together, ineffably sad, straight-backed, stubborn, and belligerent, incessant as the clouds straggling above.

At the grave — a field of chest-high rushes that Father laid down angrily with the scythe — I looked for but could not find the drowned graves of Grandfather and Grandmother. Father said they'd used tall rowan branches to mark their resting places, but those, too, had sunk. He unraveled long iron bars from a tarp in the back of the trap and cursed that they, the brothers and sisters, never returned from America to place headstones on their parents' graves. Now where they were was anyone's guess. I wondered if Grandmother and Grandfather moved about below cursing as well, unable to find their resting places, or each other.

Father tipped the trap and, using rope and harness, slowly and softly dropped the pallet and its stone from its narrow, precarious rest. I pulled at an edge of the stone, tried to lift it upright, eager to show Father that I could. No, he said, you'll break your back that way. Use the bar as a lever. Father pried the bar beneath the headstone and the pallet, and I did the same. Slowly we raised it together and moved it forward an inch at a time, side to side, to the left and then to the right. I pretended that it was easy, although each time the weight was on my side I feared I would let it fall. Father watched me. Sweat beaded my upper lip. My arms were trembling. You're doing a grand job, he said. We're almost there. His forearms were limbed and hard as thick branches; his legs were strong, somehow noble, rooted in the bog.

Da, I groaned, Da — to warn him that I was about to let it fall, that I could hold it no longer, but he was driving relentlessly forward and I was stumbling and I heard a clang of metal and a pained sound whistling through his teeth and his feet continued to move and then the stone was sliding and slipping seamlessly into the narrow trench he had dug for it, black bog muck sucking hungrily at its edges. I dropped the bar and sat heavily on the pallet.

I didn't think it could be so heavy, I said and rubbed my arms.

Father winced and shook the fingers of his right hand. It was a while before he opened his eyes. Aye, he said, it's a heavy old bastard all right. He exhaled long and hard. But I won't begrudge Rory that, not after Mammy and Daddy. He grunted as he settled the stone, fingers reaching, scrabbling for a grip. Blood washed the marble, dropped thick to the fresh turned earth.

Your hand, Da.

It's nothing, the bar caught it is all. I'm fine.

He stared me down. It's nothing. I'm fine.

He continued rocking the stone from left to right, his face pale and wan, blood seeping from his fingers, and I stared at the blood as the stone sank deeper, and wondered how long it would take for the ground to swallow the stone whole — perhaps only as long as it took for me to return with *his* headstone here. And I imagined Rory turning beneath us, his bones shifting with the bog in the years to come, as he waited, restlessly, for my father.

From across the channel: a great gray wave of rain moving upon the water, and, driving before it, wild-wheeling cormorants and shearwaters. Father looked out at them, and I knew that he was judging the movement of the birds and the drift of the rain.

Rory almost died with the red fever when he was eight, Father said suddenly. They didn't think he would live at all, they gave up on him. I remember, at the time, just waiting for him to get up out of the bed, and Mammy and Daddy and all the lads telling me it wasn't going to happen. But I knew it was, I just knew. Honest to God, I knew. Eight days, eight bleeding days with the priest and Mammy moaning over him like fools, but I knew. Jaysus, sure they even gave him the last rites, so.

He stared at his hand and fingered the wound absently. When he spoke again his face was pained. Rory never did go back to school with the rest of us. Something had happened in his head, and he couldn't take to the learning no more. He began to go out with Daddy on the boat to the islands, and I don't suppose Daddy had much choice in the matter.

Father laughed, and even he seemed surprised by it. He shook his head. The wee *puckawn* would hide beneath the tarps until Daddy was out to sea and there was nothing Daddy could do. I'd rarely seen Daddy so mad. When they got back that night, he wanted to give Rory a thrashing, but after Rory's sickness, Daddy didn't like to beat him. And it was no good anyway, so. The next time Daddy went out, Rory did it again until Daddy *had* to give in. Daddy used to say there was something special about Rory out on the open water, like he'd never been sick at all — like he'd never been sick a day in his life. He used to say Rory had the work in him of two men, and I believe it.

Father smiled and stared back toward the channel. Come on, *a mhac,* Father said and gestured with his head toward the road. Let's get home.

I reached for his hand but he was already bending for the iron bars. He threw them into the trap and the sound was loud in the stillness, almost deafening, and I felt as if I was waking from a deep sleep as we moved again. I could still feel the weight of Rory's stone in my shoulders and the long walk to the grave in my legs, and I wished Father would just rest for a while.

The donkey was lathered with sweat thick as brine; it streaked its matted coat as if it had been cut by the whip. We paused at the rusted village pump at the outskirts of Ivneen. Father drew the water slowly, his hand moving the handle up and down so that water rushed in the sluice and spilt to the drain, where he urged the donkey to drink. He removed the mouthpiece and bit. The trap rocked weightlessly as the donkey leant forward. It lapped at the clear water with its long gray tongue and Father removed his old wool jumper and wiped down its body with it. His hands moved with a tender force as if he were lost in thought. The reins rattled in his hand. The donkey trembled with his touch but did not move away. Only when the animal was done did Father lean forward and, with closed eyes, wash the wound of his hand. Shards of white bone poked from the pink flesh. The shock of such damage frightened me, but I did not say a word. I watched as he scraped at the loose bits of matter, and the water was still running with blood when he wrapped his hand with a tear of his jumper.

My grandparents' cattle had been sold off, or had fallen and been lost in the bogs, and, with them, the sheep, the goats, the few hens and bantams. I expected that if the bogs were turned upside down and the world put on its ear, all my grandparents' lost livestock would emerge and, perhaps, my grandparents, and Uncle Rory with them. The land had been rented out as grazing pasture now, although the fields were barely more than bog and marbled rock. Situated above a bare rise that looked down upon Grandfather's boat moored in the shallows, it was a place where the wind never stopped.

Movement on the dark skerries caught my eye. Gray seals were gathering and calling to one another in the fading evening light the way a family might when coming across the fields at the end of the day. So human was the sound, so lonely and disconsolate and full of longing, that I couldn't help but think they were calling to us and waiting for some type of response.

Da, I called. Do you hear the seals out there? Beyond Grandfather's boat.

Father paused, and the trap rattled to a stop. He cocked his head toward the north, lee of the wind, and waited. It began to rain. There was the sigh of sea, a feeble baa from sheep rutting in the thicket, and the jangle of the donkey as it shook its blind. Then the song came again, louder than before, from the farthest end of the promontory where a great gray seal rose itself and called out, and then was answered by every seal along the skerry's length. It brought the hair up on my arms with the pleasure and the unexpected joy of it. I grinned when I saw Father smile. He nodded with the sound and then urged the donkey on again and I followed, glancing back at the skerries and the seals until they were gone from sight.

On the horizon clouds swirled in perpetual circles and rain fell through soft-tonsured sunlight. There was a quality to it that suggested prayer, worship of the sky and the sea and earth, and I thought of people praying here once, coming up from the bogs or the dense woodlands that would become bogs to light fires on the high ground during the feasts of Samhain and Bealtaine, a thousand years ago.

As we came down the lane to the house, the dog caught sight of us and barked, crouched to the ground, tail thumping the muck furiously. Her coat was matted and her shanks were crusted with hard black shit. Father called her *Maúr na Caoirigh,* which meant Shepherd of the Sheep — which I liked best — or *An Sean Mada Salach* or *An Gruaimín* and sometimes just *Spota,* as if he'd forgotten her real name or put all the dogs he ever knew as a child together into this one. It didn't seem to matter what my father called her; the dog greeted him and knew him in the way that it seems only some dogs can know some people.

Father flexed his right hand and grimaced. By God, that dog's been alive forever, he said. He patted his thigh and the dog came running, her rear swinging out behind her through the rain. He shook his head and squatted on his haunches when she came up to him, pushing her trembling snout into his cupped hands. Her teeth were worn and blackened. One of her eyes simmered soupily with a cataract. He cradled her head and ran his fingers from muzzle to stop and then back again. She closed her eyes.

The rain fell harder and the donkey shook its bridle. I moved from foot to foot. When Father looked up, he was smiling. He squinted into rain falling in silver crescents across his face and climbed to his feet. I held the donkey as he unhitched the trap; the torn wrap of jumper around his hand was sodden with blood and the rain sprayed it across the worn leather-and-metal tack and then washed it clean again. The donkey pushed quickly past me as I opened the gate, the barrel of its stomach knocking me aside as it hurried to its foal, a small, barely discernible shape huddled at the bottom of the field.

Come here, Father said, I have something to show you. He followed the narrow, rutted cow path down past the drinking well and the dung heaps to the old sunken byre and then glanced back over his shoulder. You made me think of it back there, he said, with the seals and their singing.

What is it? I asked. The light was fading quickly. He opened the latch and pushed against the door. The timbers were rotted and he had to lift and push it across the stone with his injured hand. Standing next to him, I took hold of the door and lifted and pushed when he did, still thinking of how I'd let Rory's headstone fall. Gradually, the dark interior of the barn opened itself to us. The smell of cow shit still present, glints of blue-green phosphorescence alight on the rotted dung and straw.

I stood at the threshold as Father made his way through the barn, hands sweeping the darkness and tentatively guiding the way.

Where are you? I asked. I searched for him but could find nothing.

Hold on, he grunted. We used leave the lamp here. There it is.

I heard the sound of paraffin sloshing as he shook the lamp, the scrape of glass as he removed the lens. His face was suddenly illuminated by the flare of a match, an orange oval flickering in black space. He ignited the wick, and when he'd placed the glass around it, he raised the lamp so that his corner of the barn was filled with warm light. Father reached down and pulled back several burlap sheets that were laid against the wall between ashen stacks of turf. Rain tapped upon the roof. The dog sniffed the air and then nosed the old straw beddings.

I took in the room slowly, in the small glimpses that the lamp allowed: the beams and rafters that rose to a second tier where hooks and pulleys dangled amongst thick spiderwebs, the metal rusted, the wood cracked and brittle. The bowed roof, sunken like a galley across its nave. Stalls that once contained animals. A hoofing anvil, a cracked metal gambrel, dented milking buckets. An urn for turning milk. And then the light fell upon the wide black eyes of a seal staring out of the darkness at me. I cried out and stumbled backward.

Michael, Father called, it's me, it's me. I looked again and Father was holding the body aloft as if it was still swimming yet, swimming toward me through the darkness of a deep undisturbed sea. Jaysus, I whispered. The lamp flickered across its unwavering sloe-colored eyes, its small flared nostrils that were once moist, on the dull, slightly shriveled skin. Yet I could clearly see the life that it once possessed. At first it seemed so small, barely more than a pup, but as Father lay it back down within the burlap, its sunken length stretching across his extended forearms, I realized that it was an adult fully preserved by the bog.

Father looked at me, unmoving. It is something, isn't it. You'd think it was still alive, honest to God.

The dog sniffed at an end of the seal and my father belted her lightly. Go away!

How long has it been here? I asked.

The seal? Oh God, years and years. I don't know why in God's name Rory held on to it but he did. Father stroked the skin of the seal almost tenderly and then looked up — They say if you have a Selkie's sealskin it can never go back to the sea.

Father pulled back the other tarps, and I saw how, over the long time that Rory had waited, the bog had slowly given up all manner of long-dead things: a fully preserved cat, the small shriveled remains of a curlew, fetters and bindings of a horse trap, a woman's ragged red shawl turned black, a doll's head, parts of a hurley, and a slane, a cast-iron ladle, knotted remnants of fishing line, the strange hard shell of a bone corset — all arranged on the old stone.

I looked at the red-black shawl curled like hemp rope. It glittered reddish-gold, mica or mineral from the bog, I assumed. Father pursed his lips, the way he did when he was about to conduct business or when he had a story to tell. He said that the shawl belonged to a woman who'd come across the bogs at night to meet her secret love but who'd fallen and, like everything else, it seemed, been lost in the bogs.

I don't believe you, I said.

He smiled and shrugged, squeezed the knees of his trousers. I swear to God, it was the truth according to Rory.

Who was she?

Her name was Gráinne. She was from a small village on the other side of the lough. Father straightened and placed his hands on his lower back. They never found her body, he said, and when I looked at him, he added, only the seal's.

I stared at him and then at the garment, threads of its buried color highlighted by the low paraffin flame now sliding down the turf stacks as it began to flicker and ebb, so that for a moment the shawl resembled something golden and then something as hard as twisted black metal.

I saw the woman making her way from her village, rushing down the mountainside to be with her love, hurrying across the soft slough with thoughts only of him, then her feet slipping and the muck pulling her down and only time for one desperate scream before the bog rushed in and filled her open mouth, her hands clawing uselessly at the crumbling banks, the red shawl sliding from atop her head and spreading upon the dark surface before sinking as well. Then gone and only bog, blacker than the starless night, remaining.

The dog waited beyond the door and peered in, rain lashing her face so that she looked as if she were frowning. I curled the shawl into a pocket of my anorak. Father rolled up and covered Rory's artifacts, and then let the lamp extinguish itself. For a moment we stood in the square of gray light from the door, staring at the dog squatting in the rain.

Up the lane, the dog barking, we raced through the rusted wrought-metal gate. Rain rattled on the tin roofs and I smelled the metal of the sea. The shed door was flung open and banged loudly with a sudden gust of wind. My shirt whipped at my back. Fog moved in from the narrow tree line and sound filtered across the bogs seemingly without origin: trees splintering and falling into the sphagnum, birds crying, cattle and sheep moaning, men and women's voices as they worked the peat — all commingled in distant echo.

From the kitchen window I watched as the storm came in off the Atlantic. Someone had better bring the dog in, I thought, and I looked beyond the road to the north fields in the distance. Through the gloom I could see that one of the gates was swinging free and I went to move but then realized there was no longer anything left to care for there — those fields were empty but for the gate clanging against the cement posts and ringing for what seemed an eternity.

Father struggled from the outhouse. The door rocked with the wind as he entered the scullery. After he had pulled off his cap and jumper and hung them on the peg to dry, he rummaged beneath the sink for the bottle of Dettol, then slouched toward the living room, coughing harshly.

I looked at his hand. Da, that must hurt, so it must.

No. No, not at all.

Should we not go to a doctor?

Not at all. It's fine, he said and wiggled his fingers to prove it.

He eased himself into the chair by the fire, its embers still bright and glowing from the turf we'd stacked upon it earlier in the morning. He stoked the fire, added more turf, and then began to arrange the basin of water and disinfectant, but he seemed distracted.

How is your mother? he asked.

She's well, I lied. I was surprised he'd asked at all; it meant that he was thinking of her and, I hoped, of Molly and me. Perhaps this meant that he was considering not returning to America after all.

She's looking forward to seeing you, I said but paused when I sounded too eager. That is, if you're coming down before you leave. I shrugged.

He stared for a long moment at his boots.

That is, if you are. You might not be.

Musha, musha, he sighed, and began to undo his laces. I knelt before the fire to help him with his boots but he waved me away. It's been a long day, Michael. It's time you were in bed.

I rose to go fill the buckets with water from the well when Father called me back to him, and for a moment I thought he was still angry at me. He loosened phlegm in his throat before he spoke. You were a great help to me today, he said. You worked as hard as any man.

Outside, the storm front had passed. The air was cold and the fog turned to threads with the chill. The buckets were large and heavy and I thought of the weight of Rory's headstone. I stumbled but would not let go. I staggered to the door, water sloshing cold on my jeans, and finally put the buckets down.

When I returned Father had begun to clean the wound. I placed the black cast-iron kettle over the hob and sat back on the settle. Father unraveled the dark sodden cloth and stared at his hand. He wiped at the hardened blood, poked at the wound to ascertain the damage. Again I had to look away from the shock of exposed bone, but he seemed unconcerned. His jaw was set, his eyes narrowed in deliberation of the work as if he were sewing a wool jumper or repairing fishing line. When he threw the bloody rag into the fire, it blackened and curled into itself, and with a spit of sparks the fire flared up. He reached for the Dettol and bared clenched teeth when he poured it over his hand. Exhaling slowly, he leant his head back, exposing the pale stubble on the underside of his neck.

After he had bound his hand in fresh bandaging, he worked his stockinged feet before the embers and sleepily watched the fire die out. He pulled a rag from his trousers and blew his nose into it, opened the rag, looked at the snot there, rolled it all up, put it back in his pocket, and closed his eyes.

Good night, Da, I said.

Good night, son. Try and get some sleep.

The Angelus sounded on Radio Éireann and we blessed ourselves. I counted the slow bells, smelled the muck on Father's Wellingtons, and listened to it dropping off his boots in the heat of the fire.

There seemed to be little keeping us here now, but Father was reluctant to leave, to return to America the way his brothers and sisters had done a week before. He spread the dung heaps around the stone walls at the farthest edges of the courtyard for fertilizer and planted seeds for beautiful flowers. Mounds and mounds of them so that it would take him days. I looked at the colored photographs. I read the wonderful descriptions of Araceae, Amorphophallus, Cruciferae, and Caladium, and I wrote them down, said them aloud, practicing my spelling and my pronunciation. And then there were their common names: Chinese evergreen, Devil's tongue, Resurrection plant, Angel wings, Peace lily, Jericho rose, Sleeping mother. The Hanging Jesus's tears that would grow like a vine, up surrounding trees and walls, and shelter everything within it. I read about the conditions needed for their survival: none of the seeds Father planted here would survive. All that would grow were of the family Bryaceae and Caliciaceae — moss and lichen. We took two trips into Galway City in the rented car to buy more seed, and then more and more seed, until all the silage was spread and every space of two inches within the dung was planted a suspension of exigent exotic bloom.

⊗

Father banged the buckets in the scullery and checked on the stew brewing over the fire. He'd already put the dog in the shed for the night although it was still yet early; he must have been awfully tired.

He took the accordion down off the shelf and sat before the fire. It was the first time I'd seen him touch it. He rested it in his lap and immediately drew his hands away. He held them out at his side as if he did not know what to do with them. Together we stared at the music box, at the way the fire played in gold on the red and black and silver. Gradually Father's hands returned to him. Carefully, he unhooked the clasps, slid a thumb into the thumb strap, and paused with his large hands cradling the cherrywood sides.

He looked at me. Rory was my twin, you know, he said.

I nodded. This was his, he said. I gave it to him when we were twelve. He was always better at it than me. Daddy was proud that I'd done that. I think it made Rory very happy. He nodded to himself. Daddy bought it from a Carraroe man who needed passage to America. I'd done well at the Board Exams, and he was very proud of that, he was, thought one of his sons would be something. He laughed. He probably wouldn't have bought it if he'd known it was to be my last year. Had to work on the farm after that and then took off to England and became a laborer, a feckin laborer. Oh ho, Daddy with his stories.

I don't know if the man ever got to America, he said. We never heard from him again, so. Perhaps he did, perhaps he didn't. Father gazed at the accordion, his eyes lost in some distant memory as they roved across its lacquered surface. The tendons in his hands rose up as he clutched the accordion to him. I think it made Rory happy, he said.

Father removed his thumb from the strap, fastened the clips so that the bellows was bound once more, rose slowly, and, without a word, carefully placed Rory's accordion back upon its high shelf. Then he stepped out into the courtyard, closing the door behind him. His feet sounded on the cobblestone, and long after he was

gone, I continued to hear his footfalls on the path, and then returning again, as if he were merely traveling in circles.

I heard Father's whistling before anything else, and when he came
in with the dog and stamped his feet on the mat in the scullery, I
tried to joke. Ah, I said, would you whisht with that awful racket —
you'll even drive the poor old dog away. I grinned.

He looked at me and then at the dog. He was slow hanging his
jacket on its hook. It's not the dog that minds it, he said, and peeled
off his Wellingtons. Didn't think you were so bleedin sensitive. Just
like your mother.

My throat was suddenly tight. Sure I was joking, I said. Whistle
all you want for all I care. I felt the heat of blood in my face.

Do you need a hand with your boots? I asked, but he didn't
respond. The dog followed him to the fireplace. That's a grand fire,
Father said, and I nodded.

I suppose we'll be going soon, I said. Now that everything's set.

Soon, he agreed, soon enough.

What about the dog, what about the furniture and beds, what
about Rory's old accordion?

He rolled his eyes toward the ceiling. I must go put the dog away
for the night, he said.

I'll do it.

No, the dog doesn't know you. It's hard enough me putting her
in. He rose from the chair with a grunt and slapped his thigh, calling
the dog to him.

I'm not like my mother, I said, and he looked at me but said
nothing.

After the door closed I took a towel and lifted the kettle off the
hob. I'm like you, I said to the empty room. I'm like you. She always
says so.

I heard Father talking to the dog as they made their way to the cow shed, of things only the two of them knew; it was a tender sound full of caring and intimacy. I pulled the curtains closed and stood there in waning light sensing rather than noticing the room growing dark. I looked at the red accordion and imagined its sound in this dark, dim-lit house, down through the final years of Uncle Rory's life: the hiss of the paraffin lamps as the oil ran low, a meager fire crackling in the hearth because all the turf had been sold off, and nothing beyond the windows but the sea and the promise of a wet day just the same as the last.

The room grew darker, and I didn't bother to light the lamps. I pictured the accordion's solid cherrywood, and the running board of keys, sleek melodeon black. I heard its handmade Italian reeds, its distinct Irish tuning. When I was younger, I was told that the buttons of Rory's accordion were made of Basking-shark bone, the gold flake that burnt in the red lacquer smelt from rock, and the marble patina rubbed and daubed and buffed to a high polished sheen with Father and Rory's own birthing caul. The way everyone talked about it, you'd think it was magic.

I took the accordion down from its place on the shelf and I was surprised by its weight. I cradled it gently, watched the light at play upon the marble and wood, this instrument that was Father's present from Grandfather, that allowed a man to buy his way to America, that became Rory's and was now Father's again. I thought of everything it meant to my father and I wondered when Father left if he would take it with him.

Suddenly, I was filled with such sadness and anger I didn't know what to do with it. I raised the accordion above my head and threw it down as hard as I could. The cherrywood cracked, the accordion's innards splintered. The bellows groaned as it distended. For a long moment I stared at the damage, unable to believe what I'd done, and I was too scared to move, thinking that if I didn't move, if I held my breath I could somehow hold time, that I could even undo what I'd done and make things right, but when I did breathe again nothing had changed. The accordion remained on the floor as it had moments before, and I knew there was nothing I could do to make this right.

I picked up the accordion and turned it over. The wood was split along its undersides. When I shook it something loose tumbled inside. I smelled the richness of cherrywood like something thick that had seeped from an open wound. When I closed the bellows and clipped it shut I was glad that it made no sound. I placed the accordion back on the shelf, my hands trembling, and then the rest of me began to shake as well.

The bog gives back what it claims, Father said. Always, all things come back to us. Ten thousand years ago things fell into the bogs and they are still coming back. If you waited long enough everything returned. I thought of the bog giving back Rory, his arms breaking the bog surface and rising toward the sun, purple heather erupting in blossom from his cracked and bloodless palms. I pictured him treading from the grave, walking the long road from Oughterard, the mangy flesh of his feet giving way, and only the thought of the accordion in his dead head and the need for revenge urging him, stumbling on, mile after mile. Would he be black or stripped of skin, his bones polished and shining brightly? Would his soul be intact?

The dog howled from the shed and I knew Father was making his way back across the courtyard. I looked toward the living room and then toward the scullery as if for a way out, as if I could run all the way back to my mother in the South, and as if I was half expecting dragging footsteps on the cobblestone and the heavy sound of fleshless bone striking the latch of the door. What could be worse than that? But I knew what could be worse. It would be to see Father standing there with his smashed accordion, and not Rory at all.

We spent the next day cleaning out the old cow byre. To keep us warm, Father got a small fire going in a rusted milking bucket, and its light threw the shadows of the hanging gambrels and chains and hooks across the walls as we worked.

The dog stayed beyond the door in the sunlight, every once in a while glancing in, and only later when it became cooler and the sun had gone down did she wander into the warmth. She groaned, a bored human sound, and settled herself onto the straw. Father laughed and shook his head. Go on you, he said and the dog looked at him, her ears alert. You would think he'd said, C'mon, girl, let's go find those sheep. When she saw that there were no sheep to be got, she lowered herself onto the straw and closed her eyes. Father stared at her for a moment and then began to tie up the bundles of Rory's possessions.

When we stepped out of the barn it was dusk, the twilit rock walls glowing like ashen coals as our eyes adjusted to the changing light. Starlings were skimming low over the rocky fields, racing along the tops of stone walls. A gray-blue stretch of sky was holding the last of the low sun, and it reached like a bough over the bay toward Rosmuc.

Father called to the dog but there was no sound of her. We turned back toward the shadows and father raised the lamp. Her long body lay stretched across the straw as if she were chasing something in her dreams, and although he called again, *Spota,* she didn't move. Father sank to the straw next to her and then she opened her eyes to him, whined to him — a sound that was imploring and pleading and strangely human — licked at his fingers, still, it seemed, so eager to please, her tail thumping a broken cadence on the stone floor.

Talk to her, he said. I have to fetch the gun from the house. And I talked to Spota, I told her of where we'd all be off to after we were done with the shed and what we had planned for all the days before Father left us again; I told her, *When you're hurt like this, in the country, we must kill you — it's the only way,* and then I stroked her head, and she let me. When Father returned I smelled the oil of the gun first, and then the looming black shape of him framed the doorway and the length of gun was an extension of his hand divining the space of sky at his back and the earth and everything between. He stepped forward and knelt and the image was gone. He touched Spota's head, talked to her until she closed her eyes. Then he rose, stationed the barrel at the back of her head, and fired one shot into her. The sound was muted in the close shed — the lanyards jangled although there was no wind to move them — nothing more than a dull pop, a shudder of air, and Spota was still for good.

From the gun, acrid white smoke, no wider than a candle flame, curling in the graying space. Father stroked Spota's matted fur, cradled and squeezed her head roughly with affection so that her head lolled and she seemed alive and eager to be up and running. Good girl, he said, good girl, you're a good girl, as he ran his hand down the lean body in longer and longer strokes. As if he were merely coaxing and comforting her toward sleep after a long day. I imagined her rolling over onto her back and exposing her pale belly with the pleasure of it and with the trust and love she had for Father.

Slowly, he wrapped her body in a burlap tarp, folded the edges and bound them with rope the way that he had wrapped Rory's possessions, then rose with the dog bundled in his arms. Come, he said, and I followed him up the hill, with the sky turning purple around us, toward the blackened stack of wood, the edges of the burlap overhanging his arms, dangling as if it were a child in a gansey, bundled against the cold weather.

The dog should've seemed larger wrapped within the thick burlap, but atop the woodpile she looked very small. He poured the last of the paraffin over the blackened timbers and the tarp, and when he threw a match upon it, it exploded into a huge billowing flame that took the breath from our lungs and only slowly folded into itself. We stepped back and watched the black shape of the tarp burning brightly and quickly becoming smaller. A wind came up and carried the embers and the smoke toward the north, and I was glad for it because I didn't want to smell the dog.

Father stooped, gouged a handful of muck from the ground, and threw it onto the fire. He said something in Irish that I didn't understand and it didn't seem important that I should and I felt no need to ask him what it meant. On top of the hill, the air, the space that we occupied, the enclosed stillness that we were wrapped within had the quality of a church, of cupped hands holding us close, and I didn't wish to disturb it. Father wiped his hands on his trousers and then picked up the empty paraffin canister, but we stood there still, for a long time watching the fire burning down and, at its edges, glimmering like steel, the dark countryside beyond.

Three weeks passed and the days became warm and fine. Knowing that the weather would not last, Father took long walks around the property; in wider and wider circles he traveled outward and then, shortening his circles, he returned in the evening once more. Now that Spota was gone I joined him, and though we were mostly silent as we climbed through gorse and over stone walls, I no longer minded this silence; Father seemed content, even happy that we were together.

We were passing the lough when Father gestured toward the small islands at its center. When we were children, he said, Rory and me used to row out there and make small camps. We'd light a fire of turf and cook up fish we caught in the tide pools. We wrapped them up in seaweed so as not to burn them. The dog would be barking from the far shore at us. Sometimes we brought her with us but she'd get so restless over there she wouldn't stop until we brought her back again. He laughed. I think she just wanted the boat ride, never saw a dog like her the way she took to water.

He walked toward the field's edge and began to make his way down to the rocky shoreline. It used to make us feel like we were adults, going out there, he said. And here's where we used to swim. The water always stayed the warmest here, it caught the last of the sun.

I followed him down to the rocky edge. There was no shoreline really, just rock upon rock. Father sat on a large one that jutted out over the water. He took off his Wellingtons and his jumper and then began to undo his trousers. Within moments, he was standing on the rock in his underwear. He seemed taller without clothes, all lean muscle, as straight and angled as a pale blade driven into the earth. The only darkness on him was around his neck and on his arms; everything else looked as if it had never seen the sun. Father bent forward, slipped smoothly into the water, and disappeared beneath it. Moments later he surfaced, about ten yards out, the roped muscles in his shoulders glistening. He began to kick farther out but then quickly turned on his back and floated. Father didn't swim. He bobbed up and down on the swells as if he were driftwood, sea wrack waiting for the tide to wash him to shore.

I rushed down to the rock where Father's clothes lay and quickly undid my own. I struggled with my Wellingtons and nearly tore the ear off me trying to get the jumper over my head, and I knew if my mother were there I would have gotten a good belt for that. I eased myself over the rock ledge into the water and was surprised by how cold it was. My breath caught in my chest and I pulled my legs up. I hung there off the rock, with my knees pulled up to my chest, swinging in my underwear.

Father drifted closer, paddling with his hands. Michael, he said, just let yourself go. The water is deeper than you think. You won't hit rock. Just let yourself go, hold your breath, and before you know it, you'll be back on top again. It's only cold for a moment.

I closed my eyes, took a deep breath, and shoved myself backward off the rock. I opened my eyes. There was blue sky and high white clouds and a gannet beating its black-edged wings and then I was under. By the time I was sputtering on the surface and flailing my arms and legs trying to stay afloat, I wasn't thinking about the cold any longer. I splashed toward Father, who had floated out again but who had turned to make sure he could see me, his feet kicking, his laughter deep and pleasant and resounding off the rocks around us.

We stayed in the water until the sun had fallen away to the west and shadows stretched across the lake and the water turned cold. When we climbed out, gingerly feeling our way along the rocks, I wished we had thought to bring towels. I stood there shivering, wondering what to do, and Father said, Never mind, sure the walk home will warm us up, so. Just put your clothes on, and use your jumper to dry yourself off as best you can. We can change again when we get in.

I toweled myself off with my jumper so that I was mostly dry, but I was already cold, my skin tightening and turning pink, then purple. Father and I walked the fields briskly and I wanted to run but my legs felt too heavy. I worked hard to keep up. He held barbed wire apart so that I could pass through, and standing astride stone walls, he waited for me and then reached for my arms and swung me over. Soon I'd forgotten how cold I was. Father began to sing "The Green Fields of France" and his voice was loud and strong and I joined him for the end of the long chorus, where the young soldier is put in the ground, our voices rising and falling breathlessly as we hurried through burnt-lit fields turning marble in the half-light.

As I undressed in the bedroom, I noticed the first of the ticks, on my thigh, another on my calf, and then higher, on my stomach. And there were more of them besides. I cursed and pulled off my underwear. Three of them, swollen and shiny, clung to my testicle. Da! I shouted. Da! I pulled up my underwear and stood there without moving, sure that I could feel them on me, burrowing deeper and deeper.

Father was in the room. What is it?

I have ticks on me, I said.

He looked me up and down.

Down there, I said, in my underwear.

Father stared at me. Don't worry, let us have a look.

I pulled down my underwear and looked away. Father took hold of my arms and shuffled me closer to the candlelight. I sensed that he was kneeling and then his hard fingers were brushing my penis, and he grunted, Dirty little bastards, and I was glad for the tone of his voice, as if he were merely discovering a tick on the dog. I had seen him be gentle in that, too, seen his concern for the dog and the direct way in which he applied himself to the task of removing it.

This will hurt a bit, he said, and it did. He held the loose skin firmly between his fingers and then, using his nails, he squeezed, pried first the head of one tick out, and then the others, working as quickly as he could. I clenched my teeth, closed my eyes, and willed myself not to cry out.

Got you, you bastard, Father said and then his hands were no longer on me. He patted my thigh and I pulled up my underwear, my testicles throbbing. I couldn't look Father in the eye but was glad when he squeezed my shoulder. In his other hand he held the ticks in balled-up tissue paper.

Well we won't go swimming there again. He grinned, and I tried to smile and wanted to laugh but thought if I laughed I would cry instead; I was so grateful to him for not being ashamed of me.

Can you manage the rest? he said and I nodded and he stroked my head, and when he left he closed the door behind him. The other ticks came out more easily, once I got used to applying pressure beneath their mouths and pushing upward. The fatter they were the easier it was. One burst between my fingers and I had to dig again to pry its small head out. When I was done, I washed myself with water from the basin on the nightstand, then dressed and went to the door, but I didn't want to open it. I felt the shame of everything all over again. Slowly I opened the door and stepped out into the living room. Father looked up and rose from his chair. He poured some *poitín* into a cracked mug, thinned it with warm tea steeping over the fire, and handed it to me.

Here, he said, this will make you forget all about it. Drink it slow. I took the cup and he watched me as I sipped, and then grinned when tears came to my eyes and color flushed my cheeks. The slow lasting burn in my throat made me forget everything else. Made me think that I might even laugh along with him, with the pure joy and relief of it.

The animal sheds were boarded up, the cottage walls and floors washed, the windows and doors left open to air out rooms and to allow everything to dry. Father replaced broken and missing slates and fixed the gutters, painted the windows and replaced the putty in the frames that blackbirds had picked clean. We were working in the courtyard, clearing it of grass.

Father had given me a small hand scythe and shown me how to swing it while he used the big scythe to cut the deep stretches around the well. I moved my scythe back and forth, copying Father's large thrusting cuts. He twisted from the waist and he was a gyre of torque propelling arm and scythe. Sunlight caught his blade and his arc was a prism of shattered light as he cleaved the grass in two.

Father watched me as well. That blade is sharp, he said. Watch your leg and arm on the backswing, and so I did, and I was too busy watching him, wondering how he could make it look so easy when already my arm and my back were aching, that I didn't notice the two old men come up the lane until I heard them at the gate arguing, one of them hacking phlegm, and Father was crossing the field to join them. *Dia anseo isteach!* they greeted him and the three shook hands.

Father asked them inside for the tea but they declined and passed their tobacco to him but Father didn't smoke. They'd come to see about The Leaving on Friday; it was the first I'd heard of it.

How's young Michael? I heard one of them ask, and Father looked toward me, looked at me as if he were looking at me for the first time. I dropped my scythe and pretended to be engrossed in the work of tying bundles of wood and of stacking turf, of hacking a stubborn gorse root with an ax. He smiled and it brightened his face. *A mhac,* he called and I looked up. *Conas tá tú?* How are you?

Tá mé go maith, I said in my terrible Irish, and in hearing my own voice, I felt blood rush to my face. *Fáilte romhat,* I said, and *Tá sé fuar inniu agus ar mhaith leat cupán tae?* If not, then, *Slán leat,* for I have work to do before it gets dark, and the old men laughed and the eldest clapped his hands. The other, who had a dirty gray-stubbled face, said, *O Dia, a buachaill,* he's the spittin image of himself sure, and isn't it a great comfort you have in him.

It is, Father agreed.

They puffed on pipes as they spoke the Irish to Father and after a while they banged the pipes against the wall and placed them back in their pockets. One of the old men gathered his bike from the ditch while the other waited on the road.

We'll see you Friday then, he said and raised his hand in salute. God bless you.

Father nodded and wished them farewell. I came up to the wall and watched them make their way down the hill. Their figures became narrow silhouettes glancing through the light of the sun as it set in the bay, and still I heard their voices trailing behind, rising and falling, and then gone and only the low purple sky remaining, a last sliver of light raking across the water with night pressing down from above. A flock of greylag bellowed as they crossed the sky, black darts spearing west across the waters to America.

I'm leaving, Father said. It's time I was back. The job won't wait for me forever. I'll put you on the train to your mammy Saturday morning. I'm sure she's missing you something awful. You'll have to thank her for me. He tousled my hair, rested his large hand against my head and held it there. I don't know what I would have done without you here these last few weeks. The next time perhaps you'll come out to America to visit me — would you like that?

I nodded.

Good. It will be under better conditions than these — I promise.

He stared at me. You believe me, don't you?

Yes, I said. I wanted to believe him very badly.

I smiled and Father grinned. He pulled me close and squeezed me against the side of him, and then, taking my hands in his, he surprised me by beginning to spin me in a tight circle, something he hadn't done since I was a small child. Trust me, he said, and I wrapped my arms about him and held on, my legs swinging out wider and wider until I was completely airborne and in risk of being spun out over the fields, tethered only to the earth by my hold upon Father, and by his hold upon me. And then, at the edge of my sight, as if it had been there all along, a flaming red bush of Jericho rose burning in bright bloom from the dark mottled sedge.

Someone had strung a large banner over the mantel that read SLÁN AGUS BEANNACHT and I wondered whether they were saying farewell to Uncle Rory or to my father, for Father was merely returning to the country of his emigration. And because I didn't want to believe that America was Father's home and that he would never be returning, I thought this farewell must be for Rory.

There was food and drink for everyone. Men brought salmon and trout, and *poitín,* which they passed back and forth commenting upon its various qualities, laughing and teasing as they judged one man's ability at the still over another's. Women brought barmbrack and poultry, fresh eggs, vegetables from their gardens, and soda bread so that everyone could make sandwiches. The two old men who'd come to visit Father sat by the fire and told stories with the older people, although truly, there were no young people there. Whenever I passed, they reached out to touch me and look at me and I knew that when they did, they were thinking of Rory. The one with the face like ash-bearded coal muttered something in Irish and his speech was slurred, his eyes glistening. He stared at me and when I didn't respond he repeated in English, We'll be sorry when you leave, and it sounded so sad that I didn't know what to say. I smiled and shook his hand and moved away.

I kept the fire going well through the night and was glad for the attention and the distraction, the simple noise of people, of whiskey-warm breaths filling the room, and then as it got later I made a big pot of tea for those who had stayed. The guests were slightly drunk but pleasant and every once in a while I'd see a woman go out into the courtyard, and, leaving the door swinging wide behind her, she'd squat at the very edge of light cast from the door. Half in light and darkness, pale knees and thighs shining brightly, a splatter of urine upon stone, and then up with her stockings and quickly back in the house again amongst the music and the laughter.

A few of the men who brought their accordions were playing loudly and they kept cheering for Father to pick up Rory's accordion, teasing him to show them all how it was done. Father smiled and his cheeks glowed. He seemed happy and eager to please them, as if a weight was lifting off of him now that he was returning to America. Chairs were pulled back, women lifted the hems of their skirts, and people began to dance in the center of the room.

The men who were sitting began to sing and stamp their feet. I watched as a couple spun in the center of the room, round and around, gyring faster and faster, the man leading, the woman clinging to him and looking as if the wind had been knocked from her. Her hips were wide and her face was deeply lined and flushed; she seemed old and young at the same time. She had her head thrown back and was laughing. Her slender pale neck caught the candle glow and as she spun her rich black hair spread out behind her into a thick ropy fan. And I was cheering and clapping and then someone had taken Rory's accordion down from its ledge and placed it in Father's lap and Father took up the accordion and everything seemed to move slowly after. The smile faded from my face, a tightness squeezed my stomach, and I felt I would be sick.

I closed my eyes as he lifted the melodeon, and I waited for him to see the damage that I'd done. But when Father's fingers worked the buttons and keys and he opened the bellows, all this beautiful sound was rushing, spilling out, so beautiful that it seemed it could not possibly have come from Father nor belong to this room.

This is what I wished to happen. But in the silence I heard only Father crying. I turned to him and his hands were curled into claws poised above the ivory buttons; he depressed the keys but nothing would come. He raked at the silver, unable to open up the accordion to its beautiful rich sound as both he and Rory had once done. All the dancing, the foot stomping and hand clapping had stopped. Everyone in the room was looking at him, and his mouth parted as if in pain.

I can't, he sobbed. For fucksake — I can't.

He began to rock himself slowly back and forth, and I saw Rory with the face of my father sitting huddled by the dying embers of the fire, praying or singing as he died quietly, eyes fluttering like beautiful dark moths, black lung-blood bursting from his mouth, and nothing to see beyond this little kitchen, no lights no sounds no music but the wind the wind the wind — and the red accordion spilling, tumbling down from his hands.

the road to emain

September 1979

My aunt was peeling the spuds, her large body shaking with the effort of it. The kitchen walls were perspiring with steam, and the smell of carrots, turnip, cabbage and fish; hot, freshly baked bread; and salted, freshly churned butter seemed to drip from that steam so that I could almost taste it. The lids of pots were clacking — tap tap tapping as they boiled on the cooker. Mother checked the fish and then turned to me. I hadn't seen her as active in so long, and she smiled as if she enjoyed the work. Her face had regained some weight to it; it was no longer gaunt and sad looking. She wore a plastic bonnet on her head, tightly bound at the front and back. Chrissy Malone from up the road was down that morning doing her hair. *Fixing it in a style,* my mother said, mimicking Chrissy, who was a Corkwoman, *more fashionable,* and she curled her mouth to draw out the words that rose high at the end, *for the city than the hospital.*

A light seemed to burn from her insides. She slapped my aunt on the backside and my aunt jumped. Jaysus, Moira! she hollered and the knife she had been using to peel the spuds clattered into the basin.

Ah, go on, sure you've got meat enough on you for that, and besides, when was the last time a man had a go at you — by God, that's what you need now, Una, a fierce go with a man, you quare old cow, you.

Mother laughed and slapped her playfully again. I laughed and spit the milk from my mouth. My aunt shook her head. Jaysus, Moira, Jaysus. Don't be saying things like that in front of the boy. You're an awful woman, altogether, sure, you are, awful!

When Mother grinned I could see how long her teeth had grown, or rather, how her gums had pulled away with the illness — the new fullness to her face couldn't hide this; I suppose that it was a mark of her condition, little scars that were left as a reminder. But she was better now and that was all that mattered.

She looked out the window toward the fields and was still; a rain shower moved quick and dark over the land, the sun spilling down through it in shades of broken light, and then it was past and the fields shimmered bright and wet again. She shook her head incredulously with the wonder of it all.

There were fields that stretched for miles across wide, low valleys, fringed by smaller glens and woodlands, and stone ruins. My uncles were beyond the far rise of the valley where the Nore and Suir Rivers ran, in the field we rented from Flaherty. Beyond that were the Flats, a marshland where the rivers merged below the high rocky scree. A mile or two beyond was the town on the banks of the Barrow, and farther still, there was the sea.

How many haycocks did you say they'd baled, Michael? she asked, still staring across the valley. I can't believe your man has us doing this this late in the year.

Flaherty was supposed to have had the field topped and baled for us that summer; and though the field had been cut, the hay had been left to rot there. I looked at my hands, at the red, weepy blisters there, and tried to remember how we had arranged the hay in the field. I counted on my fingers.

I think it was five?

Those men, bloody loafers, so, she said, but even this seemed to entertain and amuse her.

She left the kitchen and my aunt's eyes followed her; together we listened to her quick short footsteps on the lino, the squeal of the rear door, and then her feet crunching the gravel and her voice as she called the cats to her.

Michael, she called, go get Oweny and Brendan out of those fields. The work will still be there tomorrow.

She called to me again: Fetch some water while you're there, and tell Brendan to clean his mouth out before he comes in the house. The saints give me strength, where did I get a family like this at all?

My aunt smiled. Praise be to God, the *geis* has been lifted from her, she said. Her words filled my head with a silence so great that only slowly did I return from it to the sound of water rushing from the tap. My aunt, a big burly country woman, unused to displays of tender emotion, stared toward the space Mother had occupied moments before, with such a strange look that it took me a while to understand it was a look of love that could not be expressed in any other way.

After the soft rain, the fields were full of amber light; the unharvested grain threw the sun back in sheets. A wind swept down from the hills and bent the stalks back and forth; rain-blackened scioc shuddered stiffly amongst the yellow gorse. Children's voices at play somewhere, perhaps miles off, were intermingled with the noise of men and the churning of threshers. A herd of Jerseys, mottled black and white, lowered their heads to drink at the falls below Delacey's. Flax dripped through the air, heavy, dry on my eyes and the back of my throat.

In the glen, the trees rose high, higher than in the surrounding fields, and the sound of the falls ebbed, murmuring softly through the underbrush. I descended through trees, the air was cool and moist, and things scattered in the gorse. All sounds fell to a muted hush, with something like reverence.

When I was younger, this was a favorite place I would come to of a twilight. Beyond, everything moved as it would, but here, time was stilled. I'd watch the light fade deep in the woods and the mist of dusk rolling silent and thick through the trees. And once, when I was ten, I even saw the spirit of Peadar O'Suilbháin's widow, the witch that haunted the glen.

My uncle Oweny often talked of the O'Suilbháins' little house, a hovel really, with the pig and cow quarters backed up to the side of the house the way they used to be. It was still there, down the small overgrown boreen deep in the bottom of the glen, and within it lived the widow Ní Suilbháin, whom everyone called a witch. It was said that she had killed her husband and children. Her love had been so great, so possessive of them, it had poisoned and consumed them, and they died with the fever of it. Now she wandered the glen and could never know love again.

I was in awe of the story, not really frightened by it. It seemed sad and odd that the local folk could think that the widow's love, being so great, had not sheltered and comforted, as one expected love to do, but rather destroyed everything close to her. If it had truly happened as they said, how sad that must be — to lose everything just because you loved so very much.

It was autumn then, too, and near the end of the day, and I'd just come from running across the hills. A wind moved across the treetops, and it was the sound of waves breaking softly upon a shore. I closed my eyes and let the sensation of the place rush over me: soft moss beneath my feet, sunlight flickering down through the treetops, glinting shafts flickering and trembling in reds and oranges across the insides of my closed eyelids.

And then, I heard the dry snap of twigs, so unexpected and loud in the hush, I stopped and my breath caught. I opened my eyes. Distance in that place was hard to judge, but there, before me, it seemed not more than twenty feet away, stood a woman, with a basket of small shrubs and berries cradled against her bosom as if she were protecting them. A red shawl was tied about her head, and she wore a stiff black dress, the type the old people wore at funerals.

At first I thought her old, and wizened, her back bent by the years, but I realized she was merely stooping to pick wildflowers and had paused in midstride, as if somehow she could avoid detection if she remained as still as a wild doe. When her face rose I saw that, though it was thin, it shone with the color of youth. Her eyes, though I don't know how I could possibly see them, being as far away as I was, were a bright blue. A damp wisp of red hair slipped from her shawl and curled on her brow.

I stood still: it was the witch Ní Suilbháin. I held my breath and waited. Eventually, she began moving through the trees once more. And I sensed that I could hear her singing then, like the wind singing through the high treetops. It became darker and from the deeper woods came the cry of nightjars, which always gave me the shivers. Only then did I wake and begin to move, wondering if I had seen her at all or if it had just been my imagination. I had no idea how long I had been standing there, but I kicked up the dry combs and leaves dampening the mossy floor and sprinted from the glen.

And after, even though Molly and I often dared each other to take the path at dusk, I never would again.

When I jumped the stile into the field, Uncle Brendan was standing atop the sixth haycock, tamping down the layers, laying them like thatch, so that the rain would run off and the hay would stay dry. He shifted his weight easily and gracefully atop the high mound. Short, stocky Oweny practically raised a bale of hay to him with each heft, his wide legs planted on the flatbed like small oaken tree trunks. Before I was halfway across the field, I could hear the swears out of Brendan's mouth. Oweny smiled, and nodded, and continued to heave the hay up to him, reserving his strength for the work. A cigarette dangled from the edge of Brendan's mouth. This is quare daft business altogether, sure you couldn't give this hay away. It's good for nothing. It'll start to ferment as soon as we have it indoors. We'll have feckin Farmer's Lung. I can feel it in me throat already.

Oweny grunted. That's your smoking, Brendan, not the hay. This is rotted already — it will do fine as bedding. Someone will take it off Moira's hands, so.

Brendan's eyes squinted through the smoke as I approached. Ah, for fecksake, Michael, where's our tay?

Mammy has it on, I said. She wants you to come in for it. She and Auntie Una have cooked up a huge meal.

Is that right? Did you hear that, Owen? Sure, Moira's in rare ole form these days. By God, I knew it, too, I knew she'd have the old sickness bet, sure what do the fuckin doctors know about it at all, the fuckin thievin hoors.

Oweny nodded.

And when was the last time Moira McDonagh let her brother into the house, now, tell me that?

The last time you were in the house you picked up the cat and swung her by her tail around the room, Oweny said. You broke all of Moira's good china. And, he continued, the time before that, you were drunk and argued with Padraig before he left for America.

Brendan grunted.

Before that, the Guards were chasin you, and —.

Well, never mind now, sure that's all in the past. Moira understands all that, so. Isn't that right, Michael?

Mammy says to clean your mouth out before you come in for the tay.

Oweny laughed.

And by God, Brendan said, isn't she a fierce woman altogether, a great Christian altogether, worried about the sounds that come out of a man's mouth now.

Oh ho, Brendan Dolan, Oweny said, you'd be singin a different tune if she were here.

Brendan grinned and pulled on his cigarette. His long fingers were yellowed by the tobacco, and even though his hands were callused, I could see the bloody damage the threshing had done to them. Swallows swam over his head, calling to one another excitedly, sweeping low over the threshing and the windrows. Never mind Saint Patrick, he said, still grinning, it was that woman drove the bloody snakes from Ireland. He jumped easily to the ground, landing like a thin wiry cat, and threw the pitchfork powerfully into the base of the haycock where it quivered, rooted to the ground.

I raced my uncles back to the house, trampling the long rushes underfoot, hurdling the stone walls. Out of breath, I stumbled into the house, preparing to take off my Wellingtons, but as soon as I stepped through into the scullery, I sensed something was wrong; I did not hear Mother's voice. There was an unnatural stillness in the air — that absence of life that I could read with my nerves, it had become so familiar.

Radio 2 was playing old band tunes; the sound drifted ghostlike down the hallway as if coming from far away. Where's Mammy? I called, and to my ears, my voice crashed against the ceiling, clattered against the walls. The lino dripped with condensation.

Aunt Una turned from the sink, her face flushed from the heat. Is she not with you? I thought she was gone to bring you lads in. She waved her knife in the direction of the fields and then went back to her peeling.

I ran from the house toward the pastures. The fields were burning with the setting sun. I saw my mother as she had been when her illness was in full sway and before we knew how sick she was. When she walked the fields or the glen or made her way down to the river at dusk and wandered the countryside in silent pain as Molly and I prayed for her. A time when she'd leave the house each twilight and we feared she would never return.

I sprinted toward the glen, stumbled over a sty, and ended up in a nest of thorns and brambles. Berry juice and blood streaked my arms. Brendan and Oweny would be taking the high path through the fields. I had not passed her coming home; she could only be in the glen. I ran as hard as I could, my ribs pressing sharply against my lungs. I splashed through the water at the Falls; startled cattle broke into a run.

In the glen, the air was warmer as if it had been collecting the heat of the day; now, near dusk, it was moist and heady, the way a hay shed would be, full of the smell of heated seed, dank moss, animal, and sweet fennel. I leant against a tree for support and waited for the pain in my side to subside. In the graying, the tree trunks stood dark against the light at play on the glen floor. I looked back the way I'd come, and in that moment I saw her, illuminated by the peculiar light.

It was the witch of the glen, Peadar O'Suilbháin's widow. She looked up, a faraway gaze in her eyes, the shawl falling loosely about her head so that her hair spilt out. She was singing, her voice young and filled with happiness. In the last of the light she looked radiant and completely lost in some dream.

The woman put up a hand to shield her face from the glare of the sun sweeping through the trees and squinted toward the treeline where I stood. It was my mother and it was the witch, and she was lost and far away and did not recognize me at all. I began to cry.

My mother squinted until the flax cleared. The sun dipped further on the horizon and the light in the glen paled.

You fool, she said, what are you doing standing there?

C'mon here and give your poor old mammy a hand. This basket's getting too heavy for me. I approached, and when she looked up her face was bright and flushed. She smiled. Sure, what are you crying for?

I shrugged. I thought you were a witch.

She laughed. Tears came to her eyes. Oh God, I am that.

I thought you were the witch Ní Suilbháin.

Mrs. Sullivan? Ah, Saint Jude have mercy on us, sure, she was no witch, the poor old crature. Mother shook her head. I don't know which she had it worse in — the livin or the dyin. I hope I don't end up that way.

She handed me the basket and pressed her hair back beneath the shawl. Her fingers were swollen from nettles. She sucked on them absently. I took her hand. She looked about the glen. It's beautiful here this time of the year, she said. I used to come down here a lot when I first met your daddy, and she stared at me. Y'know, you look just like him — the spittin image. And for all that I say about him, it's not a bad thing. He was a handsome man.

I passed the basket from arm to arm. I stared at the forest floor. She often compared me to my father when she was angry and I'd always assumed she meant I was ugly. I doubted that I had been in any part of her thoughts for some time.

The odor of chemicals was strong in my nostrils; I wrinkled my nose. Is that the smell of the perm? I asked.

Do you not like it? She beamed. I know, sure it's rotten, isn't it? But I think I've gotten used to it. Chrissy said I had to keep it covered until it's set. I'll wash it before we hit the town.

The town?

Sure the lads are taking us into the dances this weekend — did you forget? Perhaps I'll pick meself up some rich fella in there. A doctor from the Rouer or Inistogue, perhaps a rich Yank, what do you think about that, then? Perhaps I'll get a young fella for meself, wha? She nudged me with her hip, and I stumbled and almost dropped the basket.

Mother raised her arms and pirouetted across the flat grass, the dead wood, and the dark leaves, one hand gracefully curved against a man's, who spun all the while, invisibly. The setting sun sparkled through the trees. I imagined the way she used to dance with Father when they were first married, before her illness and his America had taken them away from each other.

Come here, she cried, give us your hand, and I went to her. She took my hand in hers as if she were changing dance partners and spun me effortlessly as if I were her small boy again. Birds rose in startled flocks from trees like sparks off tinder. We danced and the light came across the fields in a flood and then the two of us were falling, holding each other tightly.

Spring 1980

My mother spoke with the dead. After the doctors declared her cancer free, she could feel and hear their ghosts, see them as clear as day. It was a reprieve, she said, and it was consolation, a constant reminder of what she should not forget and never take for granted. But in the country, the essence, the sense of death was everywhere. It was a fox half buried in muck at the side of the ditch; it was a dog floating in the river. It came in the form of disease like mad cow or hoof-and-mouth or rabies or distemper or encephalitis that left rabbits dead in the road, their faces grotesquely contorted, twisted from the inside out. It was the odor of pig slaughter that drifted over the fields from Milo Meaney's, of blood and feces and lime that destroyed the remains of carcasses. Death was Gerald Power turned about, sucked in and out of a combine harvester and spraying the field red with bone and gristle. It was Patsy Prendergast jumping into the Barrow after the pubs had closed because there was nothing better to do and no promise that things would ever change. Or poor queer Brigid Long, who had been found wandering the fields and taken up the country, a place you'd never want to go, and her babbies left all alone without her. That was a kind of death as well.

Mother made sure that, whether she went or not, we attended Mass every Sunday. She'd walk with us the four miles into town and wait outside with the men while the service went on. It made the men uncomfortable — they shuffled their feet, sucked on their cigarettes, and coughed loudly; they were talking men things and her presence was an intrusion into this world. But my mother was beyond caring; and I'm sure her world was much more interesting. A world that vacillated between rapture, humor, and despair.

Howya, Moira, they would say in chorus and I'd hear her voice, a laughing singsong of *Howya, John. By God, Sheamie, you're looking well. Lookit you, Mulligan, and poor Peg in there offering up blessings for your soul, you blaggard.*

The first time our mother trusted us to go to Sunday Mass without her, Molly and I only made the pretense of doing so. Dressing in our Sunday best — or rather, the best that we had, which only meant that our clothes were freshly washed and not threadbare — we headed off down the road, and once out of sight, we slipped through the fields and spent the next few hours in the woods. When we returned, she was sitting by a roaring fire of coal and bundled up in jumpers against a cold only she could feel, for it was still summer, and warm. She asked us what it seemed she already knew.

Did ye go to Mass?

We couldn't lie — we knew she knew the truth, and so we told her. We could not understand the pained look in her eyes, how badly we had disappointed her. She nodded and stared back at the flames, sadly and strangely subdued.

When Mother came to church with us, she circled the holy water font like an aged cat sniffing something that has been dead on the road for days. When I asked her why she hesitated to bless herself with the holy water, she stared at me. Her face was close to mine.

I meet God in other places, she whispered. She tightened the shawl around her scalp and sat at the back of the church silently, mouthing words to prayers that were different from our own. Her demeanor was one of confidence and sublime calm. Often she went to the church alone, when there were no priests and no parishioners, and sat amongst the candles lit for the souls of the dead. Her coins clattered in the tin and then she lit her own. She never received Holy Communion and always rose late for the liturgy and responses, seeming startled from her peaceful reverie. Yet, on the long walk home through the fields, avoiding the roads, she'd laugh as she picked herbs and plants for seasoning the late supper.

It was an early spring morning; the chill had left the air and all kinds of smells were coming up from the warming earth. I held Mother's hand as we entered the churchyard. The men stood gathered on the gravel smoking, but Mother no longer saw them.

A bleedin ghoul, John Delacey muttered as we passed, just like me dead wife, but it was at me he glared as we mounted the steps — he could not look my mother in the eye. I thought of Mag Delacey's gray headstone in the dun field beside the church and wondered how or why he would say such a thing: my mother was no ghoul. But thinking of Mother alive and Mag Delacey dead and the difference between the two of them, between living and being buried in the ground with the worms and the muck, made me hold my mother's hand all the more tightly.

It was Sunday again, and Mother had stayed home, sullenly staring into the fire. Molly and I lit candles for her, offered up separate prayers, and were grateful when Uncle Oweny picked us up on the long road coming from Mass. Our aunt Peggy had run off, taken the night boat from Rosslare to England with an American doctor. He knew she would be back — this was the third time and she always came back — but he wasn't good at the cooking and he knew there was always good food to be had of a Sunday when people had to be Christian and charitable.

Oweny looked about the kitchen table, pushed buttered potatoes and bread into his mouth, chewed vigorously, and washed it down with tea.

'Tis some fair weather we've been having, he said, and nodded enthusiastically.

Jay, that's fine tay there, he said, grinning at Molly and me. Molly, smiling sheepishly, rose to bring him the pot that was steeping on the grill.

Are you a hand at readin the leaves yet, Molly? he asked.

Molly shook her head as she poured the tea. Only Mammy, she said.

Oweny nodded, food bulging in his cheeks. He gulped the tea. His boot thumped the floor in time to the music on the wireless.

Moira, you're lookin awful tired, so.

I am awful tired, Owen.

You've not et?

I'm not hungry.

Mother placed her elbow upon the table and rested her cheek in her hand. Outside a soft rain spilt through the sun and, in dazzling, color-lit streams, fell sparkling on the fields. Miles away, I could make out three interlinked rainbows sharpening in color over Rowan. There could have been countless more, receding as far as the eye could see, linked like dreams all the way from the valley to Sliabh Coillte in the East. I thought of Mother's moods, which seemed to move with the weather and the tides and the moon until there was no discovering where she was or where she would be.

I'll go out on the river this weekend, Oweny said. Bring you back a fine pair of salmon. That'll get the color back in you. Daddy used to say a salmon would cure a dead man. Daddy used to say —.

You weren't old enough to remember Daddy, Mother said. She held her head as if it were hurting her; she sounded very tired.

Our knives and forks scraped on our plates. The room grew warm from the cooker. Mother's eyes fluttered closed, her breathing deepened. It was as if she were asleep.

Christ, Moira, sure what's wrong with you? Oweny asked. He stopped chewing, his knife and fork poised in his hands as if he were ready for battle.

Mother came back quickly; her eyes opened and they were bright with pain. She reached for her mug of soup, wrapped her shaking fingers tightly around it.

Is it the sickness again? he asked. Sure, what have the doctors —.

Fuck the doctors! What do the doctors know of anything! Mother shouted, slamming her mug upon the table with such force that it cracked. Ceramic splinters scattered across the table. Hot soup splattered on the cement floor. She sank back into the chair.

Molly scooped up the broken shards of mug with the broom and dustpan. I poured my mother another mug of soup and placed it before her, more out of the need to do something than just sit there and gawk at her and because there was nothing else I felt I could do. The radio seemed loud in the quiet that followed. Oweny nibbled at his food, his body stilled of activity, until he could bear the silence no more.

Aye, sure the salmon is just the thing. You'll see. The wonders a salmon can do now, by God, you'll see.

Mother clutched at her mug as if she were losing her hold on everything tangible and real about her.

The bands of color were dissipating, becoming pale and washed out over Rowan. The rain clouds had moved east. The fields were so green, the sun so bright I had to close my eyes from the brilliance of them.

∞

On Fridays during Lent our mother made sure we ate fish, that we blessed ourselves before every meal and as we passed before every church. During confession she waited outside the confessional, the final leveler of due soul wage, counting the minutes of our sins, and then the minutes of our contrition. Before confession we prayed for guidance so that we might disclose all of our sins to the vulpine shadow within.

But she never went into the black box herself. Again and again Father O'Brien would come out to talk to her, but she would already be leading us by the hand, genuflecting before the Eucharist, and then walking swiftly up the aisle, her heels and her voice echoing, trailing in lilting farewell, and filling up the vastness of the church's high vaulted ceilings.

Ah, now, sure, wasn't that awful quick, she'd say once we were outside — Are ye sure you told him everything?

I certainly did, Molly said.

How many Hail Marys did he give ye then?

Four.

And Our Fathers?

Four.

And what else?

Nothing else.

Are ye lying, because I'll know if you're lying.

I'm not lying, I swear to Jesus I'm not lying.

There's no need to be swearing to Jesus like that, you'd have a good mind to go back in there to Father O'Brien this very minute.

Sorry.

It's not forgiveness from me you'll be needing at all. And what about you, you devil?

I blessed myself, rolled my eyes heavenward, pushed my face into what I imagined contrition looked like, the look on all the adults I'd seen leaving the confessional. She squeezed my hand and laughed.

By God, I don't know what the world's coming to then. You never got out of the holy church with that in my day.

Father O'Brien was a plump, well-fed little man from Cork, with full cheeks and a flushed face — I often imagined him at the altar or in the confessional, wondering what the maid had prepared for his supper and the progress of the Cork match that would be playing on the color television in the presbytery after the Mass on a Sunday. He had receding red hair and heavily hooded eyes with pale eyelashes that gave the impression of boredom, and small fine white teeth that he sucked on in contemplation, as if they were sweets, before he spoke.

When he saw my mother he called, Moira! We must talk before it is too late! And, as my mother fled up the sacrosanct aisle, his voice rose to a high pitch at the end, giving it a sense of authorial despair, like a parent scolding a child. He wanted her confession of what he must have believed were dark and exciting sins. He wanted everyone to recognize that she was a sinner who, unless she confessed and received absolution, would never know salvation. She would never give it to him, she said, not even on her deathbed. God could take her as he found her, if God would take her at all.

You were sleepwalking again, Mother said in the morning. Her eyes were wide and unblinking, but I didn't think she was seeing me at all. Her voice sounded as if she were speaking from a dream.

Rashers were spitting on the grill. The heady odor of strong tea filled the kitchen. The walls and windows were covered in condensation; beads of moisture reached up into the corners of the ceiling where the plaster had darkened with rot.

I woke with the moon beaming through the curtains, she said. It was filling up my whole room like a great pale eye peering in on me, so I got up and looked out the window, and there you were, walking across the field, down by the woods, toward the marsh.

She glanced toward the dark corners of the ceiling and hesitated. Her eyes no longer seemed to respond to light. All the electric lights in the house had been turned off so that she could see properly, and it seemed she was always waiting, longing for the natural gray of twilight to descend with the promise of night.

I kept losing you between the trees, she continued. You were like a ghost and at first I thought you were a ghost, but then I says to myself, sure, don't be daft, isn't it only Michael, and it *was* you, and I just sat there and watched and waited for you to come back in because that's what the doctors say, leave a sleepwalking person alone and eventually they'll wake up. She nodded, pleased with herself.

You passed right below my window, she said, and before you came in, you looked up, stared straight at me, and for a moment I was scared again because I thought, it doesn't really look like you at all, and your eyes they went right through me, so pale and lost they were. But then the clouds shifted before the moon, one of Flaherty's dogs bayed, and everything was right again. It was you, as you had been, and it must have been a queer trick of the moonlight for me to think anything else.

I almost had to laugh at me own silliness, she said, and then you came in so, climbed the stairs and fell into bed. And straight to sleep. It's strange so, how it is that you sleepwalk like that. And that I could have thought you were someone other than yourself. Strange.

Molly and I looked at each other; we chewed our toast quietly, supped our tea, and then Molly rose and cleared the table. She turned on the tap and bent over the sink, her shoulders rounded and trembling, the sound of running water filling the silence.

I have to feed the dogs, I said and went to the door while my mother stared at her tea leaves. But in the hallway I leant against the cold wall, closed my eyes, and cried.

I did not sleepwalk and neither did Molly. In fact, we woke each night to watch that ghost tread back and forth across the moonlit fields. We watched the ghost return to our house every night, track muck and twigs and shit across the carpet, climb up the stairs to its bed, into which it clambered with barely a sound. We watched and prayed because the ghost that roamed the countryside every night, walking the dark fog-shrouded fields, searching, looking for something that in the light of day was lost and forgotten, was our mother.

On the school bus Cait's eldest brother, Martin, led us in song. And when Sheamie Walsh or Brean McDonagh or Tessy Furlong got off the bus, they continued singing, their voices a rising and falling swell of sound following them down the boreen as they waved good-bye and disappeared into the gray twilight.

Cait had the strongest voice besides Martin, and when she arched to reach a note her breasts swelled beneath her raggedy school jumper, her lips parted, and I saw her sharp uneven teeth, the chipped enamel from fighting with her older brothers. Scars from the barbed wire shone long and pale on the underside of her raised chin — a shattered cobweb of fine white strands. She punched Martin when he missed a verse or when he sang her part and they laughed.

Come on now, why aren't you singing? Cait shouted during the chorus.

I shook my head and said: I can't sing.

Go on out of that, sure I've heard you — you're a beautiful singer. Her eyes were the same dark blue as her blouse and skirt and the sky falling outside.

Ah, go awn, sure you have the voice of a little angel, Sheila Power mimicked and Patsy Whelan jeered and blood warmed my face. We reached a rise in the road, the valley falling away below us, the bus shaking and shuddering, Fitzy cursing, struggling with the stubborn gears, and the sun burst against the glass and Cait dissolved in amber light as Martin bellowed out the words to "The Gypsy Rover."

At the Falls Cait and I were the last off the school bus. She pulled me back as the others walked ahead. Wait, she said, and stepped into the bower, lazily picked wild blackberries and raspberries from the hedgerows, pushed them into her mouth. Let them go on, she said.

They rounded the bend in the lane, and Cait leant her hip in toward me, pushed moist, dark-stained lips on mine. We stood there, resting our lips on each other's, pushing, and testing. Our lips parted and our mouths opened. Our hands tightened within each other's grasp.

A dog barked. A tractor was making its way up the lane. There was a gun blast from across the fields, someone out hunting hare. I could hear my heart. We were breathing hard together; everything was moving around us and beyond us but we were still. I reached up and touched the center of her chest with the palm of my hand, my fingers splayed on the rise of her breasts, and I could feel her warmth and her heart there, as loud as my own. When we pulled back it was to catch our breaths. She opened her eyes, and the lashes curled darkly to her cheeks. We stared at each other, and the world seemed very far away.

There was a sudden rustling amongst the scioc and a man stumbled off the sty and out into the road carrying a shotgun and a gunnysack. He wore a belt of gun shells, high hunting boots, muck-encrusted jeans, and a raggedy green jumper. Startled, we stepped apart.

Carry on lads, he said and scowled at us. Carry on. He passed into the next pasture, cursing as he clambered over the loose stone wall, blood-spattered ears poking from his sack. From the wall, we followed his progress until he was a dark figure on the rising horizon. We stood smiling across from each other, watching the other's expression, and waiting.

You taste like jam, I said stupidly.

Cait grinned and took my hand again and together we walked back up the lane without a word.

Blaggard. That's what Mother used to call my uncle Brendan. By the time I was thirteen he'd been blacklisted from almost every pub in town and had been sent down for numerous fishing violations on the river; he collected the dole yet worked openly; he populated the town with his offspring so that you saw familiar shaggy-headed blue-eyed babbies everywhere; and he joked that the welfare allotted for the extra children made him the drinker he was.

The truth was that most of Brendan's children were children lent from one family to the other, so that the whole town had a surplus of unidentifiable boys and girls wandering around. One day their name was MacGuire or Power, the next, Furlong or Dylan. The council workers couldn't keep up with their faces and names, not in New Rowan. I assumed that one day the children would forget who their real parents were just as the real parents would forget to reclaim them in the end, and then they would be true exiles, roaming endlessly across the quay, up and down Mary Street, searching the pubs and betting offices and churches, and wandering forever like some lost tribe of Israel.

The back door slammed and Uncle Brendan came running down the hall, his boots clapping the lino, and we cheered from the kitchen table when we saw his flushed face, his wide grin, and the sack he'd taken from his shoulder. It was less the salmon and more the surprise of him, of his misadventures, his close escapes with the law, and his imminent capture that excited us, and about which we created imaginary stories long after he was gone. Brendan threw his sack onto the table and the fish slid out, bloodied.

There you are, Moira, two for you and four for Quinn the fishmonger. The next time you're in town you can settle with me. The boys are on me tail today, haven't been able to lose them the last hour.

Brendan Dolan, if they had any sense, they'd have given up on you by now. Mother took the two fish and placed them in the sink.

If they had any sense, they'd just let me fish, the effers. What comes from the river is for anyone's taking.

That's not what the law says.

Fuck the law.

Brendan threw his cap on the table and pulled up a chair. Mother had already placed a cup of tea before him and a plate of rashers and eggs and he attacked it, knife and fork flashing, with the force of someone who hadn't eaten in days.

He shoveled the food into his mouth, plowed the plate clean with bread, then wiped at his mouth with the back of his hand. Whisht, he said and bent his head like a dog. We sat still and listened to the silence. Faintly, when the wind banged against the door, there was the sound of men's voices.

For fucksake, Brendan said, the effers haven't given up the bloody chase yet. It's that fucker Mitchell and his gang, he's been policing the river for twenty years and it's his own private vendetta to get me. He put back his tea and pushed away from the table, looked at my sister and me. Well, lads, I'm off. He pulled his cap low over his brow, then picked up his sack. I'll see you in the town on Thursday, Moira, and we'll settle?

I'll be at the co-op at nine, you can wait for me outside if you like.

With the women? I will in me arse. If you want me, I'll be in Sullivan's on the quay with the lads.

You and your lads. Mother shook her head.

You always stand by your lads, they'll never let you down — isn't that right, Michael?

That's right, Uncle Brendan, I said.

Brendan winked, then clattered down the hall. A gust of cold air blew in and then the door slammed after him.

I imagined Brendan running across the fields, long legs moving him forward through the unthreshed fields so quickly he is a blur amongst the green, the sack of salmon banging his back. The sun is lighting in the west and he's been running for half an hour and there's still no slowing him — if anything he's running faster. The fishing authorities are far behind. He can no longer hear their curses, their rants of rage. He hurdles a low wall and lets out a holler — he knows they will not catch him — not today; today he is much too fast. The green fields spread out before him. Light bends and arcs in the V of the valley. Along the riverbank, down small dead-end boreens, through pigpens, and across farmyards, dogs snapping and snarling at his heels, Brendan never stops running, and we're glad for him — this bandit, this outlaw — he is one of us, he's family.

Will they catch him? I asked Mother, and grinned.

Catch Brendan Dolan? She considered this for a moment, looked out the window over the distant fields.

She shook her head. They won't catch him. But someone will.

he Grand Hotel lay half a mile outside of town, crumbling slowly into the riverbank. In other days, boats and barges had docked there to enjoy riverfront dining, and had then continued down the Barrow to Waterford, or up further, to the three rivers. It had held fine banquets and even finer dances. Mother often spoke of it, of how Mickey Boyle and the Dublin Brass would come down from the city of a weekend once a month. She said that if the dances at the Grand Ballroom had continued, she would have been married off long before she ever had the bad luck of meeting my father.

That summer, when the old, dilapidated, and long-vacant hotel was purchased, no one gave it a second thought. Properties around New Rowan had been bought before with the promise of work, of renovation, and of jobs, but the money had never made it to the town; the developments never happened and the Barrow continued to churn dirty and lazy down to the Flats; nothing changed. But then, a prospective land developer had never come to actually live in New Rowan either, not until the American, John Longley, came with his wife and young daughter.

In church of a Sunday, you couldn't help but notice the Americans. They came up in their new Range Rover and they always wore different clothes. Mr. Longley passed through the throng of men smoking and stamping their mucky Wellingtons outside the church, and, as always, he said hello and wished them well. Some of the men, or perhaps their children, worked for Mr. Longley at the hotel, or on his acreage with his horses and dogs. Some were builders or contractors who'd worked on his house and the remodeling of the Grand Hotel. Some were farmers and fishermen whom he deferred to in matters of breeding and hunting. On weekends he sometimes went to watch the dogs coursing, or he might even be seen with his daughter at the stock-car races that were put on in large fields, where young farmers raced old Leyland Minis and Morris Minors and Fiats around the muck and grass, thumping and grinding endlessly into one another to hundreds of local cheers. He seemed to be open to everything and he wanted to know all the things that he did not. In that way, people believed him different from other Yanks, and they respected him for it.

On one side Mr. Longley held his wife's hand, on the other, his daughter's. Her bright blond hair was thick and curly and shone with the unnatural sheen of a wig, but the girl herself seemed pale and sickly. Her footsteps were measured and slow, and her father hugged her to his hip. He did not seem concerned about the way people looked at them, and there was a grace in this that I envied. But they were also outsiders, so talk could never hurt them the way it did if you were from the town or the country. If you were an outsider, you could escape the tongues because they did not hold you to the same rules, secret laws, and exactions. The Longleys seemed far removed from all that as they trod the gravel to Mass. As Mr. Longley raised his daughter up, held her in the crook of his arm, and together they dipped, extended their arms, and reached their hands into the dark holy water font, I saw them as hope and as a reprieve from everything I knew, from all the mute estrangements that the country imposed.

Whenever I lit candles at church for my mother, and for my father — wherever he was in America — I also lit one for the Longleys' ailing daughter, and I did so with a faith stronger than I'd had before. Good things were happening and they were happening for a reason: we all deserved it. Certainly the Longleys seemed to deserve good things happening to them. And because they recognized the goodness in us, and were aware of everything that was good here, they reminded us of it as well.

The Longleys seemed to have such a grace about them that it was, at first, not easily recognizable, for it was not something I saw in any other. In a way, they seemed much too kind and tender to be in the country. They seemed exotic and untouchable, and suggestive of all the kinds of things that were possible if only you were American. But while that sense of possibility was beautiful, it also seemed naive and dangerous. No matter how much we wanted to believe in such a thing, we knew that, ultimately, we met the Longleys with disdain, for they reminded us of the softness of newborn things in the country in spring, before they learnt to grow hard and coarse and mean, if they were to survive at all.

the hidden country

unt Una used to say a lack of moonlight meant that witches were at work. If the cows did not give milk, and they sometimes didn't, she'd say the Host were on the wind and no one was safe out on the roads or fields that night. On such nights, if you were caught unprepared and you could see no lights, you shouldn't listen to the sound of your footsteps in the dark; it was a trick the Host used to make you go round in circles until you were outside of this time and lost to the world forever.

Una said it was easy to spot those who'd once counted their footsteps at the urging of the Host. They were always walking in the wrong direction or looking like they had somewhere else to be. Their minds were never in the here and now. They took to the fields instead of the roads and they often forgot where their homes were.

She said that was the problem with my mother — she'd once followed the sounds of her own footsteps in the dark and now she was so often confused because she was under their spell. Only by going to them completely, by stepping out of this world and into that other, would she be herself. But there was no coming back from that. Once there you could never return. And although she never said it, I knew that my aunt considered that a kind of death as well.

Once, as she'd recited this tale, I'd shouted, as if I had caught her in a lie, You said Mammy was cursed because she'd broken a sacred promise! You didn't say anything about footsteps!

Aye, I did, she said. There's a *geis* on your mammy, and she must have broken its demands upon her. She must have —.

Well then? What about the footsteps? *You* said it was the footsteps that made her the way she is.

I don't know. Bless us and save us, Michael, I wished I did, but I don't.

You don't know anything! I screamed. I was on the verge of tears. Mammy is not cursed, so she's not. She's not. She's not! You're just a thick, stupid old woman!

Aunt Una stared at me, wide-eyed, lips trembling. Then she stared at the ground and paled slightly. After a moment she went back to her knitting, but she wasn't counting, or watching her rows; she was staring at the glints of light the fire threw across the rods. Her breath was coming in gulps from her mouth, her chest heaved, the knitting needles clicked and clacked violently, and in her large, fast hands, the rows continued to grow and the ball of wool unraveled on the floor like a mealy maggot from a rotten apple.

I stood with Milo and Lugh in the cowshed watching Matt DeBurgh struggle with a birthing cow that was in trouble. He had both arms thrust into her, his face pressed close to her shanks, and he was sweating. Red faced, he cursed and shifted his weight. The cord's around its damn neck! he hollered. It's too feckin still. Why didn't you call me sooner! Jaysus, Milo, sure you know this one never has an easy time of it.

Milo Meaney's face colored, and he shifted his feet, and finally rested with his weight on one hip. Like DeBurgh, he was a big man who didn't know what to do with his body when he wasn't working. Ah, sure I know, Matt, don't I know myself I should have called you sooner.

The cow bellowed and tossed its wide beautiful neck; its eyes rolled, its legs moved weakly. DeBurgh worked and worked at turning the calf in her womb. The veins stood out on his throat and his neck bunched. It seemed as if he were holding his breath and at any moment he would collapse and lie gasping next to the cow. The cow's stomach bulged and tremored with unnatural movement. DeBurgh inhaled sharply, cursed, and held his breath again. Something moved violently in the cow's stomach and then, slowly, DeBurgh eased his arms down the cow's slick channel. Fluid spilt around his arms and shoulders.

Hold on, he said, hold on now. Here you come, wee one, come

on now. Cradled in his hands, the head of the calf, brown and slick and matted, emerged. Once the head was through, the rest of the body slipped out — unmoving limbs wrapped in the mucus sack. A large white patch showed above its pink, still nostrils. Its eyes were closed.

Michael, grab those towels and start rubbing as hard as you can! DeBurgh shouted. DeBurgh held its mouth and parted the pink lips. He cleared the nostrils with a syringe, lowered his head to the calf's, and breathed as deeply as he could. I grasped at the edges of skin that enclosed it and moved the towel vigorously back and forth across its chest and stomach as hard and as fast as I could. DeBurgh's big frame shuddered with his breathing. Minutes passed and the sound of it filled up the shed. The cow was quiet — it seemed to have sensed its loss and given itself over to it completely. It stretched its neck and stared toward the wall, grunting deeply.

The calf snorted, blew mucus from its nostrils; fluid dribbled past its lips. Its eyes fluttered, and its legs began to kick.

DeBurgh fell back, breathing deeply. The calf bawled. Beneath my hands its stomach rose and fell and I could feel its heartbeat thrumming with new, raw life. I gasped and watched it clamber to its feet, tumble, and rise again. The cow bellowed and turned its head toward the calf, and both moved to each other through a beautiful undeniable instinct.

DeBurgh wiped his hands on his apron and shook his head. It's a sight all right, makes you think there's a reason for everything, wha? And he smiled his big stained teeth at me.

he Ball at the Grand Hotel was just for the people of New Rowan. It was held in the stately Leintser Room, which seemed bigger than any football pitch I'd ever played on, and it looked as if half the town were there, although in truth there could only have been about five hundred or so. Everything was decorated with green bunting and there were small white lights, like the type you put atop a tree at Christmastime, sparkling off the polished mahogany and brass. Four giant chandeliers made the room seem as if it were lifting up and stretching further and further skyward.

Dancing across the wide shimmering floor of the ballroom, Cait and I stumbled into and around each other; we dipped and we swooned. Her hands were warm in mine and we were both sweating slightly. When we grazed lips, her upper lip was moist, and she laughed as someone dimmed the lights and a spotlight sent a shower of stars spinning across the ceiling.

Perhaps it was from the cider we'd stolen from her older brother Martin, or from the champagne we'd been stealing from the serving tray, but I felt giddy and sick. Cait was all angles of white skin and at first I didn't know where to look. I had a sense of her body through her dress, a light blue dress with thin straps that kept falling off her bare shoulders and which she had to set right again, first one strap and then the other. She'd bought it in Waterford especially for the gala, especially for our dance together, she said, and we laughed with the thought of her buying a dress for *our* dance. I waved to my mother across the room and we took more champagne from the tray and no one stopped us and Cait spilt hers down the front of the dress in her hurry to drink it before we were caught, and we laughed because the dress looked as if it might be ruined, and then we danced some more, pressed tightly together so no one could see the stain.

When Mr. Longley made his appearance, it was to shouts and hollers of appreciation. Lugh began to sing "James Connelly" and someone told him to shut up, that he'd ruin the mood, and so he quieted, but Mr. Longley raised his glass and shouted, Up the rebels! and everyone cheered, surprised but strangely pleased.

Mr. Longley's face was flushed and a small group of men standing at the front, none of whom I recognized from the town, began clapping him on the back. They looked like strange businessmen, with their unkempt hair and dark turtlenecks beneath polyester suits, but he shook their hands with enthusiasm.

Broken strains of "James Connelly" came to us at the back and the men looked in that direction, and someone told Lugh to shut up again but everyone was laughing and we began to sing "Auld Lang Syne" even though it was the middle of August and the crowd lifted their champagne glasses and toasted Mr. Longley. After giving his own thanks and a short but modest speech, he left with his business companions, and everyone continued to dance and drink. I held Cait's body close to mine and we spun laughing across the floor through a glitter of light that stretched the distance of the ceiling and made everything resemble the hard stars of a dark night in the country.

No one had lived in the old Greelish cottage for as long as I could remember. It lay down an overgrown boreen that ended at a rusted gate before wild fields and marshland. Beyond the house stretched woods, dark and shadowy and, once dusk came on, full with the song of nightjars. And beyond that, only the river. I often set snares in the surrounding fields, walked through the dilapidated and rusting sheds, surprising the odd sheep or crow, but now, this was my first time coming with Cait, and it was as if I were seeing the place through new eyes; the house with its red stained corrugate, its blasted whitewash, its crumbling walls, and the land it occupied: hedges and dikes and black-limbed woods, all once owned and worked by hand.

There had been a murder here once, a killing, when my mother was still just a girl. It was during the worst snowstorm the country had ever seen. Late one winter evening, a man came trudging down the boreen through the thickening drifts of snow. Michael Greelish and his family were just sitting down to dinner. There was a knock and Greelish rose to welcome the visitor in out of the cold. When he opened the door, he was shot dead. I imagined the door swinging back and the gunshot resounding in the small space, Mrs. Greelish with her child huddled over Mr. Greelish, and the gunman's figure, a black shape falling with the white light down the lane.

Do you know the story? Cait asked.

I nodded. Sure everyone knows the story. We kicked our way through the scioc to the door.

Ay, but you don't hear anyone talk of it. What was it all about?

They said he was an informer.

What happened to his family?

I don't know. It was a long time ago.

It's awful, she said, and we peered through the slats of the boarded windows. The house was dark, the glass panes long shattered by schoolboys of another generation, the frames rotted and pushed in by the wind and rain.

Your grandfather had a part in it, she said. That's what they say. And your Brendan, too.

I laughed, shrugged. Brendan's harmless. Sure to hear people talk everyone has a part in it.

Cait shook her head and grinned. Not like your bleeding family, they don't.

Have you ever stood outside Walsh's at closing time? You've never seen more patriots for the Cause in your life. They're all dying for Ireland, and falling in the river after — feckin drunks.

Cait banged the boards and the wood rattled. Something inside the house shifted amongst the rubble and scurried away.

Your Brendan is no innocent. Sure everyone is scared of fishing the same river as him.

I thought of Brendan, of his easy smile, his quick banter, the shaggy-headed, grinning poacher. He owned the river above and below New Rowan and no one but he could lay claim to it; all the local poachers knew it and they went far afield to avoid him.

That's the river. It's different.

Well — Cait shrugged — he's your uncle so, I suppose you would know.

We stared at each other and Cait grinned. Shall we take a look? she said.

Inside, the air had movement and was surprisingly cool. Sunlight spilt through cracks in the plaster and in the roof, yet everything seemed dry. There were old chairs, a red-and-white dresser that had once held fine china. A crumbling settle in which jumpers and shirts smelling of mildew still remained. Upon the plaster a St. Brigid's cross hung, now black and dry with age. A mattress lay upright against the far wall and, together, we dragged it outside and beat it with boards, coughing in the dust that came off it. Then Cait doused it with water from the well and we lay it in the sunshine.

Cait found an old paraffin lamp and after she had cleaned the glass she lit it. She raised the wick, and amber light pushed back all the shadows. I swept an old stiff broom across the cambered cement floor, through bird shit, straw, and muck. I swept until I could raise no more dust from the floor and my arms were tired. I swept until there was the sense that we might have been the first people to ever have been there. I thought of the Greelishes and felt as if I'd stepped on their grave.

I told this to Cait and she rolled her eyes. You're bleedin daft, you are.

Do you not believe in ghosts?

I do not.

I cleared the hearth of debris and brushed an inch of black coal soot from the walls; I built a small fire and the chimney's draw was still good. We dragged the mattress back inside and lay it before the fire; the room grew warm and the bedding was quickly dry. As the light grayed above us, we lay down together.

Twilight settled a purple tinge on the world outside. I could hear a lone car way out on the Rowan road and, far away, Flaherty's cows lowing because Lugh was on the bottle again or off down at the river and hadn't brought them in from the low pasture to be milked. I thought of Father's fishing tackles, husks of torn line and rotted eel creels, his oversize Wellingtons that Mother left still turned aslant of the fire, his foot so impressed into the sole that they were forever shaped to him no matter how much I wore them and returned them to that same spot every night; of his shiny, rosin rosary beads hanging untied and open in preparation of prayer; and of his large oiled shotgun gleaming dully and dutifully, sacrosanct above the mantel.

A stillness fell over the cottage and I blinked, realizing I'd fallen asleep. Cait lay warm against me. I could hear a soft rain on the roof and wind moaning in the rotting eaves, a crow cawing from the fields; I imagined pigs and cows chuffing and snorting from the shed backed up against the wall and the Greelish family sitting down to their supper. The roof joists groaned and I felt that I could hear worm grub sloughing through the old wood. Snow clomping from the roof edge and wetly thumping the cobble. And a man slowly making his way up the path from the boreen.

It was Thursday and I went with my mother into Rowan for the dole. We heard Uncle Brendan before we saw him, a black shape dancing at the edge of a roof high above the quay with the low sun at his back. He was acting the goat, as my mother would say, jeering at the passersby, throwing broken slates down onto the road, taunting the Gardaí, and exposing himself to the women.

Is that our Brendan? My mother raised her hand before her eyes, craned her neck back.

Katty Kinsella left down her shopping and stood in the road to look up. Shattered tiles lay strewn across the pavement. People passed to the other side of the street, fearing something might come down on their heads. Traffic coming over the bridge slowed as drivers leant out their windows to watch.

Katty! Ye fine big thing ye! Uncle Brendan shouted down. He laughed and wriggled his crotch. Katty! Do you remember that day at the back of the jacks when you taught me how to kiss? He raced across along the roof edge, jumping roofing bales. Katty! Do you hear me? Are you listening? Sure I've always fancied you, woman!

It's your Brendan all right, Katty said and grinned.

He's drunk, my mother said, sounding surprised and offended.

Aye, Katty said, him and half the town now that they've got their dole. She smiled and, with the faintest touch of melancholy, said,

I always did like your Brendan. He was one of the good ones, y'know?

Mother looked at her as if she were mad. What the hell are you grinning at? she snapped. You're as soft as the rest of them.

Uncle Brendan was laughing, his curly hair raking the sun as he leant over the edge, his face lost in the blackness of shadow. He swung and climbed and leapt between the stacks of tiles held suspended against the side of the roof, and then, as he reached for a joist, his feet slipped, his grin faltered, and he was sailing off the rooftop and out into the blue sky high over the road.

He struck the ground like a wedge of wood split by a maul. There was a loud splintering sound and he toppled to his side. I held my breath — we all did. I couldn't believe what I'd just seen; over and over again Brendan was a silhouette against the sky, spinning, tumbling down, wide eyes, stretched limbs, open hands, and curly hair whipping about his ears.

Mother of God, Mother said, but none of us moved. All traffic stopped on the quay. There was silence and then after only a moment, or perhaps it was minutes later, we heard him groan. A shudder ran the length of his body, and he held back his head and stretched his mouth open like a wounded animal. Everything was still, and then, in the way a tremulous ripple spreads across placid water and grows and grows, we heard the startling sound of his sob-broken laughter howling and breaking across the docks.

The lights in the pub, just off the Wexford road, were dim. My uncle Oweny's face was a blur, as if I were looking at him through my Coke glass.

You killed Blackie? I asked him.

He nodded.

You told me you gave him away.

I know, but sure no one would take him. Ah, he was a lovely dog, he was, but you couldn't train him and you can't have an animal like that in the country, sure you can't. He was after Flaherty's bleeding sheep every minute of the day, and your poor mother was run ragged looking after him while you were at school. You'd have to have eyes in the back of your head with that devil. Eyes in the back of your head.

You told me you gave him away.

Oweny finished his pint and a coughing fit took him. He held the back of his hand to his mouth while the other squeezed the bar. When he was done he leant back, breathing heavily; his forehead shone with sweat. After a moment he moistened his lips and lit the cigarette.

I didn't want to tell you because I didn't want to hurt you, but now —. Forgive me, Michael.

He stared into his glass. He was a lovely dog — his voice

trembled — a lovely dog, but there was no other way, no other way —
I'm sorry.

Lights twinkled dully off stained wood and on the mirrors
behind the bar. He gestured to the barman and tilted his empty pint
to his lips. Men were hollering in the back room. There was a soft
thunk of darts striking the corkboard, the clatter of a pool cue
driving a billiard ball into a rack of balls, the tinkle of glass against
glass, the hum of the jukebox. I imagined how Blackie must have
bobbed to the surface of the river all those years before, weeks after
he'd been drowned. Maggots curling over one another in the rotted
meat of him. His tongue lolling gray. And the hollow sockets where
his eyes had once been glaring black.

Oweny wiped the sleeve of his heavy work jacket across his eyes
and held it there. His rolled cigarette smoldered to a nub in the ashtray, its end moist from his lips. He reached for it, pinched it
between yellowed fingers, and inhaled. The tip blossomed red.

He pushed his tobacco pouch across the bar to me, and I stared
at it. I went to roll a cigarette for him, but he shook his head. He
pulled me close, his jacket smelling of porter and the sea. His heavy
hand rested on my hair.

Hush, Michael, hush, don't cry. Please, say you'll forgive me. He
held out his cauterized hand and I stared at the three trembling fingers and at the empty space where thumb and forefinger had been.

On Sundays Oweny started driving by the Dolan grave site on the
way to Wexford. The car crawling the hills, the blue-gray stretch of
shadowed Sliabh Coillte looming before us, him praying and cursing the car on: *For the love of God, come on now, girl, come on now, ye
hoor,* and then the car roaring down the other side into Christchurch, the bald tires smoking and screeching to a stop at the shop,
where he'd always pick up a bag of Bullseyes for me.

He pointed to where my mother's parents, Sheila and Martin Dolan, were buried. I'd never known them and knew nothing of them; they died of consumption, Oweny said, one after the other as if Grandfather couldn't help but follow Grandmother into the grave.

He was awful little when his daddy died, but he remembers the snow and the animals bawling on the other side of the wall and Daddy choking to death in the room down the hall. And how Moira — Your mammy, he said and looked at me — brought him up after, how Moira schooled and fed them all.

Then there was his own son Declan, whom the river took, and he pointed to my mother's future resting place and then his own. He pointed to where his own family would lie if they wished. He stood before his son's grave for a long time and I couldn't tell if he was talking to me or to him. When he didn't look up I walked to a corner in the sun and sat down, looking back on his dark shape.

A large oak overshadowed the site; it seemed like the only part of the graveyard shielded from the sun. It was cold, and the tree limbs swayed and groaned. And you have your place here, too, Michael, he said, if you want it. When he looked at me, I already knew that I didn't. I wanted nothing to do with this place, nothing to do with its hold over him and my mother and the desperation they felt because of it. I would not have a place here, but I couldn't tell him that.

he week before school began, I was helping Lugh bathe the sheep over at Milo Meaney's farm. It was late in the season and cool; in the metal dipping pen I splashed in the slough and shivered. Wearing a waterproof rubber mac, overalls, gloves, and Wellingtons that reached up to my thighs, I still felt as wet as a fish and I thanked God that the day was almost over. I saw Toby Deane out of the corner of my eye leaning over the railing above the ramp leading from the pens. He'd ridden up silently on his new bike, a sparkling red Raleigh Racer, with black tape wrapped around the curled handlebars. When he saw that I had caught sight of him, he grinned. The bollocks was always grinning.

I hear you're going with Cait Delacey! he shouted over the bawls of the sheep, consonants and vowels rounded like marbles in his English mouth. Lugh was in the pen and didn't seem to take any notice of Deane. A cigarette dangled from the corner of his mouth; his forearms tensed and his shoulders shook as he wrestled with the sheep. Lugh suffered from the sheep-dipping chemicals and this was as close as he'd come to the dip; even still, tonight he'd be shaking uncontrollably and scratching his skin and moaning with the pain in his head and body, and he'd go on the drink to alleviate it all. We referred to it as *dipping flu,* as if it was harmless and would pass, but mostly nobody ever spoke of it because we all knew it was much worse than that.

When he had led the sheep down the metal ramp and into the trough, he drew on his cigarette and spat, looking at Deane as he exhaled.

I struggled with a big black-faced ewe, its eyes wide in fear.

She's not half-bad-looking, mate, Deane continued, and I hear she's a fierce ride, too. Just like her ole mum. I hear your old bloke and her got caught together and that's why he ran out on you.

I put my weight into the sheep and it began to thrash violently. Its legs were buckling under me and clattering against the pen and still I strained and pushed against it. I smelled piss and shit and the chemical on me. I looked up and Deane was grinning; his short-bristled hair gleamed in the silver half-light. I'd plow that proper, mate, he said, show you how it's done. He grabbed his crotch and wiggled.

Go fuck yourself, Deane. I released my hold on the animal and kicked it up the ramp, its legs bowing and then steadying. My own legs were weak. There was a rusted tamping bar against the shed's wall, and as I clambered from the pit I reached for it. Breathing hard, I looked up but Deane was gone; I heard his laughter, the whir of his bike's chain.

Lugh herded another sheep down the ramp, its black hooves skittering and clacking, shit dropping from its behind, splattering the ground. I dropped the bar into the sluice, where it rattled hollowly.

Was that your man Deane from the Albatross?

I nodded, leading the sheep from him.

A right little maggot, so.

I grasped the shackles of her neck so that she calmed, and eased her slowly into the green-brown foam. Evening shadows encroached on the shed and the pens; gray mist settled on the tin roofs.

The water grew darker and muddied with slough and clumps of wool. The sun had gone from the day; my lips were blue, my feet numb, my scrotum tight against my body. I was hoping that Lugh would call it a day or Milo Meaney would come down on the tractor from the farmhouse and tell us to pack it in. I felt tired and weak.

Was he lookin for a bathe in the medical then? Lugh laughed.

I grunted, felt the sheep's warm heart through her wide rib cage. Jaysus, I said. He could do with one all right.

Lugh grinned. Wipe those freckles off the little knacker's arse!

He'd been off the bottle for two months and was in better spirits for it. The hell with the devil, he said, and the hell with the priest for that matter as well. He hesitated.

You and Cait Delacey then? He raised an eyebrow as thick as a beetle. I tried to fight it, but a smile broke at the edges of my mouth; I couldn't help it. Blood warmed my face.

I nodded and turned to push the sheep up the incline and out of the wash. The stubborn thing didn't want to go; I pushed and pounded on its hindquarters and finally it bounded up the ramp, shaking itself and spraying me with muck. Lugh pulled a pack of Players from his dirty overalls, lit a cigarette, and tossed the match into the pit.

Cait's a fine young one. She comes from a fine family. Don't let any eejit tell you otherwise. Too many people around this town love talkin shite. Never mind what they say about her mammy and your daddy. They'd do half as well as the Delaceys if they'd only mind their own bleedin business. It's that feckin Cork culchie prattlin from the altar every Sunday that started the whole thing. By God, I'd like to get my hands on him, so, wring that fat neck of his. I'd throttle the whingy bastard.

Lugh shook his fist at the air and then, holding his hands out before him, mimicked choking Father O'Brien, the tendons in his forearms quivering. And then he mimicked Father O'Brien being choked, his head shaking between the hands on his neck, his tongue lolling from his mouth, his eyes rolling. Father O'Brien's shrill, high-pitched Cork accent whinged out of Lugh's lips: *Oh dear God, no, Luuugh, sweet Jaysus and Mary Mudder of Gawd, Luuugh, all the saints help us, saaave us, and preseeerve us, Luuuugh, don't kill me, pleeease don't kill me.* I hacked with laughter. My knees were weak, my eyes tearing.

Oh God, stop, I said, clutching my stomach. Stop, I'll feckin die, so I will.

Lugh leant against the wall to catch his breath, laughing. What a cunt, he said, taking a long drag on the cigarette. The ember sparked bright as a flaming coal. After he exhaled he pointed at me, the cigarette between his middle fingers dropping ash; his features seemed pinched and sallow in the fading light.

And don't mind that little bollocks, he's got way too much feckin time on his hands. A good stint in the army would put him on the straight and narrow. When I was in the Guards, we had a way of dealing with boyos like that.

We passed the cigarette back and forth — a chill breeze brought the sound of tractors, the smell of wet muddy earth, moss, and pending rain. Crows as black as forged metal, like dirty coat hangers, drifted low on the slate sky — and though I didn't smoke, I understood then why someone might.

We'll do the rest of them tomorrow, Lugh said and rubbed his hands together briskly. I have to bring the cows in for milking. He gestured to the sheep in the draining pens above the wash. Put them in the shed, put the heaters on, and I'll see you in the morning.

Will you be all right?

Lugh looked at his hands, held one steady, and smiled; I thought the skin looked raw and blistered but he seemed proud of his ability to hold it straight. As if to reassure me, he said, I will, and if not sure John Powers will lend me a hand. He winked and handed the fag back to me, pushed the sheep between us back into the holding pen with a kick of his Wellington, and loped to the milking sheds, his boots silent on the moss-lined cobblestone.

I exhaled the cigarette smoke contentedly, although if my mother smelled it on my breath she'd skin me alive. Warm, amber electric lights clicked on and hummed mechanically. The compressors of the cow-milking units thumped into life. Flaherty's hounds were at it again, bellowing away as someone passed on the road below. The sky was graying with twilight, and the queued sheep, now mere flickering outlines, pressed against the pens, waiting expectantly.

Oweny died in his old Morris Minor at a crossroads leading from the pub. He'd just won a match of darts; the three large salmon he'd caught before dawn glistened in chromium blue on the floor. As he squinted into the sun there must have been only a slight quick pain high up in his chest that seemed to race up his throat and out his eyes until his vision clouded and there was nothing but fading dancing shapes like silver arcs of water skittering across the dark surface of a rushing river. But when he fell forward onto the steering wheel, and the clutch slipped, and the car lurched forward into the crossroads and eventually stalled with his head hanged across the dash, and the car smelling of the sea, he was miles and miles from water.

I stood below the single oak in the graveyard. His sons Canus and Joe lowered him into the black ground. It was a cold day although the sun was full in the blue sky. Mother looked pale and shaken. She held onto Molly's hand as if Molly were a buoy keeping her afloat.

I hated my uncle then, hated him and loved him, and desperately wanted him back. But they had begun to cover him — earth rained down on the coffin like hailstones. The spades clanged hollow against each other. Wind whipped the trousers around my legs. The field was a green river pushing this way and that. The oak groaned above and I looked up into its pale limbs reaching toward the blue sky. I blessed myself and prayed for Oweny, and for Blackie, for Father in America, and for the rest of my family, and lastly, I prayed for myself, although it seemed like the most selfish thing in the world to do.

September 1980

very Friday we walked single file, a column of God's holy soldiers, down from the school into Listerlin Village to the church where we performed the Stations of the Cross, dutifully, carefully, meticulously. With the master and the nuns hovering behind us, we reenacted the tortuous ordeal of Christ, the anguish and the betrayal. At each station we had to contemplate not only our prayers but also each cruelty imposed upon Jesus. If the proper contemplation was not observed, we would be forced to repeat the Stations from the beginning and so revisit Jesus's sufferings for our sins all over again. It was never ending: we were constantly sinning, we always had been, and we always would, and others would pay the price by suffering for our sins. It was enough to make you sick with anxiety and fear. I did not want to see Christ die again and again, and imagine that I was responsible. Fridays at lunch I did not eat, for when I did I'd usually end up vomiting it all up again at the edges of the hurling fields behind the toilets, and, as long as small babbies were dying of the hunger in Biafra, that was a sin, too.

Lugh would come and get me and drive me home in his dented, muck-stained lorry that smelled wetly of Bran, his wolfhound, who sat high on the torn leather upholstery surveying the country like a bored and regal sentry. If Lugh had touched a drop at all, he'd be singing — some familiar Irish song about rebels or emigration and the never never of coming back; songs about the loss of land, the

loss of love, but most of all, songs about forced exile and longing for
Ireland. Then there were older songs, retellings of heroic sagas and
woeful lamentations. I didn't know which was worse. We were
betrayed by the land, the clergy, sometimes by each other, but
always by the English, on and on and on. I groaned and Bran stared
at me, his thick matted coat stinking to high heaven, and I wondered
what in God's name he'd been rolling around in and how Lugh
could put up with it.

Lugh was a lean wiry man, his face as blustery as the winter in
the country, the hue of beets spilt on a road white with snow. He
enjoyed the chance to get away from Flaherty's and often took roads
I had never traveled upon; it sometimes seemed that not only had
we journeyed through all of Tullogher, but also most of Wexford
and Kilkenny. Whistling, he eased the lorry lazily around the narrow
twists and bends of the country roads, up and down so that my
stomach rose to my chest. He didn't seem to mind at all that I was
sick or that Bran and his lorry stunk like a bogged-up jacks.

He pointed out historical sights, towers and church ruins, a
graveyard overrun with wildflowers and long grass, a stone fortifica-
tion, hills, the sites of famous, important deciding battles that had
shaped the history not just of the Nore Valley but of Ireland itself.
There was Celt this and Viking that and Norman this and Anglo
that, not to mention the Fenians, the Great Hunger, *An Gorta Mor,*
when people died in the ditches wasting away from starvation, their
mouths green with trying to eat the grass, and the English eating like
royalty off our food. There was rebellion after failed rebellion, the
Uprising, a Treaty, the Free State, Civil War, the death of Collins,
and finally, Dev's Republic, and the mess it was, too, with the right
fucking *that* bollocks had given it. The whole time Lugh spoke, I'd
be groaning, pressed against Bran, who was nestled against me as if I
were a pillow for his giant stinking head.

You know, Lugh said as he uncapped a small metal flask that he'd
pulled from his waistcoat, during the Famine, Frederick Douglass

came to see the state of the country himself, and he couldn't believe the squalor and the death. Men and women and children starving in the ditches with the green grass juice running from their mouths, their skin like paper and their bellies hard as stone.

Lugh took a sip from his flask, smacked his lips together, and shook his head as if to clear it. He thumped the dash with his fist. A grand champion of a man, he said, Frederick Douglass, sure, Daniel O'Connell could have taken lessons from that man. He took another sip and began to hum but his voice broke.

Are you crying, Lugh? I asked.

A'course I'm not bleedin crying. My brain is just peeled and me gut is in a brutal state. He handed me the flask. Here, have some of this and we'll see the tears come to your eyes. I took the whiskey and it warmed my mouth and throat. My stomach roiled and then calmed. When I handed back the flask, he grunted admiringly. That's good whiskey, I said, and Lugh laughed. Michael, he said, you're no longer our wee gossoon. I smiled but suddenly Lugh seemed very old; he'd been drinking so much lately, and for no reason that I could say, I was frightened for him.

According to Lugh, there were ancient bones buried in the sphagnum that could tell us all we would ever want to know about ourselves. Those bones spoke to us, if we listened close enough. They had their own tunes, lyrics, and songs, haunting melodies that belonged only to us, to the spoken Irish and to the old ways that persisted whether we were aware of them or not. He pointed to a rook settled upon a stile and said clearly, *Préachán,* his voice like a damp wind carrying heavy stones upon it, it had with it such undeniable authority and grace. I imagined the word before I saw what it meant and in the imagining I saw wonderful things — brilliant colors and a keening, thrashing sound — but when I looked, it was merely a bird, and not even a colorful one, just a rook, and a dull black one at that.

I repeated the word slowly, and he nodded and smiled. A bird, I said, but he shook his head. No, *préachán*. His meaning was lost upon me, except perhaps that in naming it, Lugh was giving the object of that name significance and meaning, and that the chosen, spoken word was what was finally the most important.

I knew Lugh had almost been married once, to an Indian woman during his years in the war. He'd served in the Irish Guards, a regiment of the British Army. His wife-to-be had died of cholera in Calcutta with tens of thousands of others, but Lugh only spoke of that when he was drunk. Instead he talked of the trips they had planned on taking together, to Brittany, Venice, and Umbria. But then he had been a scholar and those types of people always visited exotic places, places I imagined I would never see. To me, Umbria had the ring of ancient Alexandria to it — he often mentioned Alexandria on the rides home — a place of great thought and books and where all races of people came to learn. I didn't like school much, but the thought of a place where you could learn as much as you wanted in whatever way you chose with no one telling you what was right or wrong sounded rare and special.

Flax hung in the air above the ditches. We passed open fields, and barbed wire stretched into the distance, clumps of wool dangling from the barbs where sheep had rubbed up against them. Dog leaves glistened from a recent shower that had come and gone, passed before we reached it, and I could see it still, moving steadily ahead of us. Cows and sheep stared big-eyed and bored, chewing as we passed. Color erupted from the ditches and the hedgerows where wildflowers bloomed. The fields were bright green and lit by the high sun so that everything appeared soft and warm and full of light.

I always wondered that Lugh never asked why I was sick, that it never seemed to concern him, but I supposed he had enough of his own reasons for leaving Flaherty's, for driving the back roads through the country aimlessly, talking to himself, but always aware that someone other than Bran might be listening. The more I thought about this the more it saddened me. He wanted to be somewhere other than where he was now, and I wondered if it really mattered that I was here at all.

Lugh sighed long and deep as the sun began to settle over the horizon before us. He pressed the accelerator slightly, and we moved farther and farther and faster away from any roads leading home. I thought that it didn't really matter where we were headed or where we would come back to. As long as Lugh did not stop, and only continued speaking, I could believe in exotic places and in bones that sang from the peat moss and in rooks that could be transformed into angels with magical words. I could believe that the two of us were on a journey to ancient Alexandria or the plum-sooted hills of Spanish Umbria, that the sandals of the Danaan had marked the ground our own footsteps trod, that we came from something wonderful and were heading toward something even better, and that this was reflected in the landscape and in the way Lugh twined through the countryside.

A pheasant broke suddenly from the ditch, its plumage flashing blue and green, and for a moment I thought we might strike it. My breath caught and I waited for the dull impact as it broke into bloody pieces upon the lorry's bonnet — I sensed Lugh's foot poised over the brake — but then its wings were a wide beautiful arc spreading before and over us, and the pheasant rose and rose and left the lorry behind.

Lugh whistled through his teeth. The colors of the pheasant's wings, the satin upon its breast, were still dazzling in my eyes, and as the image faded, I blinked to retrieve it.

Lugh laughed to break the silence and Bran's ears went up. A bit of pheasant, ready plucked, he said. A fine meal for the supper, wha?

I grinned and he shook his head and rested his large forearm upon the windowsill. He stared in the direction the bird had flown and searched the horizon with a longing I knew he could put no name to, but which I felt I understood.

October 1980

oming from the pictures in Rowan, Cait and I were caught in the rain. Our clothing, the threadbare country type that were often hand-me-downs, was quickly drenched and we raced across the fields and down the boreen, its ditches overflowing, to the shelter of Greelish's with everything turning to muck around us. Cait's face was bleached white and when we held each other she was shivering. I closed the door behind us, fixed the latch, and we waited as our eyes adjusted to the soft gray-floating light within the cottage. Rain thrummed loudly upon the roof; light and shadow flickered. Cait quickly undressed. Her wet clothes fell to the dusty, raked boards and then she stood only in her underwear.

A fading yellow bruise glowed dully on her leg. I watched the tightness of her thighs, the muscles clenching, as she stooped and burrowed into the blankets. I undressed and tunneled in next to her.

She pulled me close, rested my head on the muscle of her chest, wrapped her thighs about me, and we curled into each other to get warm. She was all hard angles, bone and sinew.

I pressed against her. Shhhh, she said, tightening her legs about me. Be still. Close your eyes and listen to the rain. She stroked my head. I watched as a bead of rainwater traced the small rise of her right breast and shimmered on its distended nipple. I wondered what she was listening to in the rain, what its soft patter upon the corrugate reminded her of.

Do you miss your mammy? I asked suddenly.

She frowned. That's a queer question. What of her?

Do you miss her?

Cait looked upward, through the beams and crumbling arches to the low roof of the cottage where the rain sparkled through the splintered slats like small, distant stars. Her eyes were unblinking and dark.

I don't know that much about her. I guess I do miss her, sometimes.

Do you not remember the lambs?

She stared at me.

That spring your mother died, all the lambs that froze to death. They filled lorries with them, so.

I don't remember, she said, shaking her head. Daddy doesn't talk about Mammy. He doesn't speak to us, hardly ever. Just around the holidays, or on our birthdays. He always gets us something, he's always good about that. He won't even bring the strap or the switch to us. I think he's afraid. He won't speak to me at all — he hates me.

You? What did you ever do to your father?

Nothing — she shrugged — as far as I know.

She shuddered, crushed her breasts against me.

I'm going to move to Waterford when I'm sixteen. I can get a carpenter's apprenticeship with Anco. She chewed her lower lip. Maybe things will change then; maybe it will be easier.

At the top of the cottage rain clattered on the corrugate and we listened to it rushing down through broken gutters, sweeping against the old stone walls.

I think he killed her, Cait said matter-of-factly, and I stared at her. Mammy, he killed Mammy. Sure I know he killed her.

I found it in the cupboards after. He had it in a milk bottle and it was diluted so that it didn't smell like anything at all. Only when I poured some of it out, then you could see it, see the way it curdled, and you knew there was something wrong with it. You could smell it, too; it smelled sweet. I remember how they used it on the sick calves when they were close to dying. I'd seen him feeding it to Mammy in her tea for months. In the end she was too weak to get up or to argue.

Jaysus. Weren't you afraid?

She considered this. No, she said, perhaps then but not anymore. Sure there's nothing to be scared of anymore.

Why do you think he did it?

I don't know, probably because of all the talk. All the talk that she was hoorin around on him.

Do you believe that?

What difference does it make what I believe? She pulled at the blankets angrily. I barely remember her. She closed her eyes and I stared at the angle of her blue-veined neck, the livid white scar beneath her chin. She said, Go to sleep. I turned my head into the crook of her breast and shoulder and listened to the rain, imagining what might be passing before her closed eyes, and Cait tossed her head in irritation. Jaysus, Michael, be still, would you. The blankets grew warm beneath our bare undersides, and, after a while, Cait fell asleep. Listening to the rain and to Cait's breathing, feeling her body wrapped within my own, I stared up through the slats and raindrops shimmering there at the edge of the roof and the gutter, at the edge of night, and felt all the things we could not say pressing down upon us.

Brendan lay on a ratty, threadbare settee in a pair of ridiculous-looking casts. He smelled stale: of sweat and sleep and old beer. One bare bulb hung from a ceiling cord in the center of the room. Each time Brendan moved, the settee sagged further and further beneath him so that it seemed as if it might swallow him completely. He shifted, trying to get comfortable, but it was useless; he cursed and groaned and sipped from a bottle of Guinness.

Brendan's wife, Sheila, sat in a chair by the fire breast-feeding Darragh, their youngest. Aunt Sheila often joked that the boy was two going on six; he looked that big as well, with a head on him that could break rocks. His legs and arms were covered in raw-looking flea bites.

Sheila drank from a bottle of ale as she fed; a cigarette smoldered in a full ashtray on a side table next to her. Every time Sheila spoke, I looked up and saw her shriveled breast and felt my face growing red.

Brendan told Sheila to get up and put on the kettle for tea and she told him to do it himself, couldn't he see she was feeding the babby.

Babby me arse, Brendan muttered, it's a sick connection you have with the boy.

You shouldn't be talking that way about your own son, Brendan Dolan, Sheila scolded.

I never saw a Dolan that looked like that, Brendan said and

gulped from his bottle. When Sheila didn't move, he shouted, Would you put the effin kettle on! Put him on his feet and give him a bottle of something, for fucksake, he should be drinking out of a cup, not sitting on your lap sucking on your tit.

Margaret! Sheila crowed, Margaret!

My cousin's footfalls banged on the stairs. She came into the living room but didn't look at us.

What you want? she asked.

Put on the kettle so's we can all have a cup of tea.

Margaret stomped to the kitchen.

And say hello to your aunt and cousins!

Hello! Margaret shouted.

Say it properly, Margaret!

Don't be at me, sure you're always bleeding at me. Leave me alone and I'll make the tea, so.

On the mantel were bottles full of sailing ships, half a dozen replicas from the Spanish, British, and French armadas. The fireplace was painted gold, the center tiles above the flue cracked and blackened as if from some intense heat. I imagined the flames curling out of the grate and licking at the walls and Brendan and Sheila in a drunken stupor with the babby wailing and the children screaming and neighbors banging at the door. The only thing nice about the place was the wallpaper. It was red-and-gold filigree with velvet fleur-de-lis, but even that was darkened by dirt.

Sheila shrieked. She thumped Darragh's head and pushed him off her, so that he began to wail. She squeezed her breast, scrutinized the distended nipple, and then put his mouth back on her. I stared at Brendan's legs stretched over the edge of the settee looking like white bolts of cloth.

How're your legs? my mother asked. Brendan shrugged, gulped from his bottle of Guinness. He'd broken both feet and both legs, shattering them the way a wedge driven into a splint of wood will shatter the length of it. I saw him still, lying on the road and laughing

between the sobbing and the pain. He'd be in the casts for months, and then six months of rehab across in Wexford City, perhaps longer. The whole thing had only been for a bit of craic, but now the Gardaí were after him for slandering an officer, indecent exposure for showing his privates to Katty, and willful destruction of public property for the damage he'd caused to the road.

Mother shook her head. Flashing Katty Kinsella, what's next?

From way up there, sure what could anyone see at all, sure wasn't it just for the gas.

Oh, my mother said, and a right gas man you are, Brendan Dolan. Too bad you didn't land on that hard head of yours.

Sheila cackled instead of laughing, and then broke into a wheezy coughing fit. She handed Brendan her cigarette and he inhaled deeply. Sheila grinned and showed us what was left of her teeth. In some strange way I was sorry for her; I was sorry for the both of them. I knew my mother could not stand to see her brother this way. She sat stiffly at the end of her seat as if she might, at any moment, have to make a dash for the door. She often said that marrying Sheila had been the ruin of Brendan; I thought that perhaps they were the ruin of each other and that it was ruin they welcomed and embraced. At least they were together, and that was something more than what my mother had.

Where's the tay? Brendan asked.

He needs as much looking after as the babby, Sheila said, as if Brendan had not spoken at all. Don't you, my big wee mucker.

Lay off, for fucksake.

Sheila leant over and, crushing Darragh against her breasts, tousled Brendan's hair; Darragh woke and began crying. She plucked the cigarette from between Brendan's lips, sat back by the fire, and took a deep drag. She squinted at the babby as if it were a stranger, exhaled smoke slowly out the side of her mouth. And what are you going on about, my good man? she said, and pushed his head down to her breast. When he found her nipple, he was quiet again.

Men and children. She shook her head and sighed. Well, I suppose you'd know all about that, Moira.

No, Sheila, my mother said. I shouldn't suppose that I would.

Oh. Right, right. I didn't mean anything by it.

Of course not.

Never mind now, Moira, Brendan said. Sure, here's Mag with the tea. Ahh, for fucksake, Margaret — where's the effin biscuits?

We have none, Daddy. I told you yesterday, we have nothing in the house. Margaret dragged her long black hair out of her collar and sighed. Her face was flushed; I thought she looked pretty.

She glared at me. And what are you looking at, boy? she said and thumped across the room and back up the stairs. I could hear her banging around up there and then a door slammed.

So, Michael — Aunt Sheila leant close and whispered as if she had something important to say. She scratched at her calf where her nylons were torn, and a patch of scaly pink skin shone through, looking raw and sore. I'd heard that happened to old women who hadn't the strength to move away from the fire when it got too hot. She placed her hand on my knee and kept it there, kneading relentlessly. She smelled of stale sweat and urine and nappies. Her teeth were rotted away; when she grinned the two front ones shone black as obsidian.

My mother passed an envelope over to Brendan. Thanks, Moira, I heard Brendan say. This will help tide us over until I'm back on me feet. You're an angel, a real fucking lifesaver.

That's the last of it, Brendan. That's all I have.

Oh, I understand, Moira. I understand.

No, I don't think you do — that's money saved from the hay, from me knitting, from the few drills of potatoes we dug up, and from what else I've been able to hoard away over the years — that really is the last of it.

Well, like I said, Moira, I'll begin paying it back to you straight away. The lads say there's work something fierce in London. Once

these casts come off, once me legs are right, I'll have the money back to you in no time.

So, Michael — Aunt Sheila breathed in my ear. She smelled ripe. Her white breast flopped before me and I stared at the red swollen tip — I hear you're going with Mag Delacey's young one?

It was dusk and I wandered the fields down by Greelish's cottage checking my snares. They were all empty but for one, outside a burrow at the base of a high loamy bank shadowed by overhanging trees and gorse. The rabbit was only dead a short time, its white chest turned rust with blood, its eyes and mouth black with flies. I paused, wiped my hands, and slowly rolled a cigarette with tobacco from Oweny's pouch, the Old McGwyer's Brown that smelled of him. I was an expert at rolling them now, now when I no longer had him to share them with.

As I pulled the brass coil from the rabbit's bloodied neck, I heard a motor gunning down the old lane toward the cottage. I climbed the slope with the rabbit dangling from my hand, stepped through thorns and bracken, and peered across the sedge.

A van backed up to the side of Greelish's, by the old cowshed, and I was surprised to see Uncle Brendan stepping out of the cab, hobbling slightly, his familiar black cap pulled low over his brow. I wanted to laugh as I looked at him. He left the van idling and blue smoke feathered the air; the smell of petrol and oil drifted up the hill. He began unloading the contents of the van into the shed, dipping low beneath the collapsing capstone, large tarp-wrapped bundles in his thick hands.

The small doorway was just large enough for a cow to pass beneath, small enough to keep wind and rain out. Uncle Brendan

disappeared and when he emerged again from the darkness, straw matted his clothes, stuck at crazy angles from his cap. He did this a dozen or more times and then, securing the door of the shed behind him, quickly climbed into the van, spun it around in a tight circle, tires spinning up muck, and rattled back down the narrow laneway.

It took a long time before the sound of his motor was gone. I stared at the shed door, then looked at the rabbit dangling from my hand, at its raggedy, gaping neck. I knelt and worried the knife into its fur and, with a ripping sound, cleaved it from crotch to chest. Its entrails steamed onto the bright green grass.

When I was done I wiped my hands clean, took the rabbit up by its legs, and hurried home, a dusk-mist spilling quickly behind, and the small packed bones of the rabbit's soft blood-speckled head banging against my side.

We were coming by car into town from the Rouer when Lugh, weaving his bicycle almost into the ditch, brought the news. Dear Lord, my mother said, and my uncle Brendan who'd been singing stopped. He rattled the gears and brought the car slowly over the rise. The sky was purple and bruised but just above the tree line it was becoming bright. As we came down the hill, we could see the flames toward the northeast, at the bend of the river beyond the docks, and Lugh was right: the Grand Hotel was burning.

The fuckers, they've done it, Brendan said. They've really done it.

Mary Mother of God, my mother muttered.

We watched entranced as Brendan took the turn onto the Waterford road. Across the river, people were milling about on the quay, and as the hotel came into view, Brendan slowed the car and stared at what was occurring a quarter of a mile or so up the river. Cars and cattle lorries were stopped on the bridge.

Brendan pulled the car over to the edge of the riverbank, and we walked to the center of the bridge, where more people had gathered. I noticed Martin Delacey and my teacher, Mrs. Murphy. They were pointing to something in the water. It was John Longley's boat, and it was on fire. Flames had reduced it to almost nothing. Loose from its moorings at the hotel, it drifted down the river and was turning aimlessly in the water. From the top of the town came the sound of fire engines. I squeezed the sleeve of my mother's jacket but she said

nothing. Brendan moved over to other men in from the country who whispered and nodded amongst one another.

The boat moved slowly toward us, and on it I was sure I saw movement: two shapes falling and collapsing in upon themselves — a moment of struggle, and then nothing. The boat spun in wider and wider circles. The timbers cracked and splintered in the heat.

Ma, I said, there's someone still on that boat.

No, no, there's not. She was silent. The flames licked down to the waterline. The main s'l split and fell hissing into the gray water that shone white with fire. Sure, there can't be, she said. Dear God, there can't.

Brendan came back from talking with the men. He was grim. It was those bastards all right, he said. The lads were saying three of them came down from the North last night. They're probably already back beyond the border.

I looked at John Longley's boat, then I looked about the bridge, scanned the banks of the river and the quay for anyone who was not familiar.

We'll probably hear it on the news this evening.

Mother stared at him. Not like this we won't. Are you thick? Do you think they called it in? Cop on, would you. This is out and out murder, and they can't call it anything else. They know that. They'll never claim responsibility, the cowards. And I doubt your friends will talk either. Mother waved him away. Go back to your lads, with their big talk. They haven't a clue. Next it will be themselves.

Now, Moira, sure they're no friends of mine.

Mother grunted, tossed her head, and turned back to the river.

I noticed that people began to look ill — a gray pallor covered them, and it took me a moment to realize that it was the ash and soot in the air, the hot cinder falling almost invisibly.

We watched as the boat spun beneath the bridge, felt the heat upon our skin as the flames leapt up to the guardrails and licked at the mortar. When the boat passed out of view, we crossed to the other side. There was no hurry or excitement. A strange and sad silence had fallen over everyone, as if this was some tragic but inevitable end, and everyone was helpless before it.

The remains of the boat moved out into the open waters. The flames had died somewhat and I imagined I saw John Longley's blackened body curled around what was left of his wife and the small shape of his daughter. Their skins glowed wet and resinlike, their contorted mouths screamed without sound; and I sensed that I could smell them.

Do you see that, Ma?

There's nothing there, Michael. Will you stop, there's nothing to see.

But there is, I persisted.

People began praying, their hushed voices punctured only by the sirens of the fire engines and the Guards approaching along the river road.

Mother shook her head but continued to stare anyway. That poor, poor child, she said. Those savages, those bloody savages. She thumped the rail uselessly with her hand until the flesh turned red. My uncle tugged on her sleeve like I had done and led her back to the car.

People watched the boat until it was a burning speck down the river. When I looked up, night had fallen completely and the orange halogens upon the bridge were lit. I didn't recognize the faces around me; they were all strangers. Everything looked the color of ash and bruise. Even when the Guards came, people were reluctant to move. The Guards were wearing dark cloths across their noses and mouths and their voices were muffled.

They cleared us off the bridge. The smell of cordite and ash, sulfur, and the sweet stench of paraffin came off their clothes; it filled the air and I wanted to vomit. I walked back to the car, passing people I knew, yet as I went I recognized no one. Not one person called out to me, or touched me in greeting, or told me what they'd seen or perhaps that the boat was merely an empty boat and that John Longley and his family were safe and protected by the Gardaí in the barracks up the town. We would see him on Sunday at Mass, or at the next Grand Ballroom dance. Perhaps he'd gone to the Curragh for the horse races, or was coursing the dogs in Cork. But no one said anything at all. They all crossed the bridge to Rowan, or to the country, as silently and deliberately as if they were strangers to one another.

When I looked, there was no glimmer of reflection in their eyes that they had seen what I had seen, but I also knew that in that lack of recognition there was an unspoken familiarity. In it was the timeless silence that bound us all.

all the way from america

April 1981

Only on the Thursday before Easter was my mother eager, excited even, to attend church, and we knew it was for the Maundy foot washing. She wanted to see Father O'Brien bent over someone's foot, washing it with water from a white porcelain basin. The big face on him turning red with the effort, the spittle caked at the edges of his mouth, as he stroked the wrinkled and callused, corn-encrusted foot of some poor country woman or knacker with the gout.

That morning I'd seen her lugging the lavatory bucket from the out-house down to the bottom of the field, where she burnt the waste. She was wearing her Wellingtons and the yellow rubber gloves she wore when she went mad cleaning the house. Her small body swayed from side to side with the weight of the toilet. Cows came closer to the fence thinking she might have something for them. I could hear her voice from the top of the field, filled with good humor. Go on, out of that, Pat. I smiled. She sometimes called the cows the names of old friends. She would say, Now, will you look at the gob on that one, it's pure Willie Ryan, and that one there, sure it might as well be Brid Long standing there herself. I never saw people in her cows no matter how hard I looked, but I was glad that such a fancy might take her away. She was in a good mood to be playing with the cows so relaxed, and I went to get the mop so that the shed would be clean when she returned with the lavatory bucket.

From the shed she was a small bending figure in Wellingtons and a housecoat; I saw the yellow gloves in movement and then a spark, paper and tinder igniting, an orange flame, and smoke began to rise from the pit, pale and ashen, into the low gray sky.

On the day she made her way into church, she removed her shoes and walked the whole way through briar and gorse, through muck and dung, through cow pasture and sheep meadow, staying at the edges of the road when she got closer to town, waving at the people who passed in their cars, so that her feet picked up all the strew and sluice of the ditches. The sedge and the bloom and the hedgerows were thick and bursting with color.

Molly and I walked in the road, at the edge of the macadam in our clean Sunday clothes.

Mother had made me polish and wear my good shoes. She shooed us away pleasantly when we came too close and smiled and told us to stay out of the muck and to watch our clean clothes. It was the happiest I'd seen her in some time.

By the time we got to church, her feet were black as coal. She walked into church barefoot, laughing like a young girl. Her eyes shone. The slap of her bare feet echoed on the tiles. A few of the men standing by the font blessed themselves and turned away.

Molly and I shifted restlessly in the nave, watching our mother in the queue before the altar. The line moved forward slowly and then it was her turn. Father O'Brien looked up and paused when he saw her, his hand poised over the washbasin. I won't wash your feet, Moira McDonagh, he said, and his voice was firm.

Mother smiled. You're showing yourself for the hypocrite you are, then, Father. Her voice carried across the tiles, echoed off the cement. The line behind my mother staggered and shifted, bent and twisted as parishioners sought for a better view. I took my sister's hand and led her into the pew; together we sank down on our knees and bent low and small. I lowered my head on my hands and pretended to pray.

Father O'Brien poured the water quickly and I knew he would have liked nothing better than to heft the bucket and dump its contents over my mother's head, but even as she genuflected and bowed she continued to stare at him and smile — and such a smile! Father O'Brien lifted the ladle and quickly doused her feet, once, twice, three times while rapidly reciting the prayer as Jesus had done for his disciples near the end, and then he was done. He took her foot roughly in his hands and she leant back and raised it to his face so that she could watch all of him as he toweled dry one and then the other. Behind them, people shifted and murmured.

Father O'Brien's face was brightly flushed; sweat streaked his forehead and poll. His stole seemed to be choking the life from him. When he was done my mother held her foot raised for a moment and then slapped it hard down upon the tile with a damp smack. She looked down at her bare feet approvingly. Now that they were clean and shone white, she took her shoes from her bag, placed them upon the floor, and stepped into them.

Thank you, Father, she said, and when she bowed she gracefully lifted the hem of her skirt, a curtsy more than a genuflection. All eyes followed her as she made her way to our pew, all except Father O'Brien's. He rose to his feet, pulled the stole from his neck, and handed it to Father Keene, his assistant. His hands were shaking and I noticed for the first time that he had palsy, that he was actually an old man. He stared at the ceremonial bowl, at the foamy, muddied water there, then at the wet footprints upon the floor. Absently, he wiped his hands upon his chasuble. He turned and walked toward the sacristy, and the door closed slowly behind him.

One of the altar boys returned with a bowl of clean water and white towels draped over his arm. The sound of Father Keene's rich Kerry accent traveled on the stone, his voice soft yet sonorous with the words of prayer. He worked patiently and tenderly, it seemed then, and his face had the look of all the apostles I'd ever heard of in scripture. Late sunlight spilt through the stained glass, bathing both priest and penitent, so that they seemed transformed somehow, the swollen veins, the blisters and calluses, the deep dirt entrenched beneath the nails, the wrinkled flesh, and Father Keene's smooth white hands moving the soapy water gently over them.

I turned to Mother. She stood at the end of the pew watching, a smile upon her lips. And it was not cruel as I'd seen before. This was content — tender even — as her eyes traced the way Father Keene's hands graced the people's feet. She turned back to us, raised her eyebrows so that her eyes were large and caught all the roseate light in the vestibule. Shadow submerged to the edges of her, into the reaches of the church, so that her face seemed to occupy all.

Are we right then? she asked. Shall we go? And she strode up the side aisle to the back of the church and her feet passed across the tile with barely a sound. At the top of the church she turned, genuflected, took water from the holy water font, and blessed herself before she opened the wide wooden doors and stepped out into the fading light.

We walked home slowly; there seemed to be no hurry now. Cars slowed for us but she waved them on, calling out pleasantly. Vesperal birds sang from thickets and the fields hummed with such peaceful reverberations that it might have been a Sunday. Mother began to hum some tune or other, and I watched her calf muscles tensing and tightening as she strode.

I wanted to ask her about the foot washing and why the need to shame Father O'Brien in such a way, and how could we ever face going into the church again? I wanted to ask her what it felt like to have her feet washed by him, the man she hated and despised. I wanted to know if she felt closer to God now or if she believed the washing had taken away all her sins. I wanted to know if she thought she might truly be better.

And then she looked back at me, and her gaze was that of watching Father Keene bathing the parishioner's manky feet. I smiled and almost expected her to reach out her hand and gather both of us into her arms. But suddenly she turned and walked quickly on.

Mammy? Molly said, but our mother didn't slow or look back. Her pace quickened, urgent suddenly, so that we rushed to keep up. Mammy? she said again but Mother was no longer listening. She began running through the ditch, through gorse and thicket, her calves splashed with muck. Brambles tore at her skirt, scratched her pale legs.

We rounded the bend and the fields curved toward us. Cows leant against fence posts and, at the sound of us on the road, turned from rubbing their crusted shanks. My mother called to them: Pat! Deirdre! Willie! Shay! The cows, pushing their hard straining faces between the barbs of wire, stared at her, no spark of recognition, or even affection, in their eyes — and my mother, oblivious to that emptiness, still calling: Matt! Oh Sheila! Deirdre! Pat! Oh Shay! I'm home, I'm home, I'm home! And my sister and I, holding tightly to each other's hands, watched from the far side of the road as our mother rushed forward to embrace them.

The first time I called for DeBurgh it was a fine spring day. The gorse shone amber at the edges of the field. Honeysuckle lay bent by the wind further up the valley and the wild brake crowded all the paths down to the river. When I took the boat out at night, my traps were full of eels, constricted in upon one another. It was a time for living things, yet when DeBurgh climbed the stairs through the late slanting sun — so that he seemed to dissolve in light between the rungs of the banister — and stepped toward my mother's room, he paused. I thought that only Molly and I could smell the vomit that underlay the strong disinfectant smell of Dettol, but of course I was wrong. There was a smell of disease that nothing could drive out, not the washing or the scrubbing or the burning or the airing out, and on such a day it stilled DeBurgh and his talk. He stood in the doorway and wouldn't budge, and stared beyond the door frame.

DeBurgh was a big man: his head grazed the lintel and he blocked all light from the hall. And at first I thought it was fear or shock that held him.

It's the pain, I said, that's all it is. She just needs something for the pain.

I was grateful that DeBurgh didn't ask, that the sight of my mother perhaps had driven the need for questions from him and he merely reacted in the way that he had been trained to do, that he had spent much of his life doing. My mother was in pain and something had to be done. The large hands that I watched turn a calf in a cow's womb reached for her, and I had to resist grabbing for him and hauling him back. He looked into her eyes, touched her stomach gently, making a circle, squeezing it in the shape of a bread box. He checked her pulse.

She's had morphine before?

I nodded. In the hospital, I think.

DeBurgh's voice caught and when he spoke again it sounded rough as gravel. Then that's what we'll give her so, he said and wiped at his eyes, rubbed a thick forearm across his brow. I was surprised that he had needles with him: syringes, hypodermics, clean towels. He drew the morphine from a small glass vial. I looked at his hands, thought of the dirt upon them, the sanitization of the needle. He caught my eye. Don't worry, he said, it's fine. She'll be fine.

Molly looked on from the threshold as DeBurgh and I held her, as he injected the morphine. Her arms and legs thrashed, her nightdress billowed out, and she screamed. Molly turned away, pressed her face into the wall, closed her eyes, put her hands over her ears, and began to moan.

Gradually Mother stopped fighting; her breathing deepened. Soon she closed her eyes and was asleep, and Molly sat on the bed by her side.

DeBurgh shook his head. My Margaret, six years it was this Easter, and she was in terrible pain. She lay medicated till the end. I advise you to get your mammy into the hospital as soon as you can but I can't make you. You have to call Dr. French and get him up here to take a look at her.

She's been in the hospital. She won't go back. We can't call Dr. French. He'll have her put away.

Jay, they'll have my head if they find out I'm doing this. He ran a large hand through his hair. Rain banged against the glass, rattled on the empty spaces between the slates. They did fuck-all for Maggie, he said, still looking at my mother. God save us, he said and rubbed his face hard. Call me when you need to mind, and I'll do what I can.

I nodded and thanked him and looked vacantly toward my mother. DeBurgh didn't move. He stared at my mother as if he were seeing someone else, and I imagined that it was his dead wife he was seeing. DeBurgh told me that Mother would be all right, that she was strong, that everything was fine. Maggie, he said, didn't have much of a chance, and then he told me how much better the hospitals were these days, how no one needed to be sick if they chose not to, that doctors now could do all sorts of miraculous things. Then he fell quiet, and for a moment I forgot that he was there.

I can see why you wouldn't want your mammy going back there, he said finally. I can't believe how backward we are in this feckin country. He moved toward the door. Sure you'd think we was in the Dark Ages.

I woke to the moon filling up all the dark places in my room and for a moment I was still dreaming that Father had returned and that any minute I would hear him coming down the lane, or his soft footfalls on the stairs come to say good night, but then I realized I wasn't dreaming. Father was home, had been home a fortnight, and with this realization came the keen, sharp edge of pain. We had not gone to the airport to greet him, nor waited by the train. Unannounced, he stumbled home late one night, come to settle his bank accounts, he said, and auction off his share of the land. He'd already been drinking, and when he stepped through the door he looked at us all as if we were strangers — it had, after all, been almost two years. There had been an accident six months before; he wasn't well, he said, and he waved at the air as if his illness defied articulation — he neither expected nor wanted our pity — or as if we were phantoms he might simply wave away, but that was before he saw how sick my mother was, before the word *cancer* was uttered like a curse.

Still, now, I woke for him, as expectant and hopeful as a child that he would soon be home. My bones were jangling live coils and my veins felt so hot they could burn.

I rolled toward the window. Beyond our field the raked silhouettes of farmhouses and sheds, the ruin of a tractor, stood as dark sentinels and there was not a sound. No dogs barked, no cats

mewled, not a single car moved on the Tullogher road — silence;
and then, my mother's sobs from down the hall. She'd been listening to talk on the wireless of the hunger strikers in the North again.
A brief squall lifted a shale slate off the roof, scattered its broken
remains in the lichen-bloom of cobblestone below. Rain from the
night before shook from the trees and spattered the glass. It was late
April and yet summer seemed so far away.

Then there was the squeal of the rusted iron gate as it was flung
wide and Father's staggered footsteps loudly dragging the gravel.
Every night since he returned, I heard his drunken song — of a
young Irish boy dying alone and scared in a green field somewhere
in France — come swelling down the boreen. And I wondered how
long it took for Father to walk the three miles home on his damaged
legs, his sad song drifting out across the dark, mist-covered fields
and returning just as empty and alone to his ears as he stumbled on.

Tonight he was not singing. I sat at the edge of my bed, listening
to the silence, and then pulled on my shorts and spiked running
shoes. My footsteps padded the landing and I paused at my
mother's open door. The air in her room was still and stale, as if no
living thing had stirred it in such a long time. Mother had been right
all along; her grace, her stay from the illness had merely been a
reprieve, and now it seemed we were paying for the time she'd been
given. But I couldn't feel either blessed or thankful for that. I ached
and seethed with something I could put no name to.

The thick curtains admitted no light; I no longer remembered
what color they used to be. Rarely did she open them and then only
at night. Sitting before the window, she often stared out at the niter-
lit fields glowing beneath the pale hoof of the moon. The room
would be dark but for a fire burning in the grate and a small slant of
light cast across her face and lap. Her mouth would be moving
soundlessly in prayer, her hands bound in tight-wrung invocation.

Now she was a dark shape bundled beneath thick blankets,
turned away on her side. The wireless intermittently spat static with

news from Long Kesh. A small fire, barely more than embers, smoldered in the grate of the fireplace. I crossed the room and placed a log upon it; when it flared I covered it with a shovel of coal. I did not look at her face when I passed back.

I turned off the wireless, listened to her for a moment again, then, after closing her door softly, I tiptoed downstairs.

Father was sitting in the armchair by the fireplace, half in shadow; only the glow of his cigarette told me he was there. From the wireless, the closing show on Raidió na Gaeltachta: more wailing, more moaning from the west of Ireland. Three thousand miles away in America and this was what he could not let go of. Listening to this music, I knew what he meant when he said what it would do to him to return here. A kind of death, he called it once.

The smell of black porter and gray smoke rose off damp, drying wool. I envisioned a pub full of men like my father, dying in their living. In the dark I knew that he was staring at the pictures above the mantel but I did not know what memories they evoked — what it was he was looking for but could not find, no matter how much he drank, or smoked, or stared.

There was a picture of him taken in America, high above the Boston skyline, grinning on an I beam while the city spread out far below him; the curve of a slow-moving river like a bend of gray-brown rope lashed out at the sky. Next to this, a picture of him taken at the airport in his new suit. He had asked an American cop to take his picture and he looked so proud, so young and strong and smelling of America, as if he believed nothing could touch him, or us, ever again. There seemed to be no end to the money he had managed to save. But that was before my mother's illness, before he was with Mag Delacey, and before the accident in a construction tunnel that took the best of his legs.

I moved quietly toward the door and he coughed.

Are you off running? he asked. There was no sound of drink in his voice. I stared into the blackness, searching for his eyes.

I am.

You'll catch your death, Michael. I can't understand why you do it at all.

Even my name sounded awkward in his mouth, as unfamiliar as the word *Father* in my own. I stared at him as he fretted the knees of his trousers. He couldn't seem to control what his hands did anymore, not since the explosion.

Y'know, you needn't have come back, I said. Not for our sake, in case that's what's worrying you. I said this although I knew he was thinking of dead American men, crushed and burnt and buried men, and he amongst them, one hundred and fifty feet below. He was incapable of keeping such thoughts from his mind and I wondered why I was being so cruel to the man I had once loved so.

No, I didn't, he began, it's not that. He shook his head. Your mother, I understand, we do the best we can, what else can we do? We do our best with what God has given us. I've tried to do my best — I swear to God that I have, but — Michael, you just don't know —.

I don't know? I laughed and shook my head. I don't know. God, that's a gas, so. Of course I know. Sure, you've done your part, you can leave as soon as the mood suits you. Back to America. I spat the words and waited for him to respond. Can't you now?

Please, Michael, I'm leaving in the morning. It was a mistake me coming back, I know, but your poor mother —.

Don't talk about my mother. You know nothing about it.

His exhale was long and slow and pained but I wouldn't relent, not now. You made a promise to me once, I said. You said I'd be out to America to see you and everything would be better — do you remember that? You said to trust you.

And now, don't you?

No. I don't.

He stared into the black grate of the fire, at the flame-scorched brick, and was quiet. The clock ticked over the mantel, echoing and enlarging the silence that remained. A gust of wind rushed down the flue and scattered a handful of ash; it brought the smell of rain and damp, moist brick. Father shifted his legs with difficulty. I looked away.

Tomorrow he would leave as he had left before. In the beginning there would be phone calls and letters and some money but gradually they would trickle away to calls on our birthdays, cards at Christmas, and then, nothing at all. Did you hear anything on the wireless about the hunger strikers? I asked, although I knew being back in the country for just a fortnight, the troubles in the North were the last thing he cared about.

How's Bobby doing? I asked.

Bobby?

Bobby Sands. It's been fifty-two days.

Father shook his head. It's freezing, so it is, Michael. You shouldn't be going out at all.

If you could find some news on the wireless about it, I said, about the hunger strikers, something good, it might cheer her up.

My spikes clacked on the worn lino. I was already dreading the cold but not as much as standing there talking to him, or listening to her sobs moaning in the stairwell. I knew Molly was awake as well, staring into the dark, listening. We both knew that Father's return changed nothing. Mother's illness consumed her more and more each day while his legs would atrophy and be useless. Their hopes and dreams and promises to each other and to us had been broken. I resented my mother as well; the both of them deserved each other.

I'll have a fire going for you when you get back, he said, and I saw his eyes. He was staring at my legs with something that resembled longing.

Thanks, I said and closed the door behind me.

I crossed Murphy's pasture and ran the dark fields along the river. It was cold, the air had weight and substance to it, and I shivered. My toes were soon numb. I clenched and unclenched my fingers. Air whistled from my lungs. The ground fell away around me, and there was only the slightest hint of a dark sky above a darker horizon, with Venus shining brightly in the east. I breathed the land in and it carried me, and I forgot I was running at all.

At the bend of the road a trailer stood upturned, old rotted beets spilling out like severed heads piled atop one another. Father's legs would continue to weaken. He could walk for now but soon he would not even be able to do that. Someone would have to lift him, bathe him, and dress him. He would need a wheelchair. I shuddered, not at what he would become but at the fear he must feel. I couldn't imagine Father frightened.

Since the accident his hair had grown soft like a child's, and white as down. He seemed to have shrunk while I had grown. I knew Father dreamed of the accident and in his dream nothing changed: He was in a tunnel one hundred and fifty feet below the city; there was an explosion, and the makeshift lights went out. Deadly gas filled the drilling holes, swept through each chamber containing men, and in the dark his friends died around him. They moaned and cried out, choked to death on their own vomit. I would like to believe that for the first time in a long time Father thought of us.

Running past Flaherty's fields, the hounds all asleep. I imagined Lugh drunk and curled up in the small gable cottage by the road, gleaming with frost. Beneath the gutters, ice sheets the tops of his rain barrels.

Past the sleeping horses and the high crumbling peak of Flaherty's barn, through the gate, and along the old wire down to the stone walls and the small burn, barely wider than my hurdle across, cold water splashing against my calves, and on through shimmering phosphate-lit fields. Climbing the hill, old Mrs. Molloy's to my left and, behind her, the rows of tall ferns lighting the way with their bright smell.

Quickly over a stone stile, hitting the ground and then running again. Brown fields scarred by the plow line mile after mile, the dim glow of the town bobbing up and down in the distance.

Cows grunting, big bay draft horses standing asleep beneath corrugate shelters. Up through the woods and flying now, branches whipping past, up the rise and then the last hill before the town, up and over, slowing only slightly and the black of the River Barrow before me, my heart pressed hard and thrumming against my chest.

In the town, fog shrouded the streets; it climbed the worn, slick-gutted stones along the river walls and slinked along the quay. Water slapped the rocks and a buoy clanged farther up the river. Gulls huddled on the roof of the river galley, tremored in and out of shadow and streetlight like a single breathing thing. Light flickered behind the red curtains of Ryan's Pub and I heard singing within. I had forgotten that it was Thursday and everyone had received the dole money and the pubs should have been closed but they weren't.

A bottle smashed and voices whispered lustily from a dark street corner. A laugh. A moan. A rustle of clothing. A man and woman pressed and struggling against the flat of an alleyway wall behind the rear door of the pub. I saw the almost perfectly rounded moon of a woman's shocking white bottom trembling, kneaded like dough by large ruddy hands; the sudden, exposed, secret sliver of moist flesh and the swollen paleness of the other. I heard, *Hurry, Eamonn! Hurry!*

A thin Guard named Foley walked the town front checking to see that all the drunks were home and no publicans were cheating the law; he moved toward Ryan's as if he could smell it. His hat was pulled tight over his head, his face hard and resolute. Only his large ears ridiculed the effect. He eyed me suspiciously as I passed. I knew the look: *There's McDonagh's young one. Better keep an eye on him.* I hacked a gob at the ground before him and kept on running.

I followed the stretch of the river and its scudded water toward the last of the lights angling through the mist toward the dark and silent country. I cut across the fields, muck splattering wet and cold on the back of my legs. Two miles of hard running across the barren fields misted with tulle fog and I was on the hill overlooking Christchurch, my lungs burning as if they'd been blistered by a welding arc. Everything was dark and still. A row of three halogens along the mainway, opposite the church and the graveyard, cast the only light in the village — a warm circle in the center of the road leading people home to their beds, like what the soul must look like when one gives it up to God.

This was where we would all be buried, where Oweny and his son and Grandmother and Grandfather were already waiting, beyond that pale amber shade, where the wide sycamores were, their leaves stirring softly now like the faraway broadcasts from Belfast that Mother listened to.

Father's body would return to the West where he was born. Or perhaps he really would be buried in America. It was my first real moment of considering him truly gone. What kind of son was I at all?

I stopped at a grotto to the Virgin that lay nestled in the side of a hill, and I said a prayer for my mother and my father although I knew it would do no good. My words frosted the air. The Goddess's weather-beaten face, worn smooth and soft, shone beatific in the moon glow. Hers was an altar of rowan branches, wildflowers and moss heather, lichen, and pools of bog water, the type of old-country shrine that once dotted the lanes and hillsides.

Wrapped in thorns yet serene and calm, the Goddess assured me that everything would be all right, if only I believed. But the thing was, though I wanted to believe, I didn't.

My reflection shivered upon the pool's surface, resistant and numb. I tried to think of ancient things because I knew this was what Mother would do; I imagined fires burning on hilltops through the nights during the harvest feasts of Samhain and Bealtaine, that old coming together of earth and flesh, of river and sky and air, of finding God inside and everywhere about us. My mother had always drawn strength from this, but there was nothing here but the smell of ash and loam, of rotting potatoes and cow shit. I stared into the pool, trying to see the light in the darkness and the way to my soul.

t dawn the next day I again ran the fields into town, and from the hill over the River Barrow I saw my father for the last time as he boarded the bus for Dublin. He emerged from Sullivan's, where two years before I had waited in the predawn gloom with my mother for a similar bus that would take us to him. I knew from visiting the pub with Lugh that nothing had changed. It still smelled of cigarette ash and smoke-bilged wood; of the spilt beer and stale sweat of old men. A mist moved along the waterfront and at that distance Father shimmered in the smoky light, and he looked as if he were young again, as if I might have evoked him from my dreams after all, and as if his homecoming had never been.

And though I could no longer see him, I waved. I wished that I had come to wait with him; I wanted badly to have hugged him and to have said good-bye. A pale watery sun spilt over the top of the town, on the spires of the cathedral, and down the pubs on Mary Street. Father's bus crossed the bridge over the Barrow and rumbled slowly down the Waterford road past Stanton's Trucking and Fitzgerald's Fertilizer.

I smelled the chemicals of the tannery and the hops of the old brewery. Morning traffic moved sluggishly along the docks. The sun sat on the squat terrace houses above St. Mary's ruined transept. JFK had stood here once, out on the corner of Sullivan's, and said proudly that this was where he was from and where he would still be if his great-grandfather had never left and become a bootlegger in America. He'd pointed across to Stanton's and Fitzgerald's, the places where he would most likely have worked, had he stayed. I knew lots of lads who worked in both places, and I tried to imagine JFK in their places, covered in grease or lung-choking phosphates. He had returned, he said, because in one's heart one never really left.

Vendors and tinkers were setting up their stalls for market. The bird-shat statue of the pikeman from the Rebellion of 1798 gleamed dully. A drunk stood on the slimed, river-washed stones by the Old Quay, pulled himself out, and began pissing exuberantly into the river.

It took a while and I had to use paraffin, but I knew that when Flaherty's bales caught, everything would go quickly after: the ladder, the beams, the joists, the buttressed cross sections, and then the roof itself. It was sometime after midnight. The lights were off in the Flaherty farmhouse and the hounds were still. The shed was warm and moist from the heat of the day. It felt like the glen at dusk, smelling slightly as if animals had just passed through: of moss, and manure, and sweet honeysuckle and fennel. I hesitated with the sensation and, in that moment, was suddenly scared for what I was about to do, scared that even though he was gone, my father would still pay for the things I did. I beat the bales with a stick to drive out any animals. Rats rustled through the depths, and when that was done and there was silence, I threw the flaming book of matches onto the doused straw.

Father had once said that you had to pick your battles and that he'd never been much good at it. He was forever paying for the mistakes he'd made. I watched the flames spread and then consume Flaherty's shed, and I thought of Father never ever coming back. Timbers blackened and hissed and began to smoke. Corrugate metal twisted and warped and screeched as it tore from nails.

In making Flaherty pay I also knew that I was giving myself over to the country, to everything my father had despised about it, and everything I would never be able to break free from and leave behind. I had given myself over to older tragedies and the never never healing of wounds.

I knew there were all kinds of ways to find ourselves and to lose ourselves in the country, full of old ghosts and old hate. The mythologies that Master Dunne taught us in school, Aunt Una's superstitions, even Father's and Lugh's drunken songs told me this. As much as I wanted to let go of this history, I could not. When I slipped over Flaherty's borders through his ditches and his black silage, I was Queen Maeve of Connaught come into Ulster with her men, seeking revenge while everyone dozed beneath a magic spell of sleep.

I stole back across the fields quickly. There was no moon and I couldn't see a thing before me. Once over the stone wall and splashing through the small burn that dissected the properties, I felt more secure. The water was running fast and came up to my calves. It was cold and I paused for a moment to wash my face and hands of soot and paraffin.

I felt light-headed and sick, and knew that I had stayed too long after the fire. My lungs felt heavy and wet. I gagged twice and then vomited bile into the water. I was sweating even as I stood in the chill current. I bent and splashed my face with water, held my cold hands against my mouth and nostrils until I could breathe again and the nausea had passed. I exhaled deeply and straightened.

Clouds passed invisibly and then stars were shining brightly; the spring constellations were clear. Venus was at its fullest. After a moment, I looked back the way I had come. I couldn't hear the fire but I could see it. The peak of the shed rose out of the darkness, red above the black hedgerows, and in the heat, it shimmered like an illusion. Flaherty's hounds had begun to howl. Smoke drifted ghostlike over the fields but the wind was coming from the northwest, driving it as if it were a curtain falling across the stage of some tragic play. Lights were coming on in the farmhouse; they were pinpricks, like the stars themselves, shimmering through the hedges. I stood invisibly in the dark and watched with a certain satisfaction as the shed's roof collapsed into itself — ashen timbers jutted flaming from the exposed hole, and pale smoke turned black.

Flaherty came out of the farmhouse wearing an old coat over his pajamas; his hair was plastered to one side of his head. He stood in the center of the courtyard roaring orders at his family, shouting for someone to bring Lugh from his bed in the gable cottage to help douse the flames. It was Friday and Lugh would have been dead to the world after returning from the pub; he'd be in a stupor so great nothing would wake him.

I had no worries of the flames spreading to the animal pens or to the other sheds — the large cobblestone courtyard separated them and the wind was bending the flames in the opposite direction. I splashed through the burn and followed the stone wall that climbed the rise to our house.

The house was silent. I took off my clothes and smelled them, inspected them for any damage or marking, but there was none; they were just wet. The fire in the grate had not died down completely. I spooned another shovel of coal upon the orange embers, though I knew we could not afford even that, and pulled the clothes rack before the grate and hung my clothes over it. They would be dry within a few hours. In the scullery, I toweled myself with a washcloth from a basin of cold water and made my way up the stairs to my bedroom, suddenly aware of my footsteps loud and resonant on the creaking wood. Counting them: *one two three four five,* falling heavier and heavier, I clung weakly to the banister, the souring of adrenaline like brass in my mouth. I paused on the landing, and the sound of my footfalls reverberated like an echo in my head.

My mother's room was dark, and she was bundled beneath the bedclothes even though it was a mild night. A meager fire crackled softly in the room's hearth.

In my bedroom, I pulled on pajamas and, almost feverishly, climbed into bed. The sheets were cool and clean and I was glad for them. I felt immensely tired, as if I'd gone at Flaherty's shed with an ax instead of a match; I felt as if I would sleep for a week and there would be no dreams. But I did dream. Ancient war chariots were turning the earth to muck. Northern hills were burning to ash, and the Connaught rivers were running with blood. Drums pounded the air and horns cried as horses spilt their guts into the fosse and the sphagnum. I slept through Flaherty's shed burning and the howling of Flaherty's hounds and the wail of the fire engines from Rowan. In *my* dream, the Host were on the wind and Queen Maeve was screaming bloody murder and exacting revenge at last.

It was late spring and warm and I sat at the Delacey's kitchen table for the first time. The older children had left and moved into the town; JJ and Aisling were working in Waterford and Noel and Martin had taken jobs in Dublin. Rollie had joined the army and was stationed in the Middle East with the UN. Everything seemed sparse and untouched, as if not one person had sat at the table or cooked in the kitchen since Mag died; there was no trace of another's presence in the room, not even the lingering scent of cooking. A requisite picture of the Sacred Heart, the light glowing a sooted crimson, hung on the far wall, along with a picture of the Pope; a St. Brigid's cross; a Drexel fertilizer calendar showing well-fed and presumably happy cows feeding at an outdoor trough before a new gleaming red Ford tractor. Everything had the sense of being polished, as if waiting for the owner of the house to return, but when that might be, no one knew, and so everything seemed prepared for the unknown and the unexpected.

Daddy's up in Dublin with solicitors, Cait said, as if to explain why I was allowed in the house, or perhaps to allay her own fear that I was there; John would never have allowed it.

Jay, I said when I looked about the place. Cait nodded and rolled her eyes. She put the kettle on the cooker for tea. We're here to study, she said and went upstairs to get her books for an Irish language exam that I was sure to fail.

It's useless anyway, I called after her. Her footsteps were on the stairs and then on the floorboards above me — and I imagined what the room she slept in each night must look like, the bed she lay upon, the dresser containing all her underwear. And I thought of darker things, of the narrow hallway to the room where her father had murdered his wife.

I sat at the table and fidgeted; I thought of all the work it required of Cait, and of the other sisters and brothers, to live in and occupy such a space. To go on pretending nothing was wrong or, at least, nothing they could affect or change. China glared from a red dresser; even the corner boards and skirting gleamed as if freshly painted. Nothing stood out of place, no shoes or muddy boots left on a mat by the scullery door, no clothes left to dry on a rack before the old cast-iron Argyle cooker.

I expected to see pictures of Mag, but there were none. No clues to the past, to the existence of a mother at all. Nothing except for the milk bottle of Penthanol, the bovine euthanasic that Cait had told me of. Her father had fed Mag small amounts of it in her food and tea for months, and now it remained on the windowsill, catching the last rays of light. I looked away from it but it remained, sparkling amber at the corner of my eye, a reminder of what John was capable of doing if he were pushed to it.

I fidgeted some more and was glad of Cait's footsteps on the stairs. She dropped the heavy bound books on the table and sighed, quizzed me quickly, and though I knew the answers I feigned ignorance. Now that I was here with her, I had no desire to study at all, and I knew that if I were difficult, she would soon give up.

Is cuma liom. Tá ocras orm.

You're useless, is what you are, she said, but she smiled.

The day was almost done, the sun sank to the far treetops and poised there. Everything lasted longer now that spring was almost over. The sun shone through the window and bathed the room in a sudden umber light. The kettle was quietly steaming the wall with condensation.

Blinking, I looked toward the window, at the old dust-grimed milk bottle. Together, without a word, we watched the sunlight spill through the marred surface, turning its sullied contents gold, and we were caught, transfixed by it; I imagined the same color curdling in Mag Delacey's blood before her heart burst.

Would you not break it? I said aloud, not to Cait really but to the silence, to anyone who might consider the bottle at all and the cruelty of it placed there, with its suggestion of death and murder and fear that hung in all the silent, estranged places of the Delacey house. *Would you not break it?*

I lied, Cait said without looking at me. I am scared, I've always been scared. But neither of us could look away from the bottle; it was as if having two witnesses to confirm its existence also confirmed the unthinkable: that Cait's father *had* killed her mother and that Cait, knowing this, had done nothing.

As we stared, the last of the day, that aching measure before dusk, dipped low behind the trees. Everything darkened around us. I was conscious of both our breaths, and then Cait pushed back her chair and strode across the room. To hell with you, you bastard, she said and took up the bottle and smashed it on the floor, and I shuddered with the sound it made. I thought I would feel glad but instead I only felt scared for her and guilty that I had had no part in what she had done.

Cait stood looking at the broken glass and what was left of the milk that the poison had strangely preserved all these years. She sniffed the air and I did the same but there was nothing, no smell of rot or decay, no odor of corruption as there had been years before when she had first smelled its sweet and curdled poison — nothing that might have satisfied the need to destroy John's trophy, that might have made sense of any of this. The milk bottle was smashed and once it was swept up there would not even be the proof that it had existed at all, and no evidence, other than the knowledge of his children, that John had killed his wife.

Are you all right? I asked. I wanted to stand next to her and hold her but felt like an interloper spying on her grief. The room lengthened with darkness.

I shouldn't have done this, she said.

She knelt and I knelt with her and began scooping the larger glass fragments up with my hands. The bones of her kneecaps shone white. Her eyes were moist with tears. I shouldn't have done this. She shook her head. You shouldn't have made me do this.

Cait, I said, you were right to do this. It should have been done a long time ago.

A long time ago, she mimicked, and a long time ago my mother would still be alive if it wasn't for your father.

I stared at her, willing her to be reasonable, willing her to see that she couldn't mean what she was saying. Cait, come on now, let's clean this up, sure it's all right.

It's not all right. I think you should go.

But Cait, sure —.

Leave me alone, Michael. Sure you've done enough.

Go, Michael, just feckin go, would you.

I tipped my palm, and the glass shards fell back to the floor, glittering now in the fading light. When I stood she would not look at me; her shoulders moved up and down as she picked at the glass. For a moment I stared at the crown of her head, at the tender spiral of hair there, but still she did not look up. I thought of my father leaving us and my mother dying and the few small things I had to remember them by. In the end, no matter how much you loved another, they always betrayed you and left you wishing you had never loved in the first place.

The hell with you, too, I said and stalked out the door, leaving it wide to the country, to the night and the sky and the fields smelling of sulfur, and a hundred unknown sounds and imaginings in the dark, and a drizzle that had just begun that would turn to a hard rain within minutes and leave me soaked before I was halfway home, and that I was glad for because these were all things I could understand and truly believe in.

The sky looked wounded and raw and the back of Flaherty's gutted shed stood out darkly against it. His hounds were baying from somewhere beyond the farmhouse and courtyard, as they did at this time every evening when the light shifted. The farmyard was mounds of muck and silage weeping slowly across the cobblestone and sluices. Crows sat thick and silent on the shingle roof.

Lugh was working in the pigpens. Moss fractured the low stone walls, the thatch bristled green with rot. I leant over the sty wall and watched him, my nose bunched against the smell. With a thick, stiffbrushed broom Lugh pushed the muck to the edges of the pen; brownish yellow water ran around his bright yellow boots and into the gutters. Over and over again he plowed channels through the waste, and over and over again the muck flowed back into the divide he'd created, yet somehow he still seemed to be moving the stuff.

His green jumper flashed through the late-afternoon shadows of the pen and I smiled. Green jumper and yellow Wellingtons — his pig attire. With horses he wore drab colors, with sheep he wore red, with cows he wore blue. He was convinced that certain animals liked certain colors and if you wore what they liked it made them easier to work with. In truth, all of the animals seemed to like Lugh, even those who wouldn't come within a couple feet of anyone else. Pigs are easy, he said. They like yellow, Wexford color, the traitors, but sure it's not their fault, sure they have no judgment at all.

He put down fresh straw, poured grain into the trough. The big sow ambled over and sniffed with her snout. The shoats stumbled about her feet, and when Lugh picked one up, it began to squeal. The mother looked up and Lugh held the shoat against her sloppy nose. Satisfied, she returned to eating, her great shanks shaking. Lugh held the pig against his chest, its small hooves scrabbling at his green jumper. What shall we name this one, Michael?

I looked at the small thing. It was black and white with large dark eyes, its snout puffed and snorted. It looked sweet and gentle and much too fragile; the other pigs were already beneath the mother, tugging at her teats. I shrugged.

Come now, man, you must be able to think of something. Haven't you got a brain in that head of yours at all? Where's your imagination? Your sense of adventure?

You could call him Lugh, I said. You two'd make a grand pair.

Lugh laughed. Oh ho, what's eating you?

Nothing. Are you going into the pub later?

A'course I am.

Can I come?

You know where I'll be. You don't need permission.

Will you stop at the gate on your way?

Only if you give the young lad here a name. It's an awful state altogether when you have no name.

I shook my head but grinned anyway.

I think he's a Michael, don't you? Looks like a Michael to me with the sour puss on him. Lugh placed the pig on the ground and went back to work. The shoat's legs bowed for a moment before it stumbled over to its mother and struggled for purchase on her nipple.

After the Angelus I headed out to the wall but Lugh never did show. I waited until it grew dark and the moon rose high above the hills and still there was no sign of him. The light of my mother's room shone down into the courtyard and I watched her silhouette moving back and forth behind the curtains. Then the light went out but I had the sense that she was standing there still, looking out at the dark fields. I knew better than to think she was looking for me. I stared up at her window, at the slim lappet of curtain and the ghost of her outline pressed against it, moving faintly in the breeze as if she were dancing.

the route of the tain

I t was dawn and I'd just come from running along the river. I stood upon the hill and looked over at the gray town and watched the light changing as it had the day Father left. Church bells were ringing throughout the narrow lanes and streets, and I saw people running through the slips. They were coming out of businesses and pubs and shops all along the quay. Cars sounded their horns and the old lighthouse boat blew its horn in response, a great moaning bellow that washed up and down the riverbanks.

A man stepped out of Quinlan's and stood in the street, his head bowed, one hand pressed to his face, crying softly. I thought he must be drunk.

I walked up between the shop and the pub and recognized a lad from the Good Council running up the street. What's happening? I asked.

Do you not know? he said breathlessly, and he seemed both shocked and filled with a strange nervous excitement.

What?

Bobby Sands is dead.

In the Bosheen young men were setting fire to whatever they could lay their hands on. Already you could see the black smoke reaching up into the sky. I heard a young woman crying: Wake up, Bobby! Wake up! Some had picked up rubbish-bin lids and were banging them on the cement as they did in the North, filling the streets with a painful clanging keen.

I ran home along the overgrown railway cut. They had set fires alight in rubbish bins, and the flames, contained within the drums, were singular and bright. Smoke rose from a pyre of burning tractor tires and the wind bent it upon the Estate. I stared into the flames and my eyes watered; blinking, I ran on. The smoke swept back over the houses and into the country, and I pressed on through the choking black billows and emerged out into the lane with my eyes streaming and the smoke sweeping over the hills and through the valley and covering in burning ash all the long straths of blindingly bright yellow gorse.

June 1981

Mist still clung to the fields as I eased the boat out into the Flats. A sweep of black-and-cobalt sky ran across the surface of the water like shivers from a lash. Cows chuffed behind the hedgerow above the brae leading down to the cove. Creels rocked empty in brackish water at the bottom of the boat. A large bird lifted from the brake across the way and I listened to its sound magnified in the fog, reverberating down through the channel, off the stones of the breakwater and the point, and then ascending into silence.

Trying to ignore the dampness, I turned on my wireless and poured some tea from my flask as Radio Luxembourg came in, its signal splitting and then humming into life. I turned up the volume to dispel the quiet. I rowed slow against the current, then rested on the oars and listened to the country waking around me. The smell of river and furze bloom, of cow shit down near the banks where the herds came to drink of an evening. My father would have hated that I was fishing the way I was, using illegal eel pots and creating a famine of the freshwater for other fishermen, but I didn't care. He was three thousand miles away in America now. How I was fishing the river was the last of his worries, I was sure.

I heaved the pots in, worried the eels from the trap into the creel, trying to avoid their teeth. On the wireless, a man was talking about the hunger strikers in Long Kesh. He said that Joe McDonnell was now blind. Fifty days. How long it seemed. Almost two months without food. When my belly growled I thought of the sandwiches that I had packed this morning and I felt guilty.

I steered close to a rock overhang near the bulrushes and fixed onto another trap with my gaff, brought it up, emptied it into my creels, baited the pot with perch and other fish bits, then sank it again. If I could spare I'd use the whole fish, but mostly I used the heads. Sometimes I used worms, giant lobworms, cut in half and hooked four per bait. They gave off a strong scent in the water, and to the eel the stench of death and decay was everything.

⌐ As I rowed I looked for my lines and markers. Shortly before dawn gray light shimmered off the fog banks and the river was one throbbing movement of glimmer and reflection; everything was suspended, filled with expectancy of the transformation that the light would bring.

On the wireless, doctors discussed how long a human could survive without food. There are factors, they said, and I nodded. I knew factors. It depends entirely upon how much fat content an individual has and their health from the outset, but with proper body fat and proper muscle mass, a healthy adult can survive for about sixty days.

When the body is deprived of food it starts to use its own tissues to produce energy. It will start to break down the protein in vital organs. Everything will slow down while trying to conserve protein, but there will come a point when slowing down is not enough and the situation will become serious. The heart, the respiratory organs, and the liver will start to fail, and lastly, the nervous system. Perhaps this is why you felt everything as it was happening to you; you were aware of your own decay, and I thought of the cruelty of that.

Muscles shrink and bones protrude. The eyes become large but blind. The skin becomes thin, dry, inelastic, and pale — as cold as something you'd throw in the ditch to rot. I wondered, How can Joe McDonnell's family eat at all and not think of him? Does his youngest refuse her food? Would I fast if it would bring my mother back to health, bring my father back from America to stay? If by my sacrifice I could make my family whole again, would I starve myself to death?

I lowered my traps along the shore, toward hollows that caught moonlight, then moved farther out into the channel, thinking of old men that I shared this act with, and it was a soothing thought. I'd sell the eels to Quinn, the fishmonger on the quay who shipped them off to Britain and the continent. Some I heard even made their way to Asia, and I marveled at that, at the distance these eels had covered, from the Sargasso Sea to Ireland, and now all the way to Korea, China, and Japan.

Joe McDonnell would die in a matter of days, perhaps a week, and my mother would be lying on her back, staring at the ceiling or looking through her window to fields facing the North, listening to the report on her own wireless.

From the bottom of the boat I took three large river-washed stones. They were wet and cold and heavy. Carefully, I stacked them above the rest, closed my eyes, and prayed: Mother, these stones are from your belly. With each stone, I take away your sickness. With each stone, I give you room to eat and breathe and sleep without pain. Please God, make you whole, make you well again.

Starvation, a voice from the wireless announced, is a very painful way to die. Then there was silence and I could not tell whether the speaker's colleagues did not know how to respond or how to continue after such a statement, or if the broadcast had just ended entirely. The signal hissed and spat and water lapped softly against the gunwale. Mist breathed along the riverbank; my breath smoked the air. I heaved out on the oars and sloughed roughly toward the tide, my chest and stomach expanding with each lunging stroke but feeling only hollow in the space between rib and muscle and lung, where I knew every feeling of love and kindness should be.

I n church, the heady aroma of incense rose with the chorus of chants and prayers toward the vast vaulted ceiling. Father O'Brien mumbled, swished his robes, and Peter Fallon, kneeling in his altar-boy whites and grinning at some friends in the front pews, jangled the ceremonial bell loud and riotously over the words. Even as Father O'Brien crossed the altar, Peter was still grinning and ringing the bell, and when Peter turned away and least expected it, Father gave him one sharp clout on the head that left my ears stinging far up the aisle.

In the dim light I saw her sitting in the front pews; it had been two months since we'd spoken. Light fell from the roseate and illuminated the vestibule of the altar, cast shadow along the side of her face, the edge of her jaw. Dust motes spiraled down around her, holding her frozen like one of the statues that encircled the clerestory.

The Mass ended, and as we departed our pews, I found myself straggling, waiting for her. I watched from the sacristy, where an old man was offering up a candle for someone's soul. Cait's hands slid into the font; her palms cut the dark water and she leant forward to anoint her forehead. The water, dewdrops on the tips of her fingers, held the light, and when she looked at me the marks of her fingertips glistened. *That one, Delacey, is a hoor, an effin hoor I tell you, just like her hoor mother.* She came toward me then, but I passed her and trudged out to the chill air of the wet street littered with crisp packets rattling with the wind. I walked down to the quay and the river — the boarded-up barges, the still coal flats, the old rusted lighthouse boat, the black scudded water. And I continued walking, passing Matty Murphy in a bright alleyway beating a cat to death.

I walked the boreen to Greelish's cottage with dusk coming on. The tops of the sedge shone silver with mist. At the farthest edges of the horizon the sky was tinged purple; night closed and with it came rain sweeping unbroken across the fields. The door squealed open at my touch, and I closed it fast behind me. The corrugate I'd placed across the tiles no longer stopped the rain. It collected in a pool on the bowed floor.

Cait had left her underthings in the cottage and I might never have found them in the darkness if I hadn't stepped upon them. I ran them through my hands, stretched the material and brought it to my face; they were moist and dank with the smell of her and from lying in the cottage so long. It had been months since the two of us had been here and everything seemed to have been destroyed in that time. More plaster had fallen from the walls; sheep had wandered through and left their droppings on the floor. Tiles had been swept from the roof in the recent rains and lay shattered upon the cement. Our mattress was sodden and rank. I don't know how I could have imagined this place looking better than it did now.

I rooted for kindling, broke the old settle into pieces with my boot, and soon had a small fire going. Leaning against the mantel and watching as the flames bent up the flue, I drew Cait's clothes to me and shivered. For another moment I held her worn, faded underthings pushed to my face. Then I dropped them onto the fire and watched as their paleness blackened and shriveled. I stoked the grate and threw our blankets onto the coals. The room brightened with the flames but still I could not get warm.

I stared out at fields turned the color of char. Rain began to tap the window, thrum and clatter on the broken roof tiles. The boreen was turning to muck and everything was rushing into the ditches. I sat on the mattress by the fire and watched the flames dance upon the scorched brick as water trickled down the wall. The fire died down to glowing embers and still rain beat upon the timbers and lashed against the boarded windows. I began to doze when there was a flicker of headlights, and a heavy rumbling engine sounded at the gate. I stamped on the gleed, pulled up the mattress from the floor, and stretched it before the glowing hearth.

The lorry's doors slammed. Above the sound of the rain, I heard the sounds of men's voices. They stood before the lorry's headlights, dark silhouettes passing in and out of shadow and light. Someone worked the gate and then there were footsteps on the gravel, the flickering beam of a flashlight sweeping across the boarded windows, lancing the floor. I squeezed into the corner against the walls.

Through the slats I watched their shapes as the lorry waited for them to reach the shed before rumbling down the gravel, headlights shining across the dark courtyard. It was Brendan and another man talking to each other and laughing. The driver stayed in the lorry. Brendan's face shone with rain and for a moment his eyes caught mine and I imagined he could see me. Another figure appeared at the gate and both men turned quickly; one of them swore. Lugh came down the gravel with his push-bike. A smile came to my face, and I wanted to call out; I moved forward but then quickly pressed back into the shadows at the sound of another voice asking him what the fuck he was playing at — it was John Delacey.

Lugh greeted them, and he sounded drunk. Their footsteps rounded the cottage. A clatter of the lock at the shed door and muffled conversation. After a moment they returned, their voices loud and angry. They stood before the windows of the cottage arguing but I could make no sense of it. John jabbed Lugh in the chest with his finger as he spoke. Suddenly Lugh's arm flashed and in an instant he had his fingers squeezed around John's Adam's apple, his fingers dug deep into the flesh, forcing John's head back. Slowly Lugh pressed him to the ground. John choked and sputtered, flailed at Lugh's arm with his own.

That's enough! Brendan shouted, but Lugh's eyes were locked on John. Brendan's voice became low. I won't say it again, Lugh. Let go of him.

And Lugh did. John stumbled backward, grabbing at his throat. He turned in circles, glared at Lugh as he wheezed and swore. You're a fucking dead man, McConnahue, a fucking dead man.

Come on, Brendan said and took John's arm, but John was reluctant to move. Finally, he relented and they headed up the gravel. When they reached the lorry Brendan looked back and pointed at Lugh. Stay off the drink, you, and keep your head down. He had to push John into the truck. A fucking dead man! John kept shouting. A fucking dead man!

Tiocfaidh ár Lá, Lugh said and saluted, but they had already turned their backs to him. They climbed up into the lorry and Lugh stepped before it, staring at them across the stretch of headlights. Rain washed down his angular face, and he did not move. The lorry remained at the gate, idling. Then its headlights brightened on Lugh and he squinted into the glare, but still he did not move. He stood illuminated and blinded and resolute. Finally the beams dimmed and the lorry backed slowly out into the boreen, its headlights flickering through the slats and momentarily pressing back the darkness of the room.

As it turned, the lorry's headlights swept the woods before it, and there was Cait, in her hooded mac, standing at the edge of the trees. The woods and Cait faded at the light's bright edges; the truck rumbled away deeper into the woods. When I looked again, she was gone, and I wondered if I had merely imagined her. Lugh stared after the lorry, hacked phlegm, and spat into the ditch. He took his bike from the wall and stumbled off into the rain-swept night.

I pulled the mattress away from the fire, stoked the embers for warmth. There were remnants of Cait's clothing there — a sliver of lace-trimmed elastic from her underwear. Rain shattered incessantly around me, coiled and breathed as it ran down the walls. I could see Lugh and Brendan still, staring at each other across the length of the lorry's headlights, and, in the rain and the dark, the vast distance between them that its lights seemed to suggest.

Just above my head, in the failing timbers, there was a high-pitched squeal followed by another, and another, a frantic scrabbling and then silence. In that silence, I imagined the sound of rats, thousands and thousands of them, devouring each other, invisibly, in the dark.

ll through the last weeks of June and into July, Molly and I
kept a deathwatch as the list of hunger strikers from Long
Kesh grew. It was day sixty of Joe McDonnell's starvation when my
mother began wailing from her bedroom. I was shoveling cinders
into the ash bucket, my sister was on the settee knitting. Her needles
stopped making their noise and we looked at each other. Molly's
face was flushed and it highlighted her freckles. In many ways,
although we'd never spoken of it, I supposed our mother's illness
had brought us closer together. I'll get the towels and the washtub,
she said. I nodded and continued to sift the ash for coal.

DeBurgh was up to administer the morphine to mother. He lifted
the edge of her nightgown and I stood watch. Her thighs were
the color of chalk, skin so pale and bruised I wanted to cry. He
shouldn't have been able to see her that way, he shouldn't have
been able to see her at all. I asked if he would show me how to give
her the morphine and if he'd leave the vials, but he said it was
too risky should anything go wrong and I give her too much and
she die.

DeBurgh was a big man, with battered and scarred hands. He
smelled of cow shit and dead animals, and though he'd been here

many times before, I'd never gotten used to him. I was prepared to lunge at him, tackle him to the floor to get him off my mother. I thought of the different ways in which I could do it. I saw myself biting his ears, butting his face, scrabbling at his eyes, punching the hard knot of his Adam's apple and driving it deep into his windpipe. I'd clamp down on his fingers with my teeth and rip them to the bone. From behind I'd drive his testicles up into him with a boot between his legs. I'd climb onto his wide back, wrap my arms around his neck, and squeeze until he was dead.

Michael, he said, and I looked at him, my vision returning from some point just over his shoulder, from the soft skin below his ear, shaved and scrubbed raw. By rights, she should be in a hospital, he said. How long can this go on, giving her this stuff? She needs better care than this. Perhaps in a hospital —.

You know they'll not look after her in the hospital. Besides, she'll never let anyone take her back.

I squeezed the door frame; I wouldn't let DeBurgh see me cry. She always gets better, I said. She'll get better this time as well.

DeBurgh grunted and rose from his knee; it cracked hollowly like splintering wood. If you say so, he said and sighed. It takes more and more morphine to calm her. I can't imagine the pain she's in. Soon, the morphine won't do anything. It's gotten to the point now where she has to be knocked out in order not to feel anything at all.

She'll get better so she will.

Michael. He looked at me entreatingly.

She always does, I said, although I wasn't sure if I believed it anymore. I stared hard at DeBurgh and was surprised when he looked away.

I can't keep doing this, Michael. You know I can't. Your mother will be dead and they'll have me license.

Molly offered him a cup of tea but he couldn't stay, he had to go up the road to Tullogher to a sick heifer. He had looked at her last week, and it was a shame but if she hadn't improved, they'd have to put her down. As he said this he wiped his hands absently on his mucus-streaked apron, as if he were removing dirt from his hands, as if he were making them clean, over and over again.

ohn Delacey's old Ford Cortina passed me on the road. I looked down as John's blurred gaze caught my own. Just the glance and his face looked hard and mean and I wanted no part of it. I slowed and, pretending to be occupied by something in the ditch, poked at the gorse with my Wellington, but it had begun to rain and there was only the one road into town. The car pulled into the ditch, splashing muck, engine rumbling loudly, exhaust pipe jetting white smoke. I heard him undoing the latch of the door, and it swung open. I hurried to the car, pulling my coat up around my neck against the rain that was falling harder now.

Howya, I said as I leant in and slid onto the tattered vinyl seat. Thanks for the lift.

Not at all, just in time to beat the rain.

A tractor passed on the other side and we waited in the hush of the car's heater, the wipers, and the low static voices of Radio 1 commenting on the previous day's hurling matches. It was Milo Meaney on the tractor and we both waved. When the tractor had passed, a wide plow at its rear buoying it up and down like a boat at sea, its wide-channeled tires leaving muddied tracks along the narrow road, John glanced in the side mirror and pulled out. A smoking Woodbine crumbled in his fingers. There was ash on the dash, the steering column, and the gearshift. The car was much too hot and damp and I could smell melting manure. I felt dizzy. Shifting uncomfortably, I tried to control my breathing, make it as natural as I could. I stared out the window at the passing countryside, concentrated on the way the rain broke upon the glass.

You're Moira's young one, he said, and I nodded.

How's your mammy?

She's all right. I breathed slowly and stared out the glass.

Last time I saw her, God when was it at all? Must have been the spring. She was having an awful hard time of it.

She's not so bad now, I lied. The doctors say she's in remission.

That's good to hear, so. And Cait, do you see her around at all?

Once in a while, I do. More Martin, so.

He grunted at this, dropped the filter of the Woodbine into an overflowing ashtray. I can't keep track of them these days, especially the girls. He squinted through the glass. You know the way they go when they get to a certain age. He shook his head and dragged heavily on his cigarette. I nodded again, unsure of where they went or what way they were when they got there, and tried instead to evoke a sense of Cait. The car felt warmer as it rattled along the road. A faint odor of dog and alcohol, and bitter, pungent sweat emerged from clothes bundled in the back. Something else that I could not place. Something smothering and dank, and rank as if the sea had just washed in. I forced myself not to crinkle my nose.

He turned up the volume on the radio, and I thought it would be to listen to news of Joe McDonnell's death.

Are you a hurling man at all? he asked, and I opened my mouth to say not since my father left but he hushed me with an upraised palm upon which calluses formed a bridge of stone. I looked for some sign of suspicion, of crime and culpability, of deceit and maliciousness in what he said, how he said it, in the way the ashes fell from his fag, in a speck of breakfast egg at the corners of his mouth, in a whisker he missed while shaving, in the still fair hair, or in the large pores of his aged yet surprisingly handsome face. What kind of man was John Delacey? What kind of woman had Cait's mother been — the woman my father had fallen in love with? Did John Delacey's features bear the secrets? Could they tell me anything about Cait?

Whisht, he said, listen . . . listen . . . Aahh, go on you cats — up Kilkenny! His hand turned to a fist. Gleefully he looked over at me, staring wide-eyed. Oh, boyo, we'll give Galway a sound thrashin this Sunday. He thumped the top of the cracked dashboard and ash scattered.

And how's your father? Have you heard from him? He grinned and, for a moment in the dim, gray light of the car, his eyes sparked blue, as bright and young and murderous as I imagined they must have been on his wedding day.

very evening, poised over my dinner plate, I waited for the sound of Lugh's bike clattering on the lane after the Angelus had sounded on the telly, that sound which had so become a pattern of my day — and it was with this absence that I sensed his loss and missed him. I assumed he must be sick and after a week of not seeing him I asked my mother for the leftover stew so that I might bring it down to him.

She was preparing the supper and had her back to me. She'd been busy around the house and in the field preparing things, putting things in order as she always did before her next spell. These were the times when she seemed most herself, but it was also when Molly and I were most anxious and did not sleep. We knew that her wellness would not last, and we were waiting for everything to go wrong again. It was as if she had convinced herself that she was no longer ill, and we didn't mention it. All three of us pretended there was nothing wrong. Molly and I had scrubbed the walls, washed Mother's clothes, removed the soiled bedsheets and the empty morphine vials.

My mother turned from the counter and stared at me, a large ladle poised in her hand. What? For that old drunk? What do you want to bring him stew for? He won't eat it unless there's whiskey in it. All he's good for is the two arms up at the bar.

I haven't seen him for days. I think he's not well.

I don't know how that man can work a day at all with all the boozin
he does and not a speck of meat on his bones. She turned back to the
counter and waved with the spoon. Go on then, sure it's a waste, so,
but go on, I hate to think of the poor crature down there in that hovel
all by hisself. She shook her head and returned to her cooking, began
to shred rosemary over a pan of potatoes, then grunted. I'm sure the
food will go to waste, God forgive us for it, but, well, what can you do.

Running up the gravel and out the gate with the covered bowl
warm in my hands, I thought of how good it would be to see Lugh,
and how grateful he would be for the stew I was bringing him.

I remembered when old Mrs. Flaherty was alive; the laborer's cottage always gleamed with fresh whitewash, but now it was tinctured
green from mildew and moss, and the ivy had run rampant through
flower beds where only the brindled husks of bushes and rotting
flowers remained. Dried dung heaps pressed against the side of the
house. A sheet of rusted corrugate and the remains of an old cast-
iron tub, two large-ridged tractor tires. The arched window lintels
were cracked and split, the glass so dirty and dark with soot I
doubted any light penetrated at all.

Back in the time of the landlords and the big houses, this had
been the gatekeeper's cottage, but Flaherty's farm was a small frac-
tion of those early estates, and Lugh had once laughed at the irony
of that. He'd gestured with his chin toward Flaherty's pastures and
then his farmhouse, its wide Georgian columns, its large windows
full of dim burning light. Filthy rich, Lugh said, and so miserly he
thinks everyone he meets wants to take it from under his nose. I
don't believe the man sleeps at all, and if he does, it's not sheep he's
counting.

I knocked on the door of the cottage but there was no answer. I
tapped on the window, lifted the flap of the letter box, put my mouth
against it, and shouted his name. Squinting through the narrow

opening, I smelled him before I saw him — a bundle of frowsy blankets moving on the sofa. Go away, he groaned. Go away, I'm not well.

I brought you some stew, I called. It's still warm, it will do you good, sure you have to eat.

I stared through the letter box but the shape upon the sofa didn't move. I could have left the bowl for him, but I knew Mother would have a fit if it was broken or lost. Lugh, I said again and watched as he drew the blankets tighter around himself. The odor of urine piqued my nose.

I stood in the courtyard holding my bowl, the light changing over the roofs of the sheds and barns, and blackbirds stirring loudly in the trees, my toes growing numb in my Wellingtons and the chill of night coming on. From the shed off to my right I heard the rattle of Bran's chain. He gave one long mournful howl and then was quiet again.

It was the end of the week and the evening news was almost over. Martin Hurson was dead; he was the sixth hunger striker to die. On the telly they showed his coffin coming out of Long Kesh, and then the football scores — it was almost as if no one cared anymore, or as if we were all too numb to feel.

When do you think it will all stop? Molly said as we watched the telly.

I don't know, I said, unbelieving. I never thought they'd let Bobby die.

Turn it off, would you? she said, and when I didn't move she shouted, For God's sake, would you just turn the blasted thing off!

I was slouched on the sofa when I heard the clattering chain, the loose spokes and sprockets, the angled and bent rims on the macadam. I tugged on my Wellingtons in the scullery and ran up to the gate. I saw the shape of him coming up the slope of the road, the bike weaving from side to side as he stood on the pedals to get momentum to make the hill. I waited, and when he came into view, I grinned and stepped forward, but he passed without slowing.

The next evening I sat upon the wall in the dark picking the pebbles from the mortar, throwing sticks into the ditch, until I heard the sound of Flaherty's hounds and then Lugh's bike coming toward me out of the dark. He emerged from between high sycamore and beech, his old Raleigh glittering in the purple twilit shadows, and I waved and called, Lugh! but then, in the same manner as before, he was past me once again. I stood in the center of the road watching his bike recede until he was no more than a speck, while somewhere, deep in the gloaming woods, a pheasant throbbed violently.

There was no traffic on the road, and every so often I had to step into the ditch when a car's headlights came hurtling around a bend. I passed the black gates and gabled walls of silent farmhouses and empty cottages. A dog barked, then silence. Animals scuttering like darts through the hedgerows at my side mile after mile. In the town, I went from pub door to pub door and peered in. He wasn't at Shay's nor the Viking. I looked up Mary Street, in the Three Bullet Gate, then in the Tholsel Bar. Men stumbled from alleyways adjusting their zippers. Dirty-faced children from the Estate were selling copies of *An Phoblacht,* and when they noticed I wasn't from the Estate as well, they jeered and threw stones at my back.

Finally, along the quay in the crumbling Old Quarter, I peered in Sullivan's, and, through the yellow tinted window of the door, I saw him on a stool at the far end of the bar. The men glanced at me; most were from the country and nodded as I passed. Grudgingly Lugh gestured toward Brendan Walsh, the barman, and ordered me a Coke.

I climbed onto the bar stool on his left. His eyes were bloodshot and the warm smell of porter and whiskey was strong on him.

Go away, boy, he said. Can't you go away and leave a man in

peace? Sure why are you always bothering me, hanging on me like a bleedin dog. There's no bloody end to it, is there? He looked about the bar and raised his voice. Is there?

I knew all the men in the pub could hear him. I stared soundlessly at my Coke. I hadn't asked for the thing and wished he'd never bought it for me in the first place. I wished I'd never come looking for him, and when I climbed off my stool to leave, he didn't even glance in my direction. I crossed the river, and the orange-yellow halogens faded and everything became dark. It was cold. A barge sounded from somewhere up the waters, and the tops of trees bowed and shook. The land opened up and the same wind pressed the clouds. Three miles into the country, and nothing but the odd, broken beam of a car's headlights curling the tops of hedgerows far in the distance, my footsteps sounding on the macadam, and cow shit brightly sparking the black tar of the road as if it were tinder.

It was sometime after midnight when the sound of Lugh's raggedy song woke me; I climbed from my bed, tiptoed down the stairs so as not to awaken Mother, and waited by our gate in my pajamas. Soft almost invisible sheets of mist moved over everything, were momentarily framed by the courtyard light before passing into darkness again. In that darkness, carried on the same drift that pushed the mist, was the sharp smell of silage spread across recently turned fields, and Lugh's song coming from all the way down the lane.

Last night she came to me, my dear love came in,
So softly she came that her feet made no din,
She laid her hand on me, and this she did say:
"It will not be long, love, till our wedding day."

He only sang this song when he'd been thinking of Asha, and, sometimes, at odd moments, I surprised myself by humming or singing the words myself, not ever really considering that — having heard Lugh sing it so many times in that raggedy way of his, his voice cracking with the cigarettes and the drink — I knew the song by heart.

I'd often thought that it wasn't numbness or inebriation that Lugh wanted, it was death, the long slow suffering death of failing kidneys and livers, of rot from the inside, a bleeding out of himself, to mirror how Asha had died. All these years he had punished himself in readiness to face her, because he was ashamed that he'd returned to Ireland. He was ashamed that he'd lived at all.

Lugh's face was ashen with stubble, his skin beneath the color of a burst peach. There were broken veins in his nose and in the swollen flesh beneath his eyes. His breath smelled of rot and his body smelled as if he had fouled himself.

Michael, he said softly, sadly, as if he had done me some great wrong, and my anger — or whatever was left of it — was suddenly gone. Michael, he said, you're a good lad, and then in Latin, the motto of his Irish Guards: *Quis Separabit*. And more softly as if the words were taking him away to some other place: *Quis Separabit*. And then he said it again, as if it were a question: Who shall separate us, sure who shall separate us? Ahhhh, Michael, did I ever tell you of Asha? My dear sweet Asha.

I shook my head although he had told me many times. I knew that he had lost Asha to cholera in India during World War II, that he served in the British Army, that he came back the captain of an Irish regiment, educated and skilled, and ended up as this — a drunken day laborer without any family or friends, working for a bastard of a farmer. I'd heard this story before, but somehow it was different now; I knew that he would never tell it to me again.

I sat by her bed, he said, sat with her until the end. After she died — he sighed, waved his hand at the air — I lost all interest. He stared across the road toward Meaney's high-gabled hay shed, eyes searching the shadows lurching there. He licked his lips and ran a hand over his grizzled chin.

Her body wasted away to bones, he said, and I kissed her, her with the cholera. I kissed her, Michael, and I never kissed a woman since. He laughed, high and sharp and his voice broke as something caught in his throat. He looked up and down the road and then toward Meaney's cowsheds, the milking pens, the hay barn again. Only the feckin bottle, he said. It's all I've been good for.

Lugh scanned the fields and the shadows cast by the courtyard light spilling across the road. Loose lips sink ships, Michael, yes sir. Our Day Will Come, *Tiocfaidh ár Lá,* but the enemy has ears everywhere. He tapped the side of his nose to make his point. Mark me and keep it to yourself. Then he stared at me and his eyes had the look of violence to them. Sure, even you, Michael, all this time you could be one of them, an informer to the Cause.

I shook my head but Lugh was searching the fields again. Suddenly he reached for me, took me by the lapel of my pajamas, his arms darting out so quickly I could not have anticipated how fast he could move and then how strong his grip could be. My toes dragged the ground. Lugh! I cried. Stop, you're hurting me, please, stop.

What do you know! What do any of you know! When have you ever stood up for anything in your lives! Sing the "Soldier's Song" for me in the Irish. Do it! Sing it! Sure I bet you don't even know the words! Do you even know what it feckin means!

Lugh! Let go! I tried to wrestle his hands off me, but he was fueled by a feverish strength. Sweat broke out on his forehead; his eyes shone. I felt that I had to say something to him, but all that would come was: Lugh, I'm sorry about Asha.

He looked at me then, and his eyes burned in the present; his face suddenly contorted with anger. What do *you* know about it at all! he shouted. What do *you* know! He thrust me away and I fell hard against the wall. He scrabbled for his bike, mounted it unsteadily, turned to swear at me, and then rode off down the lane. I stayed on the ground long after he was gone, feeling the rawness where gravel had scoured my palms, the sense of Lugh's hand against my chest, burning still.

The door opened and Molly stood there in her robe. She squinted into the courtyard, and I climbed slowly to my feet.

What are you doing? she asked.

I wiped my palms on my knees. Nothing. I'm doing nothing.

She stared at me, drew her robe tight at the neck, and looked about the fields. She stamped her feet on the threshold and looked at me again.

What is it? I said.

It's Mammy. She was screaming, but now she's gone quiet. I was looking for you. Where were you?

I was right here, I said, angrier than I wanted to be. I wasn't anywhere.

Was that Lugh?

I nodded and spat on the ground, worked the gravel from my palm.

How is he?

He's a feckin old drunk, how'd you expect him to be?

Well, she persisted, impatient with me now, why were you out here then?

My mother's bedroom door was closed but I could hear her walking in slow circles about the room, her voice soft and bright as if she were talking to a lover. Suddenly tired, I leant my head against the door for a moment, listening — wishing her to be still, wishing her sleep. When she laughed, I shivered and turned back to the hallway. I dipped my fingers in the holy water font on the wall and blessed myself, looked out at the courtyard illuminated by pale mist, then toward the surrounding farms, their barns and sheds and milking pens, in the same way that Lugh had done, as if someone were out there just waiting for me in the dark.

When I brought Mother breakfast, her sheets were on the floor and she was writhing on the bed. The wireless hummed and crackled from the nightstand. She moaned and tossed and clutched her belly with hands riveted by tendons. When she saw me, her face went hard.

Get away from me, she growled. Get away, you bastards.

I placed my back to her as I turned the wireless off. Mammy, I said gently, more for myself than for her — I needed the security of the word, the safety of its familiarity, before I could turn and look at her. Mammy, I called again. You're in your own bedroom. You're home — please, Mammy.

Keep your hands off me, you feckin Black and Tan, she said and spat at me, then groaned and rolled over on her side, holding her stomach. I placed the tray on the floor and sat at the edge of the bed. Mammy, I said, shall I call the doctor — is that what you want? The doctor? I'll call the doctor then.

I rose off the bed and Mother turned back, tears streaking her face. No, Michael, please. She shook her head and tried to swallow. Please, no doctors, Michael, they'll take me to the hospital.

I sat back down on the bed, and with the shift in weight the bed dipped and we were suddenly much closer. I wanted to reach out and stroke her hair, but since her illness had come back I hadn't known how to touch my mother, unsure of what she wanted or allowed. Instead I touched her shoulder, the hard round bone unyielding and sure. Her breath sour like turned milk.

Lie back, I said, you need to eat. I picked up the tray from the floor and in that moment her eyes began to change — all the light receded and the iris darkened. I'd seen the sudden shift before, and although I was used to it, it still startled me. The first time I'd seen it happen I thought it looked beautiful.

The room was suddenly converging at the edges of my eyes. Everything was moving toward the center before me and I wanted to call out to my sister but there was no time. I tried to step back but Mother lunged up with her body and sent both me and the tray across the room. I landed hard against the wall. She threw herself back upon the bed and screamed again and again. Even though her body must have been exhausted from her struggles, she did not tire but continued, throwing herself against the mattress, and then, screaming, she hurled herself against me.

Molly! I shouted and sprang to my feet, flung my body across my mother's in an attempt to hold her to the bed. Molly! I shouted again and my sister's footfalls were on the stairs.

I tried to hold Mother but she was too strong. I shouted at her to stop and wrestled her back to the bed. Stop! I shouted. I swung my arm and slapped her. Stop! She fell back upon the bed and then came at me once more, screaming and raving. I slapped her again, harder this time.

Stop! Stop! Stop! I shouted and then Molly was grabbing at me, wrapping her thin arms about me. Mother lay on the bed, eyes closed, tears rolling slowly down her swollen cheeks. Her mouth, spit-streaked and bloodied, opened in pain.

I'm sorry, I cried, I'm sorry, and sank to the floor. Molly grabbed a fistful of jumper and pulled me close. Wiping her eyes, she held on to me tightly. It's all right, she whispered, we're all going to be all right.

August 1981

In the evening I stopped listening or waiting for Lugh-the-drunk; if he passed on the road at all, I was unaware of it. I sat in the living room before the telly and the fire listening to news of the latest dead hunger striker. When the room grew cold I pulled a blanket onto the settee; when the Angelus sounded on the telly I turned the volume off. I stared at the image of the Virgin Mother and of babby Jesus suckling at her ripe breast and I imagined bells ringing across the countryside and little manky children in small, dimming rooms waiting for dinner, waiting to stuff their greedy bellies as night came on, and in the North, empty supper tables and processions of black coffins shrouded in the tricolor.

Molly stood by the threshold but I couldn't see her expression in the dark. You've almost let the bleedin thing die out, she said. Mam will have a fit. When I didn't reply she said, Jaysus! It's like talking to a wall. She shoveled some wood onto the embers and then threw coal on top. Slammed the fire screen back into place and then stood there with her hands on her hips — a smaller, less confident version of our mother.

The telly showed a black-and-white picture of Thomas McElwee alongside the pictures of the other dead hunger strikers. I knew the faces by name: Francis Hughes, Raymond McCreesh, Patsy O'Hara, Joe McDonnell, Martin Hurson, Kevin Lynch, Kieran Doherty, and there was Bobby, all long hair and smiles.

The blue light of the telly flickered across the ceiling and the room grew darker still. I saw McElwee and the other hunger strikers on their death cots, blind and shivering beneath blankets piled six high, their skins so diaphanous that I imagined they were already spirits and that upon their deaths their transfigured souls rose immediately to God and to Heaven — the privilege of all martyrs and saints.

I reached into the shadows and began to pull on my boots.

Where are you going? Molly asked.

I'm going to the river.

What about Mammy?

Carefully I worked at folding the tops of my boots. She's better now, I muttered without looking up. That morning, DeBurgh had come up to administer morphine to Mother. She'd howled and screamed and tore at both Molly and me with her nails. I had to use Dettol on the scratches and bandage them because they wouldn't stop bleeding. And after, I couldn't look at Mother; I knew I had to get out if I ever wanted to look at her again. I didn't tell Molly that DeBurgh gave her twice the usual dose of morphine and that though she should not be feeling a thing, not the sheets or the bed beneath her, not color or sound or sensation, she was still in pain. I didn't want Molly to know that the morphine, the one thing we'd come to rely upon, was no longer working.

You'll see, in the morning she'll be fine. I looked up from my boots but Molly didn't look convinced. I'm heading down to the river, I said. I didn't check the traps today.

Can I not come? she asked and there was something pleading in her voice, something so pained in her expression that I had to look away. I can help so, she said, breathless now as I walked the hallway, her voice calling after me. It'll be quicker that way, if we do it together. But I was taking my jacket off its peg and Molly was standing at the far end of the hallway, unmoving, stoic now and proud — she would not chase after me although I knew I'd wounded her.

The paraffin lamps glowed warmly from their blackened glass sconces on the wall — the earthy warm smell of wick and oil and burning dust. Molly's eyes were wide and expectant, her pallor paler than I remembered. There were dark circles beneath her lashes and her eyes were small and feral. It seemed like days since either of us had slept — but if that was what I looked like I didn't want to see it. I waked and washed in darkness and went to bed in the same — and I'd wondered if, like our mother, we'd learnt to avoid the light.

I'm off now, I shouted and slammed the door behind me.

I rowed through darkness, and each slap of the oar, each ripple silvering the black water, filled my head with a welcome emptiness. Clouds slid before the moon and darkness closed in on all sides as I made my way through the inlet. A fog came boiling over the fields and leveled the banks. Sounds curved and then widened as the boat neared the bay, and often I'd thought I could just keep rowing, out to the estuary where the three rivers merged, and then on and on, across the Irish Sea, then through the straits of Saint George's Channel. Never mind England, I'd head for France and Spain and Italy.

Something splashed in the water off to my right and I stilled my oars and waited. The whorls spread wider and wider before I heard the flutter of wings and a bittern came out of the fog, skimmed the water's surface, and then with a cry rose up into the mist again. I began to draw the line in toward the traps but then paused. Half hidden at the edge of the river, in the crescent of the point, was a boat similar to my own but painted blue and with damaged oarlocks. Mist passed over its bow and for a moment it was invisible. I leant back on the oars, and, as quietly as I could, I eased the boat out of the current and into the shelter of rocks and overhanging trees along the bank. I didn't want to be caught by a poacher on the river. If I lay still until they moved on, I would be fine; otherwise I risked a severe beating. I raised my oars and lay them inside the boat.

The water in the bottom of the boat soaked through my rubbers and I began to shiver. Quietly, I hummed all the songs I knew and figured that when I was done a good hour had passed. I opened my flask and slowly sipped the remainder of my tea; it was still hot and I was glad for it. I had the mug to my lips when I heard someone moving through the trees toward the banks. I squinted into the fog. They were moving slow but steady. Branches splintered, brush crackled, and then a man emerged at the edge of the downstream bank. There was a large bundle slung over his shoulder, which he lowered slowly into the boat with a grunt. The boat dipped and rocked as the weight clattered in its bottom. The figure put his hands upon his knees, worked them as if he were kneading the muscle, then rose and stretched his back.

He unbuttoned his overcoat, rolled it up, and threw it into the boat. He took a handful of his jumper and dipped his head to it as if he were sniffing, then he pulled that off and did the same. When he bent to the water and splashed his face, he was silhouetted in fog-shrouded light and the water sparkled in his curly hair. I was frozen by the image of him.

Something in the boat shifted and the man was up and over the keel quickly — much faster than I could have imagined him moving — and suddenly there was a gaff in his hand and he was swinging it up and then down, again and again, and the boat was rocking back and forth, and with each blow I heard something wet splintering and breaking apart. Finally, the man climbed out of the boat and sat on his haunches by the water's edge, his deep breaths thumping the night like a heartbeat. He dragged his throat and hacked phlegm. My oars rattled in the bottom of the boat, and I tensed. The figure looked sharply up the bank, stared hard into the mist. After a moment, he scanned the bay, then the far rocks. A bird called to another and then was still. He looked back through the woods the way he'd come, coughed, rolled up his sleeves, and then quickly and smoothly climbed into the boat, undid his mooring ties, and slipped out into the current. The mist covered both man and boat, and but for the deft wash of his smooth oar strokes barely breaking the water, they were gone.

I waited a moment longer, fighting the urge to move. My head was filled with the white wash of the river and the image of the man lowering his dark bundle into the boat. I closed my eyes and tried to think of other things, and then, when I couldn't, I placed the oars back in the oarlocks and pushed off into the channel after him.

I wandered the narrow straits, searching for some sign of the boat. In the mist, sight and sound were transformed, distance changed. Nightjars were shrieking farther down the river. The moon broke from between high clouds and everything was still. I listened to the sound of the river, and gradually, well ahead of me, I picked up the sense of water lapping a boat, heard the scrape of oars pulled over the gunwale. I rowed slowly, soundlessly in that direction and paused when I felt close. Through the shifting bands of fog a gray shape became visible and I remained very still.

Half standing, he dropped his cargo over the side. A clatter of chains or a weighted line dragging the side of the boat. The sound of it choking on the wood then running free and fast. The bundle was swallowed by the water, and moments later, I felt the ripples of disturbance against my prow. The man turned suddenly and stared through the mist in my direction. I was convinced that he must see me, although I could see nothing of his face; there was the sound of oars swinging loosely about in their broken oarlocks and then he was rowing directly toward me. The scissors of his oars parted wide over the water, and in two large strokes he was gone.

After a moment I rowed toward the spot he'd left. Clouds passed before the moon as something broke the surface off to my right. It shifted with the current, and as it began to sink again I saw Lugh's torn green jumper. I rowed toward it wildly, my oars thrashing the water. The bundle began to go under and I reached with the gaff, caught the jumper, and strained to haul it in. Up from the water came Lugh's jumper, and then in the fractured light the pale angle of Lugh's wide jaw emerging from the black. I threw the gaff to the bottom of the boat and pulled at his shoulders, worked his torso up over the keel, and, as water spilt into the boat, tried to untangle him from the tarp and netting. I raised his head so that he could breathe, so that he could help me get him into the boat and out of the freezing water, but everything seemed soft and melting in my hands and when his body turned I gasped. Strands of orange fishing line gathered what was left of his face into a net. One of his eyes was gone, flesh and bone crushed into the vacant bloodied hole. His face looked as if it were sliding away and the eye that remained stared blindly. My hands lost hold of him with the shock of it.

His head lolled forward, and I wrapped my arms about him as best I could, pressed my head atop his shoulders and my weight against him. The moon fell over us, though everywhere else was darkness and mist. Unseen things moved about the water's edge and in the woods, and down the river the sound of nightjars grew louder.

God is always present, Aunt Una used to say. In Passing and in Light and in Darkness, God is always present. So I prayed to God, I prayed to the river, to the eels, and to my mother's cairns, but everything seemed to mock my sounds and my struggles in the dark.

Together, we spun in the flat center of the bay and the land seemed to loom up on either side of us so that I felt very small. The hours passed; I was tired and cold and I stopped crying and I stopped praying. I searched the banks and shouted and screamed for help. I closed my eyes and pressed myself against him and tried to hold on even as he slipped down into the still water. He rolled once, a tumble of chalk flesh and green jumper and bloody destroyed face. His one remaining eye, an unflinching pupil full of bright accusing light, stared up at me, and then the moon was rushing in to fill the empty, rippling space where only moments before he'd been.

he Guards asked me if I'd been on the river, they asked if I knew anything about the river, they asked how often I went out there and why I was out there this night. Foley and a junior Guard were the ones they'd sent out to ask the questions and I could tell Foley enjoyed it. Did I see anyone out on the river? he asked. How did I find Lugh's body? Now wasn't that strange how in the whole wide stretch of the riverways I'd just come across his body. And why do you suppose that was? It was quare strange so it was. The lads said that they'd often seen me with him in the pubs on the quay. Stranger yet then, that I would know the victim, too. Foley said this as if he didn't know Lugh at all — as if he was a complete stranger to him and as if it was unusual to know the people you spent your whole life living with.

I looked at him with that one, as if he were daft and did he think he was playing Kojak or something? But my head hurt something fierce and I found I could barely talk at all. Even the face on him gave me a headache to look at.

I think that's enough, Guard, Mother interceded. She breathed shallowly, and I thought she might be sick. She squinted in the light and kept licking her lips. Even I could see that she was not well, but she was trying hard not to show it. Sure he can barely keep his eyes open, she said. Wasn't he the one that found him and wasn't he the one that stayed the night with him until help arrived and wasn't he the one that got young Murphy to call it in to the Guards? Sure, he's almost done all the work for you. Can't you see he's exhausted?

Mother said this as if Lugh were resting in the back room or lying in state in one of the funeral houses in the town just waiting for us to say last prayers over his body and lower him respectfully into the black earth. Mother said this as if I did something at all, but this was not so. We did not have Lugh because I did not hold on; I could not hold on. I let him go and the river took him and washed him up miles down the shore to strangers, to people he never knew.

I want to know what he was doing out on the river, Foley said. Perhaps he might be taking after his uncles.

And if he was, so, what has that got to do with a dead man?

Foley chewed on the end of his Biro, his brows squeezed in contemplation. Again, I got the sense that he'd watched one too many American films. I expected him to throw a wad of chewing gum in his mouth and begin talking with his mouth full. You never know now, he said, you never know.

Michael often goes out on the river. It's a way to pass the time. The river is the only bit of comfort he has, sure. What else would a young fella have to do around here? A young fella needs to be out of the house. At least he's not in the town in the pubs and discos and making trouble on the streets like some of the young hooligans. Mother paused, leant on the kitchen chair, rubbed her temples. She made a slight gagging sound and the young Guard flushed and roused himself.

Sure we can come back again, missus, when you're feeling a bit better. He coughed lightly, held his fist to his mouth, and nodded at Foley. Can't we now?

Haven't you asked all you need to know? Mother asked. She sounded tired and I tried to gather myself and answer what Foley needed answering so that he'd be gone and she could get her rest. The effects of the morphine had faded quicker than I could have imagined, so quick it was frightening.

I've not been well, she said and held a small handkerchief to her mouth. Molly brought a bucket smelling of Dettol from the kitchen, and I cringed. She didn't need to tell Foley anything. I knew the satisfaction the bastard would get from this. He's been good, looking after me, she said. I sometimes think he'd go mad if he didn't have the river.

Since his father left, you mean. Foley grinned.

I sat straight in my chair, crossed my arms, and stared at him. My father didn't leave, I said.

Foley raised his eyes and his grin widened. Oh no?

I see you all the time on the quay, I said suddenly. When I'm running at night. You're always walking up and down like a hard man. I feel bad for you.

Foley's grin faded.

I've always wanted to be a Guard. It's something I wouldn't have to go to school for.

Foley put down his teacup. He rose slowly, stared at me as he straightened his uniform, adjusted the cap on his head. How old are you?

I'm fourteen.

Ay, fourteen and headed for trouble. Do you know who killed Lugh McConnahue? he asked, his face hardened and red.

I pulled the blanket around myself. I shook my head and, no longer able to hold my eyes open, lowered it to the warm wool.

Foley grunted and made his way to the door. The other Guard was already at the car. At the threshold Foley paused, turned to Mother. Your one there is headed in the wrong direction, missus, he said, and if he isn't set right soon, all I can say is, I see trouble.

My son has never done anything wrong, Guard, and you know it.

I'm just saying, he needs an eye kept on him.

You need to just mind what you're saying.

Missus, we all know you're not well. There are some who might think you're not fit to look after your children.

Then, Foley, send those people out here so's they can have a look for themselves.

I may have to inform them.

Mother laughed and mimicked him. *I may have to inform them.* Good day, Foley. Mind yourself that you don't step in the cow shit now on your way out the gate.

Mother began to push the door closed on him, but it was Foley and he had to have the last word. The detectives will be by to have a word with him as well, he hollered. Mother grunted and Foley had to move his foot quickly to avoid her catching it in the doorjamb. The door slammed shut and she turned the lock. Foley was a blurred figure through the opaque yellow glass. For a moment he didn't move but continued to stare at the door, and I was glad that I didn't have to see his face. Then there was the sound of his feet crunching the gravel as he made his way up to the gate, through the cow shit, to the car.

After Foley was gone, Molly poured more tea for all of us. Mother sat in the chair opposite and stared at me, her hands cradling her mug.

Michael, she said softly, and I looked up.

Who did that to Lugh? What did you see?

I closed my eyes, lowered my head into the wool, and wrapped the blanket tighter and tighter about me. I began trembling, and Mother, thinking I was cold, came over and wrapped her arms about me and hugged me until I couldn't breathe. Though she was the one who was not well, I felt like a sick child again, and though I was glad for her touch, I wasn't trembling from cold. Mother pressed her head against my own; her breath was warm on my neck and I smelled her sickness. What did you see? she said again. *What did you see?*

he detectives never did come. Lugh was two lines in the Rowan newspaper's obituary page: Slievecorragh man, Lugh McConnahue, drowns in fishing mishap. Aged fifty-eight. No next of kin.

I was glad that they didn't mention Flaherty, his years of labor to the man. How he worked as a swineherd, a farmer's laborer, and how he was a drunk who lived in a hovel, stewing in his own piss.

He was much more than that. And by saying nothing at all, in the end, I'd like to believe that they left him just a little bit of grace. The memory of him, that was something I could take with me.

ardly anyone attended Lugh's funeral. There were some people from Slievecorragh but even they seemed impatient and pressed to be there. Flaherty kept looking toward the stretches of gently sloping meadows as if he were tracking dogs at a coursing match, and Milo Meaney constantly fiddled with his sleeve cuffs and looked for a watch that wasn't there.

No one would buy Lugh a stone for his grave. There was a small hand-around for donations at the church, but I saw only change in the plate when it passed us in the pew. I gave all the savings I had: thirty-five pounds that I always imagined I would someday use to leave this place, to hop the night boat to England. But I wasn't going anywhere, not now. I took the fresh notes from the bank, pressed tight into a white envelope that was creased from folding it in my pocket, and laid them on the church plate.

Flaherty stared at the ground and then toward the road once the priest had said the eulogy. A light breeze came up and over the valley, pushing at the grass, rustling the leaves in the trees above, and bringing with it the sound of men working in fields in the distance. I watched the pockmarked, nervous face of the priest, a young man from another parish who had taken to doing a lot of Father O'Brien's duties since his palsy had become worse. This priest didn't know Lugh, and his words seemed meaningless to me. Even he seemed embarrassed by it all.

I looked toward Cait and she glanced up as if sensing it. Even from across the grave, the blue of her eyes was startling. But I was closed off to anything beyond those eyes, and I could not tell if it was my own distance or one of her making. I had no sense of her thoughts or her feelings as I once might have. I tried to smile but no smile would come to my face.

I studied the others: my mother, a couple of local men I recognized from the pubs Lugh frequented — old haggard men whose faces resembled heavily barked wood or crumbling facades of old pub doors that were forever closed off, locked and secured. I wondered how many pints Lugh had bought them that they now anguished they would never see again.

How many stories had he told them, how many secrets whispered over those friendly, murderous pints in that final need to express himself — perhaps to confess what he and others were guilty of — in his fear of death's imminent approach from a car idling on a street corner, or stepping out of a dark alleyway, or waiting in a chair by the black grate of his fireplace. It would be a pillow perhaps, smothering him in his bed as he slept or pushed to his mouth to prevent him from screaming, and a bullet to his temple. The fear yet the anticipation, the welcome relief that it would all be over and he would soon be with Asha again.

As soon as the priest was done people moved away; no bowed heads, no soil thrown upon the small wood coffin, no flowers left in teary *memoriam*. They headed toward their cars and their bikes and their separate footpaths. A car door opening then slamming shut, a small diesel engine turning over and catching, the whir and rattle of bike chains and sprockets, the clatter of footfall upon macadam, and then they were gone — even Cait.

Mother leant against my shoulder and I let her. She seemed small and frail and I wondered if she thought the same of me. Molly would have a large supper waiting for us when we got home, and I hoped that Mother would eat and then sleep, and that perhaps in the morning things might be better. Together we took the long way home, down by the rutted path along the banks of the gray churning river, where two nights before I'd held Lugh's body to me. It was one of the last warm days of summer. The hedgerows burst with color and my head swam with the sound of trilling birds and drowsy bees. Blackberries were bunched in rows like fat bullets amidst the dripping red fuchsia, and the sky, clear and cloudless and blue, rose up into a pale so familiar it resembled nothing at all.

It was a week after Lugh's funeral and Uncle Brendan had joined us for supper. I watched as he shoveled food around his plate with an edge of brown bread. I ate but tasted nothing. When my plate was half empty, I placed my knife and fork down and listened to the sounds of my uncle and Mother and Molly chewing.

Dusk had fallen and in the living room the Angelus sounded on the telly, followed by news of another dead hunger striker. Mickey Devine, aged twenty-seven, was dead after sixty days. Brendan muttered through a mouthful of food that someone should kill that bitch Thatcher, and my mother bowed her head and crossed herself. Dear God, she said, will it never stop.

No one rose to turn on the electric.

I looked beyond the window toward the road, but the glass was clouded with condensation and there was only the suggestion of the countryside beyond, of blackbirds gathered thickly in the trees, and the distant lights of town. Flaherty's dogs were still; the road was silent, and the familiar weight of loss, of always having everything taken away, pressed against my chest.

They still haven't found Lugh, I said, and both my uncle's and my mother's faces stiffened, yet I couldn't help myself. The river hasn't given him up, I continued. I let go of him and the river took him and Uncle Oweny used to say the river always gives up what it's taken, that's what he used to say, but it hasn't given up Lugh yet.

Michael, my mother hushed. What are you talking about? Of course the river gave him up, aren't we just after burying him.

Uncle Brendan's expression darkened. He chewed at something invisible at the front of his mouth. That man, he said through tight lips, talked too bloody much. That's the only reason he's dead. The old fool brought it upon hisself.

I continued to stare at him as I realized what he was saying, and he turned back to his mug, drank steadily from his black tea. The knuckles gripping the mug white as bone. A tightness constricted my throat.

But Lugh, I said. What they did to Lugh. Lugh never hurt anyone —.

You don't know what that man did or didn't do, Uncle Brendan said, or what he was capable of. You don't know anything at all.

I looked at him pushing sodden bread across the empty plate although he'd stopped eating. The bread moved on the china in indecipherable patterns. His fingers were blunt as pegs, thick and yellowed from nicotine. His jaws clenched and unclenched. His thick hair wired and curled as a sheep's. Gray evening light washed down his face like mist, turning it to shadow.

Were you out fishing on the river last week? I asked, my voice trembling and betraying itself.

Brendan stared at his plate, then turned to me, his face rigid and set, his eyes so hard and blazing and full of hatred that I couldn't believe it was the same man I'd known all these years.

I was in Carlow last week, doing a job, he said, a rich American who needed his walls plastered. He paid forty pounds a day, served me lunch and supper. I was there all week from dawn to dusk. Had to hitch rides back and forth on the Dublin road and never got back into the town until after ten every night. A bit too tired then to be fishing, I think.

I looked at him. He'd recited the facts as if they were a shopping list. I blinked, frightened by his stare but unable to turn away, and was thankful when he took up his mug and finished his tea in one greedy gulp, then pushed back his chair with a squeal, rose, and took up his cap.

I was out on the river last week, I said quickly, breathlessly, as if I had to speak and he had to hear it; I needed to know, I needed to know.

Uncle Brendan paused, inhaled, and worked the cap down over his brow.

Where's your boat? I asked.

Uncle Brendan glared at me. I chopped it up, he said, and used it for firewood.

You did not, so you didn't.

He stared toward the door, his jawbones whitening. As if he was dismissing me, as if I had just crossed a line from which there was no return. As if he was sorting figures in his ledger to work out an impossible balance, and when he turned away from me, I knew that I, too, had become a figure in that ledger.

There's a good lad, Michael, mind yourself now.

He waited and I knew it was my last warning. My mouth hung open but it was as if I'd forgotten how to breathe. Still, he stood there waiting, his shadow in the lamplight black and hard on the floor. My mouth moved but nothing would come, and I felt tears forming at the edges of my eyes. I swallowed and tried to breathe again. I looked toward Mother, who shook her head sadly and then closed her eyes. My uncle made his way to the door, his boots dragging on the lino. The door closed softly and then he was up the gravel at the gate, working the latch in such a familiar but strange way, this man that I thought I knew but did not know at all. My heart thrumming in my ears sounded louder and louder, and though I wanted to speak, to shout, to scream, it all felt so far inside me that I would never be able to reach the words in order to pull them up and say, *Murderer, you murderer.*

Why, Ma, I managed. Why?

But Mother didn't respond. She lowered her head and quietly began to gather up the dishes. Molly ran the hot water and turned on the electric. Outside, dusk came on quickly and mist settled upon the fields. Down by the river my boat was rocking against its ties, and the first of the nightjars began sounding from out of the woods far away.

he walls in Greelish's stone shed pressed against each other; crumbling joist posts burst from mortar bowed with the pressure of the sinking roof. I swung the light of the paraffin lamp about the shed. Angles of blackness and peaks of rotted straw rising to the low ceiling. Rats rustling in the narrow shadows.

I turned and looked about the shed and my lamp swung shadows into the low corners. I placed the lamp down and began digging through the straw, drawing up great clumps of it in my hands. I struck something hard, and when I laid back the straw, there was the oilcloth shining blackly.

I reached down and pulled the bundle from the hole; below lay more tarps, one upon the other, descending deeper and deeper. I undid the tarp slowly, drawing the oiled bindings through the grommets and then easing the covering back.

In the meager light with the paraffin spitting, the machine gun looked smooth and polished and powerful. As I ran my fingers along the metal, I heard a dozen radio announcements from Derry and Belfast, television images of bloodied shooting victims and fiery car bombs in the Shankhill and the Bogside. A hundred screams of pain and rage, hundreds of years of hatred, and my family a part of it all.

I buried the gun again, filled the hole, and smoothed the straw back over it. When I was done I sat with the smell of guns and oil, animals and mortar and damp stone, and suddenly felt very tired, as if I could fall asleep there, curled up with old murders and vendettas and so many ghosts I could not count them. I leant back against the wall. The paraffin hissed as it ran low, strange bends of light glancing across the thick metal and the darkness growing steadily on all sides, until the flame upon the wick trembled and went out. I sat there and wondered if someone were to open the small door to the shed and see me crouching in the shadows, my eyes glittering back at them from the darkness, what type of animal might they consider me?

Mother sat at the kitchen table shivering in Father's donkey jacket; she smelled of brandy and cigarettes and cow shit. You're drunk, I said. She bared her teeth, and her eyes shone. She licked at her lips and said, And you're just like your daddy. The fields were darkening behind her; long slow rolling flashes of lightning turned the sky silver over the town. Give me your coat, I said and reached out my hand. You're drenched.

I threw the jacket over the clothes rack before the cooker. Mother tottered as she pried her oversize Wellingtons off and dropped them on the mat in the scullery. The hallway seemed to recede behind her and the door looked very far away.

I'll make us some tea.

She sat heavily and chewed at her mouth; her lips were cracked and swollen. She shook her head. God, are you just like your daddy. She laughed. Do you recognize your daddy in her at all?

I stared at her.

He fucked her mother and then hopped a plane to the States. Ran away. She laughed again, crazy and high-pitched, made a flapping gesture with her hands. Left us both.

I lit the gas beneath the cooker, watched the flames. Will you stop that rubbish, I said and then sighed. It's not true. You know it's not.

Do I? Ask anyone in town, they'll tell you. You think so yourself.

Since when do you listen to them? They can all go fuck themselves.

Ah, sure, it's gas isn't it. You're her bleedin brother, Michael. Do you believe it?

That's not funny, I said.

It wasn't meant to be, it's the truth.

How would you know the truth? Half the time you don't even know what effin day it is.

I do know it — I just do.

Why are you doing this? Is it out of spite, is that it?

You could ask your daddy if you wanted, but I doubt he'd reply. There's powerful truth in silence. She stared toward the window, and I couldn't tell if she was staring at her reflection or the fields beyond. She looked back quickly, and it startled me.

What do you say, Michael? Would you like it if she were your sister?

I looked at her then, and she wasn't smiling. Her eyes were dark, unforgiving. She wanted me to say something but I didn't have the words for her. I turned toward the window.

You know, Michael, you've always had a knack for seeing what you wanted to see. I suppose you and your father are the same like that, but it doesn't matter all that much now, does it?

You're a liar, I said. She laughed and pulled from her bottle. She drank it down, and when it was empty she threw it in the sink.

Rain began to pelt the windows. The cats jumped onto the windowsill and pressed their faces against the glass, turned their bodies aslant to the rain. Their mewling sounded tiny and far away, pitiful really. I watched the rain come hard, drench them until their small bones protruded, their ears pressed back against their heads, yet still they bunched there, staring at me miserably through the glass.

It grew darker and the light dimmed in the room so that I no longer saw the cats, only their small dark shapes. Every so often, a flash of lightning turned all of them white like a negative burnt upon film: their eyes embers, their mouths small and dark and pleading. I don't know how long I remained there, but the rain seemed to have eased up, the storm moving toward the east and out to sea, and the room had turned cold. Mother had gone to bed. I stared at the cats mewling softly, at their plastered skulls, and now that it no longer mattered, I went to get them in.

he light changed only slowly over the town as I waited in the phone booth to make my call. I looked down the gray street that sloped to the river and at the men entering and exiting the pub. It was almost dusk and everything shone slick from a recent rain, and the voices of children and dogs at play carried over from the Bosheen. Mothers tried unsuccessfully to call Declan or Pat or Sean into supper — their shrill voices echoing across the Estate between flapping sheets and drying nappies. A group of strays ran barking down the hill, with two boys dressed in red-and-black Man United jerseys chasing after them. An oncoming car had to downshift and halt on the road until they passed, jeering and cursing and barking at the driver. As the car motored up the road, its engine revving high, I turned away from its lights.

I dialed the number, and when a voice came on the other end of the phone, I hesitated. Finally, I asked, Can I speak to Guard Foley?

What's it concerning? The Guard sounded bored and distracted. I imagined him glancing back to his dinner going cold in the back room, or a football match on the telly. I knew him, too. His name was Hennessey and he had big sideburns, black as tar, and wouldn't lift a hand to help anyone if he could help it.

It's concerning guns, I said and held my breath. There was a pause on the other end of the line.

Hold on, he said and then I heard him shouting for Foley.

I held the phone from my ear and Foley's name rang in my head. The line clicked and hummed and I waited, waited with the urge to throw down the phone and fling myself out the door.

In the fading light, I imagined my uncle kneeling on the floor before me. He was wearing the same clothes as I'd seen on him the night upon the river when he'd murdered Lugh. His curly hair sparkled with river wash. A growth of dark stubble grazed his cheeks. His color was high and fair and he looked very young, as young as my father was when he left us. He smelled of the river, of fish and guts, of brine and hemp and moss, of deep rich muck and woolly sweat and porter. It was the way my uncle Oweny had often smelled.

I thought of all the times he had held me as a child, how often he had made me laugh and smile — of the great fool that he was. His eyes were wide and dark as he looked at me. He raised his head back. Below the gray line of stubble his neck looked as pale as a candle.

Beyond the phone booth twilight was coming on and the lights of the town broke in staggered rows upon the far hill. In the dark I could no longer see my uncle but I could sense his eyes upon me. Foley's voice was calling from the telephone asking who was there, and For fucksake, Hennessey, sure he didn't have time for such eejit carry-on, and did he get the name of the caller and, Hello, are you there? Are you there? Are you there? In the gloaming more and more of the town became illuminated, bound around its high neck where the church steeples rose and the shanties of the Bosheen began like the silver coil of a metal snare drawing tighter and tighter. Foley's voice called urgently from the telephone as I sank down into the shadows, out of view of men leaving the pub, and I thought, *Informer, Informer, that's what I am,* the phone dangling from my hand as if it were a noose I was about to lower over my uncle's neck.

I imagined it pulling taut and choking the life from him — and still, I waited.

There's no one feckin here, Hennessey —.

Foley, I said.

Who is this?

Foley . . .

michaelmas

In the end, we didn't have a choice. DeBurgh had our mother admitted. And in truth he was right, and I was glad for it. In the end, the hospital was the only place our mother could be.

Aunt Una stayed with us through the days and nights. The staff didn't seem to mind as long as she was there. She'd already told them she wasn't shifting and they'd have to carry her out themselves if they wanted her to leave. She muttered curses under her breath but when I listened closely I couldn't be sure that they weren't spells and incantations of some kind. When she looked at the nurses they left quickly, they knew she meant business and they didn't want any trouble with her.

The hospital was an old converted army barracks, something since the last war. The walls were thick and rounded and everything was painted the same puke sheen. The windows were narrow and high, the metal frames rusted, unused to opening and letting air in. Tea trolleys rattled and clattered along the painted stone floors throughout the day until dusk, when there was an immense silence. Where there was not carpeting, sound lingered and haunted shadowed alcoves, dim-lit stairwells, wide vacant vestibules. It felt much more like a graveyard than a place that healed people, and I could sense the dead there, in sound and vibration, like heavy air suggesting the onset of rain. There was nothing surprising about it — many had died there and they did not know how to leave. I could understand this; I did not want to be there any more than they did, and I wished I could leave them to their endless wanderings.

The hospital was a tall building on a tall hill. From the windows on the north side I could see most of the city below. Dour-looking mulberry bushes straddled the entrance road from the city. The grass was dull and beaten, as if the roots were rotten from reaching down into the coal mines below; everything had the ash-graying of anthracite to it. Farther on, industrial buildings converged toward the city center and church spires raked the low clouds that seemed to cover the city and move in perpetual circles above it. Large buttressed shipping cranes arced like cantilevered bridges over the gray waterfront, and from there came the trains running east to west.

I watched the trains at night, their carriages igniting the rails beneath them like tinder, and I imagined that we could just as easily be on one of those train cars hurtling through the darkness, that my mother could just as easily be sleeping and we could be returning home to New Rowan.

I pressed my face against the cold glass toward the darkness beyond, my eyes searching up above the roof of the city. In my belly, I felt the weight of the trains upon the tracks, roiling slightly from side to side; I sensed their wheels hammering the rails and moving across them. When I lowered my eyes, we were passing wide straths of farmland, high hills darkly furrowed by strip mines: we were heading home.

When I returned to myself it was always a surprise to see my sister's reflection in the glass next to mine, as if we had been sharing the same dream and both awoken at the same time. I had the sense that this occurred frequently, and perhaps that was why we never told each other about our dreams; I didn't want to know how hers ended, if they ended differently.

We woke with the early rounds, the clatter of food trays, the giving of medicines, the taking of fluids. There was one nurse from the

Caribbean who spoke long and slow yet with so much sound — she was the gentler one. And then there was the Derrywoman whose voice was sharp and quick and high at the ends. She was always sighing, as if there was so much work to be done, and all that work was hers alone, and there was no end to it. Although she was not gentle, she, too, was kind; she couldn't help but remind us of the work we made for her, but as she complained, she rummaged through her pockets for sweets — yesterday Smarties, the day before Rolos. She had no children of her own and seemed to think even children our age needed sweets now and again. It seemed we were always hungry; nausea settled in my stomach and stayed there, and I thought of starvation. Una brought us sandwiches wrapped in cellophane from the cafeteria before it closed in the evening. They were dry, day-old things with mealy ham and crumbling cheese, but we were glad for them.

At evening, when the hallway reverberated with a quiet sob, or moan, the soft brush of a nurse's padded plimsolls, Molly and I sat in the dark watching the lights of the city below. A whistle sounded and men and women spilt from between factory gates. Dark coal smoke churned up from row upon row of small terraced houses and gray, balconied tenements. Bells were sounding the Angelus, and, absently, I blessed myself.

The hospital room grew cold; mist clouded the window. In the next hour or so, it would be dawn. We'd watch it coming over this strange town, burning off mist that had settled across the rooftops. My sister and I held our mother's hands. Her forehead was slick with sweat. Tears had left dark tracks down the sides of her face. The black sky faded, then dimmed and altered the color of the room.

I snuck into the lounge to see if anyone had left sandwiches, fruits, or Lucozade — these were the things people brought to hospitals, and I'd discovered that often they were not allowed to give them to the patients. But this time, there was nothing. The air was stale, the carpets sticky underfoot, and the Naugahyde seats worn to a sheeny luster. A young man had pulled two of the chairs together and was sleeping upon them and snoring loudly.

I returned to Mother's room. Molly had just wiped Mother's brow with a washcloth and was attentively watching her face. Mother's eyes fluttered more quickly with the paling of dawn. In my mind, it seemed I already knew where she was, or where she was heading to, and I was filled with fear. Even though the nurses had warned us to keep it open, I closed the door to her room. The dead padded the hall and broke the light at the bottom of the door, and I held my breath. In my head I thought, *Leave my mother alone, she's not dead so she's not, she's not dead,* but in my heart I felt something else altogether.

When the nurses turned on the small bedside lamp to check on Mother, I imagined our faces jumping out of the dark at them. Sometimes they forgot we were there, although we left the room rarely and only when they asked us to — when they drew the curtain around the bed and adjusted the morphine drip on the intravenous, or when they changed her bedpan, or bathed her.

On the fourth day she woke from an uneasy dream and called out our names. The change in her breathing had already woken us and we stood there waiting. She clutched at our hands almost immediately, and her grip was strong. She coughed and Molly brought her water, helped her raise her head off the pillow. She looked at us intently, as if she was back in her own room and had merely woken from some pleasant dream that she wanted to return to.

Your father, Mother said, and smiled, as if the words had special meaning known only to her. She sighed. *Your father.* And I nodded; I had always known how much she had loved him in spite of her protests. She would love him always, and I felt I should be saddened by this, resentful that she thought of him now, even though he had left us for America. It was my sister and me who were here with her now, and for all these years, there had only been the three of us. But I was not as angry as I expected to be; it seemed right and good that she could still love him. It meant that we could as well.

What do you see? I wanted to ask her. What do you see? But she had already closed her eyes again and returned to that place where there was no pain.

Aunt Una came in looking frowsy and worn, her shoes shuffling the floor. She closed the door softly behind her and lowered herself onto one of our sleeping cots. After a moment she looked at Mother and told her in a firm and precise voice that the doctors here had done all they could, that there was nothing more they could do, but that they had arranged for appointments with specialists in London who could help. Do you hear me, Moira? she said. We have to go to England. Do you understand? We're taking you home now.

Mother's eyes fluttered and then were still. Molly and I held her hands as she fell into sleep. Una muttered in the shadows, cursing the stillness, the hour, the dead. Once more, the city was turning toward night. In the distance, rain was falling from gray clouds like dark whips, horns were moaning from the docks, and ships were moving silently far across the Irish Sea.

he drab olive Land Rover rumbled along the Barrow road in the dark blue predawn. It was raining softly, and its wide tires tracked the road heavily, sweeping leaves into the ditch. The wipers thumped as uniformly and as precisely as the speed the vehicle maintained. It was followed by two armored personnel carriers from Stephen's Barracks in Kilkenny, full of soldiers sitting solemnly in parallel lines and wearing dark flak jackets and light green peaked caps or black berets, Browning guns at their sides. A fourth vehicle belonging to the Gardaí, with Foley at the wheel, rushed to keep up.

I'd like to say that I was there when they took my uncle, but I was miles away. We'd brought Mother home from the hospital the night before, and I was sitting in front of a fire I'd woken early to light because I couldn't sleep and a she-fox had been wailing out in the fields all night searching for its mate.

I looked out at soft rain that was misting everything, thinking of the river and of Lugh, then looked toward the clock over the mantel and heard in that resonant ticking the soldiers in the armored carriers loading their gun chambers, hobnailed boots snapping upon metal running boards and then macadam.

They cornered him at Greelish's house, caught him in the act of loading the guns from the shed. The Land Rover blocked the narrow laneway and the armored carriers barreled through the gates of the surrounding fields when Uncle Brendan made a run for it, sprinting off across the countryside. He'd always been good at running from the fishing authorities, he knew every inch of the land, but he didn't run as well as he used to, and his smashed legs gave out on him. He fell in the high, sodden wheat fields and the soldiers dragged him along the ground, through the muck, back to the armored cars.

I could see Brendan struggling and cursing until they'd bloodied him into submission. I was sure that Foley put in the boot a couple of times as the soldiers held him; my uncle didn't have a weapon on him, but I knew if he had, he would have taken a few of them with him. For all his talk, I knew Brendan could never stand prison, and for all his wildness, I knew he was a coward, just like me. I doubted that Mother, even at the height of pain-induced fugue, could ever have imagined her son an informer.

Someone must have tipped off John Delacey; he was home when they came. They banged in the door and stormed the stairs and found him hanging from a rafter in the bedroom where he'd killed his wife. I never imagined that he would go in such a way, I thought he'd resist until the very end, but I suppose he wanted to take one secret with him to the grave. Instead of a wife killer, he'd be considered a martyr for the Cause.

I was glad that Oweny wasn't alive to see it, glad that I could believe he had no part in the things that Brendan did, in the things that made up our family's history. When the clock chimed the half hour, I placed more coal on the fire and blessed myself. I said a prayer for Brendan as I imagined the dark cell where he'd count off the last of his days. I waited as the room grew warm, then went and brewed the tea for my mother and sister who had yet to arise, determined that I would not let anything touch us ever again.

I t was September 29, the feast of St. Michael, and our last night in Ireland. The cold woke me sometime after midnight. A hard scatter of branches thrust against leaden window-panes, wind trilling through the eaves. I climbed from the bed shivering, wondering how it could possibly be so cold. The floor was like ice, the water in the basin on the nightstand freezing. The sound of the wind seemed deadened and I stood there listening to it, waiting for a sound from my mother or sister from down the hall, or of something from somewhere in the countryside beyond. Only then did I realize that although it was autumn, and though it would seem impossible, it was snowing.

I padded the hallway and checked on my mother. A small fire burnt in the grate, a few laggard coals turning to orange embers and then sifting to the glowing ash below. Standing before the flickering shadows, I listened to my mother breathing softly; it was a warm and pleasing sound, comforting in the way that I remembered being comforted by the sound of her when I was a child.

The embers glowed brighter as wind pressed down the flue; snow shifted on the roof and thumped to the courtyard below. I moved before the window, eased the bulky cloth back. Gray light pooled at my feet, and I blinked slowly to take everything in. There was no discernible landmark anywhere. White hills rose to a black sky, from which the snow came in heavy sweeping gusts and drove down out of the clouds as if on slanted tracks. Wind rattled the glass, and I hugged my arms about me. I was nine years old again staring out at hillsides and fields covered with the small frozen bodies of lambs, hundreds of them, and there was Lugh throwing them into the back of his lorry, their bones popping like kindling.

In the kitchen I put on the tea and started a fire in the grate. In the electric light, the room seemed even colder, the space between window and everything beyond ever wider and more remote. I imagined the fields spreading back in a vast emptiness around us so that we became smaller and smaller. And the light of the kitchen was a spark in the snow-crushed darkness, pulsing faintly through the dark body of the storm.

Una stirred in the room above, stoking Mother's fire, and Molly was up washing herself with cold water from the basin on the dresser. I stepped about the kitchen as I prepared breakfast, keeping my back to the dark rectangle of window, trying to ignore the sense that, right there, just beyond the tempered glass, lay a cold, vast, inexorable thing just waiting to press us to its heart.

I closed the doors between hallway and kitchen to keep the warmth in. And to keep from looking at the suitcases already packed and staggered in rows, waiting by the back door. At the sound of distant church bells, I looked up. Almost imperceptibly, the sky had lightened. Snow lay in drifts at the corners of fields like the crooked seam within a vast quilt, and only for the drifts could I tell there were fields at all. All boundary and geography were gone. There were no longer hills and valleys. Trees bowed under the weight of snow and the wind tore at their tops so that they seemed like great silver white-capped waves cresting and then falling, crashing down without sound.

☙❧

Mother padded into the kitchen in her slippers, followed by Una and Molly, whose face was still pressed by the pillow. She rubbed her eyes and then squinted out the window as if she were still dreaming. But they were dressed and ready to go. Mother unhooked her slippers and stepped into her freshly polished shoes. Her footsteps were loud in the silence, snapping the lino with a cadence that made me think we were about to march into battle.

The back door slammed and the second door opened wide. Wind whipped down the vestibule to the scullery. My cousin Canus stamped his boots on the mat. Jaysus, it's a bastard of a day, he said and shook snowflakes from his black Crombie, ran his hands through his brilliantined hair. When he was done he clapped his hands together and looked from Mother to Una, to my sister and to myself. Are you right, then? he asked.

Mother nodded.

Canus stuck his hands deep in his jacket pockets, rounded his shoulders.

Will you not sit down and have a cup of tea? Una asked.

If I have any more tea, Una, I'll burst. He patted his stomach, then turned and squinted out the window. He watched the snow as it came down and his mouth opened and closed and I couldn't tell whether he was praying or cursing. Finally he stamped his feet again. I think we'd best get a move on before it gets any worse, he said. Sure, the boat may not be leaving at all.

Oh it's leaving all right, Mother said, placing her teacup firmly, resolutely on the countertop. If I have to get out and push it meself, it's leaving. I'll not be here one day longer. Will your car make it?

She's a tank, Moira. It'd take more than this to stop her.

Right so, Mother said and tugged at the hem of her jumper. She pulled the screen before the fireplace, then stood at the threshold flicking the electric switches off and on, then off again. We waited as she stared into the darkened rooms. Finally she said, Right! and we put on our coats, picked up our luggage, and trudged toward the cold. At the end of the hall, my mother dipped her fingers into the holy water font and blessed herself while Una mouthed a prayer to the Virgin. After a moment, I did the same, and turned, looked the length of the shadowed vestibule, smelling the damp stone walls, the kitchen and my mother's cooking, and the odor of blood-let from the gutted carcasses of rabbits or salmon that would hang there in the summers. I looked at the pegs that held our jackets and jumpers, the mat where we wiped our Wellingtons. I closed the door to the house and pulled it tight so that the bolt resounded in the lock behind us one last time.

We were going to the boat in Uncle Oweny's old Morris, which looked as if it belonged in another century, with its dull gunmetal panels, shielding, and splayed wheel wells — the wide-set heavy glass windows, the flat shed of a roof. Like his father, Canus was immutable in the face of everything. Like his father, he had been a fisherman, worked on trawlers all up and down the coast. He moved slowly but gracefully, as if he were climbing down slimed rocks to the river of an evening. He didn't much look like his father though; whereas Oweny was wide and stocky, Canus was slender as a straight tree limb.

And I'd never heard Canus tell a story. Oweny lived for the telling and the retelling of stories — tales, myths, local foolery. But Canus was a quiet young man who seemed to measure every word spoken as if it pained him to speak at all, as if by speaking he might cause himself some great injury. Yet the sight of snow seemed to force upon him some unusual urgency; this morning he wouldn't be quiet at all until he'd said what he needed to say.

He grimaced. This is bad, so. He glanced at me briefly, then back to my mother and Una. You know what happened the last time we had a storm like this. It's just bad.

Canus, Mother said, we all know what happened.

Just bad, it is, that's all I'm saying.

Well whisht with your saying, I have enough to think of. I've got a splitting headache altogether. She half turned. Michael, did you collect the last of the money we were owed for those bales? Did you lock all the sheds?

I nodded and she paused as she thought of something else to say, but then, feeling the tires of the car sliding and catching again, she turned back in her seat and held tight to her handbag. I looked at Molly, already fast asleep and curled beneath a blanket next to me.

Oweny's old Morris did move like a tank. Its motor rumbled heavy as the wipers plowed the snow across the windscreen, creating a dull quarter circle of glazed light upon the glass. The sky was boiling and the snow, wind-whipped but silent, fell fast and furious from the heart of it; so great was its projection that I had the sense of heat, of something brilliant and bright and full of burning intensity, in the way that I imagined a star would be to the touch, or poison rushing through one's veins.

Canus slowed at the bend of the road where Shea Murphy's car lay in the ditch against Flaherty's stone wall. One of the Murphys was towing the car out of the ditch with a tractor. Canus rolled down his window, and what heat there was left us in a moment. Howya, Shea! Are you set there? Shea tested the chains to the undercarriage of the car, then hopped out of the way as the tractor reared back, pulling the car with it. He nodded and waved, shouted something I couldn't make out over the wind, and Canus said, Right so, rolled up the window, and put the Morris in gear. The rear tires slipped for a moment, the car slid then caught, and we drove on. Canus shook his head. God, this is quare bad, he said. Sure, I don't ever remember anything like this before. He glanced at my mother, but her jaw was set and she remained silent.

My head rocked against the panel of the car window and it was as if I was half dreaming. I saw Cait and me in our school uniforms walking through the fields together. It had been a dry, cold day in February and the smell of coal smoke hung on the air. Great groups of crows huddled in the bare trees. The earth was brown and plowed and the farmers were spreading silage — we were almost home.

Passing a mound of yellow-and-umber straw, thatch, and leaves piled for burning, we threw ourselves, laughing, onto it. We rolled and tumbled as if we were sea wrack upon the foam. My body fell over hers, and I held her. I touched her face, traced her eyebrows, the ridge of her nose, her cheeks, her jaw. She leant her head back and I rubbed my nail against the scars on the underside of her chin. I remembered the wire that cut her and how as she waited for the hooks to be removed, she never cried. I'd always remember that, Cait not crying, not then, not even at her mother's funeral. Then my mouth was on the cold, wet angle of her neck and she wrapped her hands around my head and held me there, the two of us breathing fiercely.

Her body was warm beneath me, my legs tight between her thighs, and we were moving slowly against each other and the light was beginning to fall. Taking her hands, I blew into them to warm them, wiped dirt from her face, and she watched me, her breath turning to mist in the chill, thin air. When she leant forward to kiss me, her broken teeth bared, I closed my eyes, then felt the sensation of leaves plunged deep inside my coat, and when I looked again, Cait was up and running across the dun-colored fields, a blurred shape disappearing and reappearing and then gone. And then, as now, I felt only emptiness.

Snow howled against the old car's running boards and shotgunned in the wheel wells, sounding like dull explosive charges. Mother coughed harshly and held her handkerchief to her mouth, waiting for the hacking to subside.

Canus banged on the dash and fooled with the heater.

You right there, Moira? Una asked.

Mother gasped for air, and only with an effort did she begin to breathe properly again. Aye, Una, she said breathlessly after a moment. I am. I'm fine. She put the handkerchief back to her mouth; her chest rose and fell sharply. Canus's jaw tightened and he nodded solemnly without taking his eyes from the road; he just kept squinting and blinking and muttering, *Jaysus, Jaysus.*

A large tree limb had fallen under the weight of the snow and settled itself across the road. As Canus tried to pass he nudged the ditch with the rear tires and came to a stop. He fiddled with the gearshift and frowned. We slip into the ditch and that's that, he said. We'll need a tractor to get us out.

It seemed there were trees down everywhere. Canus said that all the electric lines must be down. Normally we'd be able to see the lights of Rowan, but not now.

Canus and I got out of the car, bowed our heads into the wind and the snow, shards sharp as gravel stinging our faces. Canus grunted, Here, help me with this, and reached beneath one end of the stump. The tree was heavy and my hands were soon numb. Canus suddenly seemed much bigger than me and for a moment I did not think I was strong enough to move it. I looked up, and through the snow and the glass and the yellow interior light of the car, I saw Mother, and her features were blurred and misshapen. She watched as we struggled with the tree limb and then lowered her head into her hands.

When we got back in the car Mother had yet to raise her head and Molly had woken. Why are you crying? she asked, but Mother shook her head and Molly leant back into her seat. Canus closed his door. We cleared the road, I said, it's fine, sure we'll make the boat. Canus sighed and banged on the dash and we started moving again. Molly pressed her head against the cold glass as I had done, and I knew she was thinking of everything we were leaving behind.

We passed a hay shed, a long gabled horse barn, an odd darkened farmhouse — black coal smoke lacing the sky like ribbons, and all along the road men working in the ditches with chain saws on fallen trees. They glanced up briefly as we passed, squinting into the snow, their saws biting almost soundlessly into the wet puckered flesh of the tree, their mouths and noses covered with scarves they'd pulled up around their faces. Strangely, over the snow, I smelled the sharp scent of pine, alder, and ash. No sound but the color of smells. The sparks of wood chips flew and churned in the wind, blinding the cutters as much as the snow itself, and then both disappeared behind us.

For the first time I noticed how dark it had grown in the interior of the car and how bright the snow looked falling across and rushing into Canus's headlights: trees and hedgerows, the fence posts and stone walls, the gutter of ditch sharply sculpted in black, and at their edges, stretching for unknown distances, fields and fields of snow.

The car made its way down the rutted lane toward Delacey's. To my right, a group of men struggled to climb the sloping rise of a field. Using thick branches as walking sticks to aid them, knees rising and falling in military fashion, their coats and wrappings black against the snow and blown about them, they resembled an ancient cathas of warriors heading to war. I closed my eyes, not wanting to see the Delaceys' home, but then, relenting, I opened them quickly, anxious that I really might miss seeing her one last time. *Slow,* I whispered, *go slow.* We rounded the bend and the house came up quickly on the right, but Canus didn't touch the brake on the bend for fear that it might put us into a slide.

The house was by us, and I turned quickly in my seat to look out the rear window, but the Delaceys' courtyard was empty, the kitchen windows dark; only a small black thread of smoke from their chimney suggested that Cait might be there somewhere in that house where both her parents died.

A flock of greylag undulated low upon the horizon, a sinuous scattering of parts like oars beating fast in a current that was carrying them swiftly away. Men and dogs and geese heading home through the snow. I wished I could take everything back, I wished I had the words to make everything right between Cait and me. Now that it was too late, all I felt was regret.

And then, I saw her. She was making her way toward the courtyard from a far gate, a coal bucket in her hands, a large overcoat bundled tight about her and her face pressed into the collar of it. I caught her eye, saw her face perfectly, and we held each other's stare for a moment. I clung to the rear window to hold onto that gaze for as long as I could. But then Cait lowered her head against the wind and snow and trudged toward the house and the car was quickly down the lane as if we'd never slowed and I'd never seen her at all.

I turned back in my seat and I was startled to see Mother staring after her as well. When she looked at me I assumed she saw only my father, but then she spoke and surprised me.

Cait's growing up to be a fine girl. She sighed, her eyes moist and shimmering. I suppose you'll miss her.

She reached for my hand and touched it with her glove. You're becoming a fine man yourself, she said. I don't tell you that too often, do I?

I looked at her but could think of nothing to say.

I'm sorry, she said.

Sorry? I whispered.

For us leaving, for the way things are —. She shook her head. I'm sorry.

Mother's words held the silence of the car. The snow came down hard and fast and everything turned dark and dim. I lay my head against the cold glass again, watching the countryside darkening, and only the sense of still-falling snow in that darkness.

By the time we reached Wexford Harbor, the snow had stopped. It was barely noon and yet a strange partial moon shimmered weakly through trailing silver clouds hurtling out over the water to the east. Gulls swept low over harsh-looking whitecaps, rose up and wheeled above the docks, their sleek edges sharp against the boat's snow-crusted gunwale. The wind was gone, darkness closing in from the sea. A single star flickered in the east. The dock lights shimmered and seemed to grow brighter now that the light of the storm was gone. The snow, already sullied and tainted by lorries and tractors, sat silent and mute. Open flats of salted stockfish, gutted and now hardened, lay ribbed with snow. The ship's stacks belched smoke. Dockworkers pushed trolleys, or shoveled and swept the snow from walkways.

I pulled my jacket tighter about myself, glanced at Mother bent in pain over the luggage like a slant of twisted metal. I saw the bight of land opening out into the wide channel of the Irish Sea, expanding like a great maw to take the whole of the world in. I stared at the starboard gunwale and thought of the way shipmen or fishermen like my uncles looked at the stars. And then, somehow, I could no longer look at the ship. I didn't want to take in its immensity, the hard resolute lines that suggested nothing but churning passage through deep water — one straight unerring line to a destination, plotted, mapped, coordinated.

Instead, I watched the sea, the distant scattering of clouds, tried to smell the far-off cow pastures, the wheat and barley. It was almost turnip season, and soon it would be beets. I imagined the last of the potatoes being picked in the country, pulled up by the roots from the rich moist seam. And I thought of Cait. How one last time, I wanted to feel the brush of her lips against mine, how I wanted the wetness of her mouth, the taste and the heat of it.

I looked out over the water, spilling vast and endless over the horizon, and tried to imagine what England might be like, but nothing would come to me. This, then, was the sea: unchanging, vast, and unperturbed — nothing could affect it, certainly not this ship's passing. A strake of light moved across the whitecaps, sharp as a shattering of bone. Una helped Mother, and Molly and I reached for the bags and we moved forward. Gulls called from their jerry-rigged nests amongst the pitons, and the ship's whistle blew. People left the ticket office or the heated lounge and the embrace of families, and together we began the long, slow climb up the swaying, snow-crusted gantry.

acknowledgments

Thanks to the eloquent heart that is Roger Skillings, and the Fine Arts Work Center in Provincetown, Massachusetts.

To some of the finest teachers I've ever known, whose passion for the form is a constant source of inspiration: Jim McPherson, Marilynne Robinson, Elizabeth McCracken; and to Chris Offutt, my friend and my teacher. Thank you for your faith.

And to Martha Collins, Tom O'Grady, Chet Frederick, Lee Grove, Professor John Tobin, and the English Department at the University of Massachusetts, Boston, for all the ways in which they guided and nurtured me many years ago.

To those who aided in the publication of this book, Richard Abate, Zainab Zakari, and, most especially, to my wonderful editor, Asya Muchnick, who took this novel on with incredible passion and engaged it as wholly and as completely as any writer could wish for.

For support, both moral and otherwise: to my sister, Máire, and Colm O'Brien, my nieces, Caitlin and Meaghan, and my nephew, Cormac; to Victoria Häggblom, Megan Carnes, Joshua Furst, Nick Arvin, Jeremy Mullem, David Ferry, Claudia Mackey, Janice Zenisek, Christa Lyons, Dan Darling, Jen Purdy, and Aran Michael Parillo. To the man who saved my manuscript from a Manhattan taxicab. I'm sorry, I've forgotten your name. Thank you!

To Michael Altobello, who drove me there and brought me home again. To Douglas Purdy, who was there from this novel's very beginning, thousands of pages ago, and who has been there ever since.

To Jennifer Haigh, whose wisdom and insight are without compare. Thank you, my friend.

To Caroline Crumpacker for your love and grace, your patience and tolerance, your incredible intellect and diligence in reading the sentences of this novel again and again and again. And to our daughter, Colette Gráinne, who has illuminated my life in more ways than I can say and for whose presence in this world I am so grateful.

Thank you, and bless you all.

about the author

THOMAS O'MALLEY grew up in Ireland and England. A graduate of the University of Massachusetts at Boston and the Iowa Writers' Workshop, he has also been a Returning Writing Fellow and recipient of the Grace Paley Endowed Fellowship at the Fine Arts Work Center in Provincetown, Massachusetts.